Three Apples
Fell from the Sky

·NARINE ABGARYAN·

Translated by Lisa C. Hayden

ONEWORLD

First published in North America, Great Britain and Australia by Oneworld Publications, 2020

Originally published in Russian as *С неба упали три яблока* by ACT, 2015
The publication of this book was negotiated through Banke, Goumen
& Smirnova Literary Agency (www.bgs-agency.com)

ISBN 978-1-78607-730-1 (paperback)
ISBN 978-1-78607-731-8 (ebook)

Published with the support of the Institute for Literary Translation, Russia.

ИНСТИТУТ ПЕРЕВОДА

AD VERBUM

This book has been selected to receive financial assistance from English PEN's
"PEN Translates!" programme, supported by Arts Council England. English
PEN exists to promote literature and our understanding of it, to uphold
writers' freedoms around the world, to campaign against the persecution and
imprisonment of writers for stating their views, and to promote the friendly
co-operation of writers and the free exchange of ideas. www.englishpen.org

Typeset by Tetragon, London
Printed and bound in Great Britain by Clays Ltd, Elcograf S.p.A.

Oneworld Publications
10 Bloomsbury Street, London WC1B 3SR, England
3754 Pleasant Ave, Suite 100, Minneapolis MN 55409, USA

Contents

PART I

For the One Who Saw

—9—

PART II

For the One Who Told the Story

—127—

PART III

For the One Who Listened

—201—

And three apples fell from heaven:
One for the storyteller,
One for the listener,
And one for the eavesdropper.

OLD ARMENIAN SAYING

PART I

For the One Who Saw

Chapter One

On Friday, just past noon, after the sun had rolled past its lofty zenith and begun sliding sedately toward the western edge of the valley, Anatolia Sevoyants lay down to breathe her last.

Before departing for the next world, she thoroughly watered the kitchen garden and scattered food for the chickens, leaving a little extra since the birds couldn't go around unfed – how could she know when the neighbors would discover her lifeless body? After that she took the lids off the rain barrels that stood under the gutters; this was in the event of a sudden thunderstorm, so that streams of water pouring down wouldn't erode the foundation of the house. Then she rummaged around the kitchen shelves awhile, gathering up all the uneaten supplies – flat little bowls with butter, cheese, and honey; a hunk of bread; and half a boiled chicken – which she brought down to the cool cellar. She also pulled her "grave clothes" out of the wardrobe: a woolen dress with a high neckline, long sleeves, and a small white lace collar; a long pinafore with satin-stitched pockets; flat-soled shoes; thick knitted socks (she had suffered from ice-cold feet her entire life); along with meticulously laundered and ironed underclothes, as well as her great-grandmother's rosary with the little silver cross, which Yasaman would know to place in Anatolia's hand.

She left the clothing in the most visible spot of the guest room, on a heavy oak table covered with a coarse linen cloth (if one were to lift the edge of the cloth, one would make out two deep, distinct marks from axe blows). She placed an envelope with money to cover funeral expenses on top of the pile, pulled an old piece of oilcloth out of the chest of drawers, and went into the bedroom. After she turned down the bedding, she cut the oilcloth in two, spread one half on the bottom sheet, lay down on it, and covered herself with the second half. Then she threw a blanket on top, folded her arms across her chest, and settled comfortably on the pillow, nestling into it with the back of her head. She gave a deep sigh and closed her eyes before getting right back up to fling both sashes of the window wide open, propping them with geranium pots so they wouldn't slam shut. Then she lay back down. Now she needn't worry that her soul would wander the room, lost, after it had departed her mortal body. After freeing itself, it would dart out the open window immediately, toward the heavens.

There was a highly significant and sorrowful reason for these painstaking and extensive preparations: Anatolia Sevoyants had been bleeding profusely for two days now. She was stunned on first discovering inexplicable brown spots on her underclothes, but then she examined them carefully and burst into bitter tears when she was certain they were really blood. Ashamed of her fear, she gave herself a talking-to and hastily wiped away tears with the edge of her kerchief. What good was crying?

It wouldn't change anything. Death hits everyone differently: it will stop one person's heart but steal another's mind with a sneer. It had apparently decreed that Anatolia would depart due to blood loss.

Anatolia had no doubt the ailment was incurable and progressing rapidly. There was, after all, a reason it had struck her uterus, the most useless part of her body. It seemed to be hinting that this was retribution being sent down because she had been unable to fulfill her primary destiny: giving birth to children.

Once Anatolia had forbidden herself to cry and fret, she calmed down and resigned herself to the inevitable surprisingly fast. She rooted around in the linen trunk, took out an old sheet, cut it into several pieces, and made herself something akin to sanitary pads. Toward evening, though, the discharge became so plentiful that it seemed as if a large, inexhaustible vein had burst somewhere inside her. She was forced to put into service the small supplies of cotton wool she had stored away. The cotton wool threatened to run out very soon, so Anatolia took apart the edge of a quilt and pulled out several clumps of sheep's wool, which she washed thoroughly and spread on the windowsill to dry. She could have gone to see Yasaman Shlapkants, who lived right next door, to ask for some cotton wool, of course, but Anatolia didn't consider that. What if she couldn't keep a grip on herself, burst out crying, and told her friend about her fatal illness? Yasaman would immediately become alarmed and tear off to see Satenik and ask her to send an express telegram to the valley for an ambulance. Anatolia had no intention of visiting endless doctors who would torment her with painful and useless procedures.

She had decided to die with her dignity and tranquility intact, in peace and quiet, within the walls of the home where she'd lived her difficult, futile life.

She went to bed late and spent a long time going through the family album, where faces of loved ones who'd been swallowed by the river of oblivion looked especially wistful under the meager light of a kerosene lamp. "We'll meet soon," Anatolia whispered, stroking each photograph with fingers coarsened from burdensome rural chores. "We'll meet soon."

Despite her downcast and anxious condition, she went to sleep easily and slept through until morning. She was awakened by the rooster's alarmed cry: the muddled bird was bustling around noisily in the coop, impatiently awaiting the moment he would be let out to stroll through the beds of the kitchen garden. Anatolia assessed the state of her body and established that the condition of her health was completely tolerable; other than the ache in her lower back and a slight dizziness, nothing seemed to be amiss. She rose cautiously, went to the privy, and confirmed with a wicked sort of satisfaction that there was even more blood than before. She went back inside and put together a feminine pad from a clump of wool and a scrap of fabric. If things kept going like this, all her blood would flow out by the next morning. This might be the last sunrise she ever saw.

She stood on the veranda for a little while, soaking up the solicitous morning light with her whole being. Then she went over to say hello to her neighbor and ask how things were. Yasaman had a big laundry day going and, as it happened, she'd just put a heavy tub of water on the woodstove. They talked about this and that, discussing everyday things while the water heated. The mulberries would ripen soon so the trees would need to be shaken and the berries gathered; then they would use some berries to boil up syrup, dry others, and leave the rest in a wooden barrel to ferment, for use in mulberry home brew. It was also already time to harvest horse sorrel – it would be too late in a week or two because the plant coarsens quickly in the hot June sun, making it unsuitable for eating.

Anatolia left her friend's house after the tub of water boiled. She needn't worry now; Yasaman wouldn't remember her until the next morning. She would be busy with the laundry until then: washing, starching, bluing, hanging it in the sun to dry, carrying it inside, and ironing. Only toward late evening would she get things under control. And so Anatolia had plenty of time to depart for the great beyond in peace.

Reassured by this development, she spent the morning leisurely doing humdrum chores, and only after noon, once the sun had crossed the sky's canopy and begun sliding sedately toward the western edge of the valley, did she lie down to breathe her last.

Anatolia was the youngest of Kapiton Sevoyants's three daughters and the only one in his entire family who had managed to live to an advanced age. Anatolia had celebrated her fifty-eighth birthday in February and this was unheard-of, an altogether unprecedented occasion for her family.

She didn't remember her mother well because she had died when Anatolia was seven years old. She'd had almond eyes with an extraordinary golden hue, and thick honey-colored hair. She was named Voske, meaning "golden one", very much in keeping with her appearance. Voske would plait her wondrous hair into a tight braid, arranging it in a heavy bun at the nape of her neck using wooden hairpins, and then go around with her head slightly tilted back. She often ran her fingers along her neck, complaining that it was going numb. Once a year, Voske's father sat her by the window, carefully combed out her hair, and neatly cut it to the level of her lower back – she wouldn't allow him to cut it any shorter. (Years later, Voske also refused to cut off her daughters' braids, since long hair was supposed to protect them from the curse that had been swirling around the family for nearly eighteen years, ever since the day she had married Kapiton Sevoyants.)

Voske's older sister, Tatevik, had in fact been supposed to marry Kapiton. Tatevik was sixteen at the time and four-teen-year-old Voske, the second marriageable girl in Garegin Agulisants's large family, had taken an especially active part in preparing for the festivities. According to a time-honored tradition in the mountain village of Maran, where Tatevik and Kapiton had lived their entire lives, the bride's family was expected to host the first part of the wedding festivities, the groom's family the second. But the heads of Kapiton and Tatevik's families, two wealthy and respected lineages in Maran, decided to work together and host one large party in the meidan, the central square. The festivities promised to be extraordinarily lavish.

Kapiton's father wanted to dazzle the imagination of his many guests and so sent his two sons-in-law to the valley to invite musicians from a theater to the wedding. The men returned tired but satisfied and announced that the prim musicians had immediately consented (who ever heard of such a thing as inviting a theater orchestra to a village!) when they learned of the generous honorarium of two gold coins for each of them, plus the week-long supply of provisions that Kapiton's brothers-in-law promised to deliver to the theater by cart after the festivities ended. Tatevik's father arranged his own wedding surprise by inviting the valley's best-known dream interpreter. For a fee of ten gold coins, he agreed to practice his craft throughout the day, asking only for help delivering the equipment he would need for his work: a tent, a crystal ball on a massive bronze stand, a table for fortune-telling, a wide ottoman, two flowerpots with a spindly plant of a hitherto unseen species that gave off a cloying scent, and two peculiar candles made from special kinds of wood pulverized to dust. The candles had already been lit for several months, spreading a musky aroma of ginger, and they kept burning and burning. In addition to the Maranians, fifty residents of the valley, predominantly respected and prosperous people, were invited to the wedding. The newspapers even wrote about the upcoming celebration, which promised to turn into quite a memorable occasion; these articles were especially prized because the press had never before mentioned festivities for families lacking noble origins.

But then something happened that no one could have predicted. Four days before the nuptials, the bride took to her bed with a fever and was tormented by delirium all day before passing away without regaining consciousness.

Some mysterious portal must have opened wide over the village of Maran on the day of Tatevik's funeral, releasing sinister dark forces. What else, if not black magic, could account for the inexplicable behavior of the heads of the two families: they held brief deliberations immediately after the funeral service and decided not to cancel the wedding.

"So that the money spent won't go to waste," Voske's father, the thrifty Garegin Agulisants, announced at the wake table. "Kapiton's a good fellow, a hard worker and respectful. Anyone would be happy to have a son-in-law like that. God took Tatevik for his own, meaning it was fated to happen. It would be sinful to grumble about His will. But we have another marriageable daughter. So Anes and I have decided that Voske will marry Kapiton."

Nobody dared contradict the men, so Voske, who was inconsolable after the loss of her beloved sister, had no choice but to marry Kapiton without complaint. They postponed mourning for Tatevik until the next week and celebrated a big, noisy, extravagant wedding. Wine and mulberry home brew flowed like a river; tables set beneath the open sky groaned under the weight of every dish imaginable; an orchestra decked out in dark frock coats and shoes polished to a shine softly played polkas and minuets; and the Maranians listened tensely at first to the unfamiliar classical music. Later on in the evening, though, once they were sufficiently tipsy, they waved off decorum and broke into a village dance, just as they would on any other festive occasion.

Few people called on the dream interpreter in his tent, since wedding guests fired up with abundant food and drink were not in the mood for that. But a concerned distant aunt of Voske's led her there by the hand after the girl found a minute to say a few words about a dream she'd had on the eve of the wedding. The interpreter turned out to be a tiny, skinny old man of a bluish complexion, who was inconceivably, even horrifyingly, deformed. When he showed Voske where she should sit, she was transfixed by his right pinkie: at the end of it was a long, dark fingernail that hadn't been trimmed in many years, curled like a clamp, bending into the pad of his finger and growing along his palm toward his crooked wrist, with the result that he had great difficulty moving his hand at all. The old man unceremoniously told Voske's aunt to get out of the tent and ordered her to stand guard at the entrance. Then he settled in opposite Voske, staring at her in silence, his legs spread wide in outlandish baggy pants and his long, thin hands dangling between his knees.

"I dreamt of my sister," she said, answering the question he had yet to ask. "She was standing with her back to me, in a beautiful dress, and her hair was plaited with a string of pearls. I wanted to hug her but she avoided me. She turned toward me and for some reason her face was old and wrinkled. And her mouth…it was like her tongue didn't fit. I started crying and she went off into the corner of the room, spat some kind of dark liquid into her hand, held it out to me, and said, 'You won't see happiness, Voske.' I woke up because I was scared. But the scariest thing happened afterwards, when I opened my eyes and knew the dream was still going on. It was *enbashti*, the darkest hours of the night, and it was so early the roosters hadn't crowed. I went to drink some water, and for some reason I looked up and saw Tatevik's sad face through the skylight in the ceiling. She threw her headband and shawl down at my feet and disappeared. The headband and the shawl both turned into dust as soon as they touched the floor."

Voske burst into heavy sobs, smearing her cheeks with black mascara, the only makeup the women of Maran used. A helpless light-blue vein beat on her temple and her fragile, childlike wrists poked out of the slits in her festive silk *mintana* dress, which was decorated with expensive lace and silver coins.

The dream interpreter exhaled loudly, producing a drawn-out, grating sound. Voske faltered and stared at him in fright.

"Listen to me, lass," squeaked the old man, "I won't explain the dream to you. There's no use in that whatsoever, and it wouldn't change a thing anyway. All I can recommend is that you never cut off your hair. It should always cover your back. Every person has their talisman. Mine" – and here he waved his right hand in front of Voske's nose – "is my pinkie fingernail. Yours is your hair."

"Fine," Voske whispered. She waited a bit, hoping for some other instruction, but the dream interpreter maintained a sullen silence. She rose to leave but plucked up her courage and forced herself to ask, "Do you happen to know why it's my hair?"

"I have no way of knowing. But throwing you her headband and shawl means she wants you to cover your hair, to protect you from a curse," answered the old man, his gaze not budging from the smoldering candle.

Voske left the tent with mixed feelings. On the one hand, she felt less uneasy than before because she had left part of her anxiety with the dream interpreter. At the same time, though, she couldn't shake the thought that she'd been forced to portray her deceased sister as almost a sorceress, but of course Voske had not acted with any malicious intent. Standing near the tent, she shifted impatiently from one foot to the other as she relayed the old man's prophecy to her aunt, who was for some reason indescribably joyful:

"The main thing is that we have nothing to fear. Do as he advised you and everything will be fine. And Tatevik's soul will depart our sinful land on the fortieth day after her death, leaving you in peace."

Voske returned to the wedding table and smiled timidly at her brand-new husband. Flustered, he smiled in response and abruptly blushed bright red – Kapiton was a very shy and timid young man, despite being twenty, a solid age by patriarchal standards. Three months earlier, when his family had begun saying the time had come for him to marry, his older sister's husband had gifted him a trip to the valley and a night at a house of ill repute. Kapiton returned to Maran thoroughly dismayed. He couldn't say that a night of delights spent in the sweaty rosewater- and clove-scented embraces of such an experienced woman who was, for a short time, entirely his own, was not to his liking. It was more likely the opposite, that he was stunned and entranced by those exhaustingly ardent caresses that she gave so generously. But he felt no peace due to a vague feeling of revulsion and the light nausea that arose in him when he glanced at her facial expressions. Even as she squirmed like a snake, produced muffled moans, and caressed him with skill and passion, she contrived to preserve an unfeeling, stony mien. It was as if she weren't making love but doing something utterly routine. With a rashness characteristic of his age, he decided that such calculatedly shameless behavior was typical of any woman in bed, and thus he expected nothing good from marriage. This was why Kapiton just nodded silently when his father announced that he should marry the younger sister after the death of his betrothed. What difference did it make? All women were essentially deceitful and incapable of sincere emotion.

That night, after the waiters had begun serving juicy slices of ham baked in spices and fluffy millet with cracklings and fried onions, a zurna wailed shrilly and the guests buzzed approvingly when the tipsy fathers-in-law led the young people to a bedroom and shut them in with a bolt lock, promising to release them in the morning. Voske burst into bitter sobs once she was left alone with her husband, but she didn't push Kapiton away when he approached to embrace and comfort her. She clung to him and instantly became quieter, but for her sobbing and odd sniffling.

"I'm scared," she said, raising her tearstained face to him.

"I'm scared too," was all Kapiton replied.

Spoken in a bashful whisper, touching in its simple sincerity, that dialogue united, indissolubly and forever, two young hearts that hungered for love. It was later, in bed, clasping his young wife to his chest and gratefully seizing on her every motion, every breath, and every tender touch, that Kapiton burned with shame for having dared compare her to the woman from the valley. In his embraces, Voske glowed like a precious stone. She radiated a warmth that filled Kapiton with a single, enduring purpose. From that moment on, Voske became the single dearest thing in his life.

A week later, Garegin Agulisants and some male relatives, bareheaded, wordless, and dressed from head to toe in black, slaughtered three purebred heifers, boiled the meat without salt, and brought it around the village on large trays. People opened their doors and silently took the portion set aside for each home, since it was forbidden to converse when someone was bringing you meat from a sacrificed animal. Voske covered the windows of her bedroom with opaque fabric and vowed to wear mourning clothes for her sister until the end of her days. She exhausted herself with never-ending fasts and spent long evenings at church, praying for the repose of Tatevik's soul and begging for her forgiveness. She visited the cemetery once a week to tend her sister's grave, accompanied by her grieving mother, sisters-in-law, and distant aunts. It was as if the light of day and darkness of night had changed places for her: at night she offered love and warmth like the sun, but by day she was transformed into a gloomy, somber creature. Tatevik never came to her again, and that fact saddened Voske very much. She swallowed her tears and confided her intense feelings in her husband, lamenting that Tatevik must not have forgiven her, for if she had she would surely have visited her again in a dream.

Kapiton suggested Voske distract herself from these mournful thoughts by working to furnish the house that had been handed down to them after the wedding. His grandmother, Babo Maneh, used to share the house with an unmarried aunt, but the two women had moved in with Kapiton's father. This left the young couple a sound, thick-walled, and rather dark dwelling. Nonetheless, it was comfortable and cozy, with a large wooden veranda, high attic, and well-tended fruit garden. But since the house was located at the other end of Maran, Voske flat-out refused to move. Kapiton, however, was unyielding, saying she would reminisce less about her sister and come to terms with the bitterness of her loss faster if she were to live farther from her grieving kin.

Voske very reluctantly ceded to her husband's admonitions and was surprised to find herself absorbed in her new activity. She threw herself so zealously into the task that she even ordered several interior design magazines from the valley. After poring over their content, she settled on a dining room set made of bog oak: an oval-shaped lunch table, four broad ottomans upholstered in dark-green velvet, and thirty chairs, since there should be lots of places to sit because the house would be full of guests. To this they added several buffets decorated with expert carving and high glass doors so they could store a fancy dinner set for twenty-four and the multitude of other tableware they had received as wedding gifts. The carpenter, Minas, who took on the painstaking job of producing the furniture, had to hire two assistants to supplement his existing three so he could meet the appointed deadline, as Voske was already pregnant with their first child and wanted to take care of furnishing the house before giving birth. She spent her pregnancy occupied with handicrafts, working with her mother to embroider several tablecloths and coverlets, two sets of bed linens, a layette, and an outfit for the baby's christening.

After the weekly ritual visit to the cemetery, Voske would call on Minas's carpentry shop to check on the work. Minas would groan and frown, but he silently tolerated Voske's visits. He always sent her home before too long, though, impelled by the thought that a woman, particularly a pregnant one, ought not to be in a workshop smelling of toxic varnish and male sweat.

Her visits to the carpentry shop were not in vain, though. The furniture was ready on time and scarcely had Voske put the house in order and taken care of the housewarming when she took to her bed with contractions. A day later she gave her Kapiton the gift of a daughter they named Nazeli. Two years later Salome was born, and another year and a half hence, the youngest, Anatolia.

Although she was affectionate and attentive with her husband, Voske spoke little. She was so reserved with her daughters that Anatolia couldn't recall her mother once using pet names for them, or speaking to them affectionately, or showering them with love and kisses as other mothers did. She never praised them but she didn't scold them either. If something displeased her, she might silently purse her lips or raise an eyebrow. The girls were more wary of Voske's raised brow than the constant grumbling of elderly Babo Maneh, their only relative who had survived the horrible earthquake that swept the western part of the mountain, Manish-kar, into an abyss.

That disaster occurred the year Salome was to be born. Babo Maneh had moved in with them in order to help with little Nazeli because it was difficult for Voske to handle the restless child, plagued as she was by severe bouts of nausea. Trouble arrived unexpectedly one chilly December day at noon when the earth shuddered underfoot. The ground began stirring and rumbling at length, and with an excruciating wail, Manish-kar's shoulder split off. Part of the mountain tumbled into the void, carrying houses, yards, and outbuildings in its wake. It swept away villagers as they choked on their shrieks; their animals, who had sensed impending doom and, confined to their cowsheds and pigsties, had gone mad trying vainly to warn their masters, were also caught in the landslide.

The part of the village that remained intact endured the blow of the elements with steadfast dignity. People held masses in a tiny chapel for the repose of the lost souls. (The church of Grigor Lusavorich, Gregory the Illuminator, which stood on the village's edge, had been first to tumble into the void.) They then returned to their own homes to reinforce collapsed roofs and walls covered with deep cracks, and to fix wooden fences that had toppled on their sides. They had not yet spoken of needing to move to relatively safe low-lying areas; they talked of that much later. The meidan emptied out after the earthquake, and boisterous festivals and outdoor celebrations were never held there again. On a few occasions, gypsies came from the valley for old times' sake and told of how some houses that had tumbled into the void were carried far to the west by a mudslide and then arrived in unknown villages. The people living in those houses were safe and sound but would never return because the fear they had experienced had stolen their memories. Besides, they didn't know they had once lived on the crown of a mountain covered by an ancient forest and fertile pastures. People listened to the gypsies gratefully and gave them various belongings and old clothes as gifts and then let them go in peace, hoping against hope that the gypsies were telling the truth and that the unfortunate residents of Manish-kar's western flank were alive. Even the fact that these people spoke other languages and wore different clothing held no significance whatsoever. In the end, the sky is always identically blue and the wind blows exactly the same wherever you were lucky enough to have been born.

The gypsies returned on several occasions. They were the first to sense the approach of a new catastrophe and so disappeared one day, wordlessly and forever, dissolving in the hazy heat of a midday sun as blindingly golden as the coins they used to settle accounts on market days at the meidan when caught red-handed for the ritual misdeed of theft.

Anatolia was born the night before their final appearance in the village. As it happened, Babo Maneh had brought her eldest great-granddaughters to a neighbor's house so the weakened

Voske could rest after her difficult labor; the newborn Anatolia was now sleeping, carefully wrapped in a warm blanket, under her mother's gaze.

Anatolia was the only one of Kapiton Sevoyants's daughters who took after her swarthy grandfather. It was he who had given their family the name Sevoyants: *sev*, after all, means "black" in Maran.

A short, plump gypsy woman with a faint scar on her left cheek entered the house unimpeded and walked through all the rooms without stopping anywhere. She did not knock before looking in on the frightened Voske, who had raised herself slightly on her elbow, shielding the baby. The gypsy woman made a calming gesture with her hand, as if to say, *Don't be afraid, I won't do anything bad to you*, then walked up to the bed and peered into the child's face.

"What will you name the child?"

"Anatolia."

"That's pretty."

The woman straightened up, folded back the edge of the blanket and sheet, gathered up her many-colored flounced skirts, and sat with her legs apart like a man, dangling her long, thin hands between them. Her pose seemed vaguely familiar to Voske, because someone had already said important words to her while sitting just the same way, with their elbows leaning into knees set wide apart, though for some reason she couldn't remember who exactly it had been. It seemed as if someone had waved a hand and erased her memory.

"We won't be coming back here ever again. Give me any pieces of jewelry you want to get rid of. You have no choice," the gypsy woman uttered slowly. Her hoarse smoker's voice often cracked at the ends of words, as if she lacked the breath to finish.

It didn't even cross Voske's mind to object to what the uninvited guest had said, since there was something in her expression and her heavy, focused gaze that inspired unquestioning trust. And so Voske pulled her long, honeyed hair out from behind her back with a habitual gesture and tossed it on the pillow so it wouldn't interfere with how she was lying, then she folded her arms across her chest and fell to thinking. She had very little jewelry, and what she did have had been bequeathed to her by loved ones who'd vanished in the earthquake. To give any of it away was tantamount to renouncing their memory.

"Open the upper drawer of the bureau, there's a jewelry box there. Pick something out yourself," Voske decided after wavering briefly.

The gypsy woman stood up slowly, smoothed the edge of the sheet and blanket, then pulled out the drawer. She stuck her hand in and blindly extracted a piece of jewelry that she concealed in her clothing before heading for the door.

"Why aren't you ever coming back?" asked Voske.

The gypsy woman stopped, grasping the door handle.

"That's something I can't tell you."

After hesitating a little, she added:

"My name is Patrina."

Voske wanted to say her name too, but the gypsy woman shook her head sharply, clearly ordering her to keep quiet. Then she carefully wrapped herself up in a warm shawl, gave a curt nod, and left. Voske began feeling dizzy as soon as the door closed behind Patrina. She leaned back on the pillow, lay with her eyes closed to wait for the fit of nausea to pass, and unexpectedly fell asleep. When she awoke, she was quite certain that she had dreamt the gypsy woman's visit, though the open bureau drawer spoke to the contrary. She asked Babo Maneh to hand her the jewelry box; a heavy silver ring with a dark-blue amethyst was missing. It was her grandmother's ring, which by all rights the eldest granddaughter, Tatevik, should have inherited. But it had been handed down to Voske.

∾

The room smelled of evening freshness with a slight scent of bitter chamomile. Dew had fallen, drawing a heady aroma from the dozing flowers and spilling it over the earth. Night would fall in another hour or two. Darkness slips down over Manish-kar as swiftly and abruptly as if it's popped out from around a corner, making it seem like sunset's rays have just begun glinting over the horizon when drowsiness floods everything only a second later and the sky is very, very low, with a generous scattering of stars and the sound of crickets singing, as if for the last time.

"I'd like to know what they're singing about," Anatolia muttered, letting out a sudden laugh. So great was her surprise at her own laughter that she found herself choking on her own saliva. After clearing her throat, she raised herself up on her elbow and took a sip from a glass – a pitcher of water always stood on her nightstand, a habit she had acquired when living with her husband, who constantly gulped down water. He drank such an enormous amount, even at night, that he asked for a pitcher of fresh water to be placed on the nightstand every evening so he wouldn't have to get up. Even twenty years after he had passed away, Anatolia poured some fresh water into the pitcher every day for old times' sake. The next morning she put it to use watering potted plants before refilling the vessel. And so it had gone, day after day, every day, for two decades.

She drank some water and very, very carefully turned on her side before fumbling around underneath herself to straighten the oilcloth. It was damp and disgusting between her legs and the painstakingly constructed pad, which Anatolia had prudently layered with oakum to make it last longer, was soaked through. Her nightgown was now so wet that it stuck to her back. She would have to get up and change her clothes. All this Anatolia did while suppressing her nausea – for some reason everything that was happening with her body provoked horrendous irritation and squeamishness. There was now even more blood, and it gushed with some sort of insurmountable, evil force, as if it were hurrying to abandon her womb as quickly as possible. Anatolia put the stained things out of sight under the bed then lay down, smoothed a second scrap of oilcloth, covered herself with it, and tossed a blanket on top, carefully wrapping her feet because they got cold even on the hottest summer days.

"If only I could hurry up and die," she sighed, shutting her eyes and giving herself up to a swirl of reminiscences. Thinking about her childhood helped pass the time more quickly.

She was seven years old when her mother passed away. Voske had started a fire in the bathhouse, bathed her daughters and put them to bed, then closed the damper on the stovepipe to hold in the heat while she was busy with them. She forgot to reopen it later and the fumes poisoned her. Kapiton was tired after working hard and had gone to sleep without waiting up for his wife, but when he woke during the night and didn't find her next to him, he broke down the bathhouse door and carried her out in his arms. Voske had caught the stove door as she fell, and it swung wide open so some of the coals (which for some reason hadn't gone out in the bathhouse's moisture) scattered, singeing her marvelous honeyed curls.

"The curse of Tatevik has caught up to us!" old Babo Maneh sobbed loudly, raising her gnarled dark hands toward the sky. She had already turned a hundred and was half blind, sickly, and spending days at a time on a divan surrounded by long sofa pillows, fondling the translucent beads of her rosary, and whispering prayers. Voske's death forced her to get up and take the burden of the household cares upon her stooped shoulders. She lived for five more years, eventually passing away during the horrible famine which took the lives of her eldest great-granddaughters. Salome was the first to fade, weakened by malnutrition. Nazeli departed the very next day. The girls were placed in the same coffin, covered by their long hair. Starvation had taken away more than their health and beauty: their luxuriant, honeyed braids, like their mother's, were gone too. Babo Maneh washed their hair in lavender water, dried it in the breeze, then combed it and laid it like a coverlet over her great-granddaughters' bodies, which had melted away to transparency.

Kapiton brought his youngest daughter to be cared for by a distant uncle in the valley, leaving them a jewelry box containing Voske's valuables and forty-three gold coins that he had saved during his years of strenuous peasant labor. Whenever

Anatolia closed her eyes, she could see her father: emaciated, with sunken cheeks and a lackluster gaze, a young man who seemed to have grown old and decrepit overnight. She would hold her breath so as not to burst out sobbing from the terrible pain that tore at her heart when she remembered how he had pressed her to his chest when he left the house.

"At least you survive, my dear," he had whispered in her ear, before firmly closing the door behind him. He never came back.

Anatolia returned to Maran seven long years later, by which time the family taking care of her had managed to squander all her mother's jewelry, leaving her with only a cameo. The piece was light pink tinged with beige, and showed an elegantly carved young woman sitting half-turned on a tiny bench. Sheltered by the canopy of a willow tree, she peered out at someone in the distance. Anatolia had learned a lot during her years in the valley, first and foremost reading, writing, and arithmetic, though she hadn't been enrolled at school because there had not been sufficient funds for her education. Her distant uncle's wife, however, had taught Anatolia everything she knew. She was probably less the mistress of the house than an unlucky woman in a servant's role who had no rights and was forced to tolerate the endless drunken escapades of her husband and sons throughout her life. She never hurt Anatolia and was very affectionate and attentive with her, protecting her from her rude and boorish cousins. She sent nineteen-year-old Anatolia back to Maran in the postal van just before her own demise, a long, agonizing death from some sort of mysterious illness that slowly but steadily destroyed her health.

By that time, Anatolia had grown into a nice-looking young woman with the dark, blue-tinged eyes and olive skin of her grandfather and her mother's long curls. By now, her hair reached the middle of her calves and looked unexpectedly flaxen, with a hint of honey. She braided it into a magnificent plait, arranging it in a tight knot at the nape of her neck, and she walked like Voske, with her head slightly cast back. When Yasaman's old mother saw her after so many years apart, she gasped and clutched at her heart.

"How you resemble both of your parents, girl, it's as if you've merged their unfortunate souls into your own!"

Anatolia was indescribably happy that the neighbors had survived the famine. Yasaman, who was twenty-two years older than Anatolia and already nannying her first grandchild by that time, took it upon herself, along with her husband, Ovanes, to help Anatolia put the decrepit house in order and reclaim the kitchen garden. They reinforced the back wall with supports, replaced dry, warped window frames with new ones, and patched up the veranda's collapsed floor. Anatolia became sincerely attached to the couple over time, a fondness that was entirely mutual. Ovanes treated Anatolia, the only surviving daughter of his neighbor and friend, with fatherly concern and attention, and Yasaman became everything to her: mother, sister, friend, and a shoulder to lean on when life became completely unbearable.

Anatolia had grown unaccustomed to grueling village labor during her time in the valley, so a fair bit of time passed before she relearned how to handle the kitchen garden, cooking, and cleaning. To simplify her life, she closed off most of the rooms in the house, identifying her parents' bedroom, the living room, and the kitchen as her living space. But she still had to tidy the whole place from top to bottom every other week, dust the surfaces and toss the heavy sheepskin blankets, and take the pillows and rugs outside to air, come rain, shine, or crisp, fresh frost.

Little by little, she acquired a few animals. Yasaman gave her a hen that continued living in the old henhouse at first so she wouldn't be without a rooster. Later, though, after the hen hatched her eggs, Anatolia took her in, along with her peeping, swarming brood. One of the chicks, a feisty male who was cantankerous from day one, grew into a distinguished rooster, a genuine rake who heatedly mounted not only his own harem but also the feathered females of the neighboring yards. This landed him in nasty fights on more than one occasion, though he invariably emerged the victor and would later crow endlessly from his perch atop the fence, inspiring fear and trembling in his conquered adversaries. Shortly after that, Anatolia was given a goat and learned to ferment sour matzoon from milk and make proper brined brynza so the cheese was soft, tender, and milky-moist when cut. At first she baked bread under Yasaman's supervision, then she became skilled enough to handle it on her own. On Sundays, very early, she would go to the cemetery and then to the chapel to commemorate her relatives. The cemetery had doubled in size during her absence and Anatolia would walk among the silent stone crosses, finding the names of entire families carved on them.

Six months after her return she found a job at the library, where she was hired despite her lack of education simply because there was nobody else for the job. The former librarian hadn't survived the famine, and they couldn't find anyone else who'd agree to spend five days a week among the dusty bookshelves for such meager pay. There were no children left in Maran because the only child who'd survived the famine was Vano Melikants's grandson, but he was barely five, so the school and library built just before the famine were practically empty. That didn't faze Anatolia, though, since life has a way of prevailing against the odds. A new generation of children would soon be born, and everything would fall back into place.

The library seemed like paradise to her, a place where she could rest from monotonous, everyday domestic chores that had become wearisome. Anatolia meticulously washed all the shelves, rubbing them to a shine with homemade wax. She went through the library cards and rearranged the books, ignoring their classification numbers and alphabetical order. Guided exclusively by color preferences, she placed books with dark covers lower and books with light covers higher. She filled the library with sweet peas, aloe, and geraniums, using as pots some of the wide-necked clay pitchers that had been abandoned in the cellar. She brought them to Minas at his carpentry shop, requesting that he drill little holes in their bases for drainage. Minas's apprentice, a short, thickset, childless widower who had buried his whole family during the famine, immediately set his sights on Anatolia. He delivered the pitchers to the library himself and stopped by on several other occasions, allegedly to ask if she needed any help. In reality, though, he would stay at the library until late, constantly watching the flustered Anatolia. A month later he came to her house, proposing marriage. Anatolia didn't love him and knew she never would, but she agreed to marry him. There were so few single men left in the village that, quite simply, she had no other option. Those men who were still unmarried were either far too young or much too old.

The marriage turned out to be an unhappy one. Over the eighteen long years during which Anatolia lived with her husband, he never once uttered an affectionate word or treated her with any kindness. He turned out to be a surprisingly callous and indifferent person; he was awkward and unresponsive in bed, and he laughed coarsely at Anatolia's shy requests for even a tiny bit more tenderness. He often took her by force, after which she would lie there smelling of his sweat and unwashed flesh, swallowing her tears and hating herself with all her soul. Her only dream was to give birth to children and devote herself to their upbringing, but that was not to be: she never did manage to become pregnant. At first, her husband simply accused her of being infertile, but he grew gloomier and less tolerant over the years, lashing out brutally as if Anatolia were deliberately trying to irritate him with her meek silence. Toward the end, he developed the habit of drinking heavily and thrashing her, throwing her to the floor and dragging her around the house by her braids with the aim of covering every single room. After this, he would lock her in the slightly damp housekeeping room until morning. He became ever more merciless and would probably have killed her at some point if not for his fear of the colossal Ovanes. After he noticed a bruise on Anatolia's cheekbone, Ovanes had gone straight to the workshop, pulled Anatolia's husband out from behind the carpenter's bench, dragged him to the yard by the scruff of his neck, and hurled him onto a tall woodpile. Ovanes glared as he left:

"If you raise a hand against her again I'll kill you, no questions asked. Is that clear?"

Ovanes's intercession saved Anatolia's life, but it also turned each day into an unbearable agony, for now her husband found wily new ways of driving her to despair in total silence. He twisted her arms, he beat her on her joints so that there wouldn't be any marks, he exasperated her with his carping, and he openly mocked her. Anatolia accepted all of this in silence and didn't complain, because she didn't want to cause any trouble and was afraid that Ovanes would keep his word by killing her disaster of a husband.

Reading was her sole outlet during those grim, colorless days. In the early years, when the library always seemed to be empty, she indulged in her favorite activity for entire workdays. Little by little, thanks to intuition and innate taste, she learned to distinguish good literature from bad and fell in love with Russian and French classics, though she came to hate Count Tolstoy, unequivocally and forever, as soon as she finished *Anna Karenina*. After assessing the intolerable heartlessness and arrogance in his treatment of his heroines, she classified Count Tolstoy with other petty tyrants and despots, and stored his fat tomes out of sight to make herself feel better. Her husband's taunting had driven her to the brink of despair, so she had no intention of letting that sort of injustice go unpunished in the pages of a book as well.

When she wasn't reading, Anatolia worked on making the library cozier and prettier. She hung the windows with light calico curtains sewn to half-length so as not to deprive the plants of sunlight; she lugged a woven wool rug from home and spread it on the floor below a wall covered with portraits of writers; and she decorated uncomfortable seats on wooden benches with cheerful little cushions she had made from assorted scraps of brightly colored fabric.

The library was now reminiscent of a reading room in a well-tended conservatory. All the windowsills and aisles between the shelves were filled with pitchers and pots containing plants that Anatolia had brought from an old estate that was now boarded up. There were eight heavy antique-style flowerpots in which she cultivated tea roses, fragrant goat-leaf honeysuckle, and mountain lilies. The roses bloomed inopportunely and their aroma lured bees through the little open windows so that they soon found their way to the plants after briefly getting lost in the folds of the curtains. They collected flower pollen and flew back out, only to return again. One autumn the bittersweet scent of honeysuckle fruit enticed an entire swarm of bees to fly through the window and make their way behind a ceiling beam, where they apparently intended to stay forever, and so Anatolia had to run around the entire village in search of the household whose bees had escaped the hive. A large anthill developed in the basement, too, resulting in crooked ant paths that meandered and stretched along the planks of the wooden floor toward the entrance and disappeared outside the threshold. Swallows plastered their nests all along the perimeter of the roof's cornice and flew in year in, year out, to hatch their nestlings. Right after the birds flew away in autumn, Anatolia had to use a broom wrapped in rags to wash droppings and other gunk from the outer walls. Once she discovered a sparrow nest in the stovepipe and was forced to wait for the nestlings to hatch, gain strength, and fly away. Only then did she carefully carry the nest to a tree. Otherwise she might have frightened the parents so that they abandoned their home forever, leaving their incompletely incubated eggs to the whims of fate.

Over time the library became a sort of Babylon, surrounded as it was by all manner of living creatures: any kind of baby bird or little bug would find shelter there, and they seemed to multiply with amazing zeal. Anatolia left saucers of sugar water on the windowsills for butterflies and ladybugs, crafted several feeders for birds, and planted a small kitchen garden in the yard, much to the delight of the ants. And that was how she spent her days: childless and unhappy, rustling the pages of favorite books that smelled of leather bindings, surrounded by innocent creatures at work, and tormented in her father's home by the hatred of her spouse.

Sometime later, the school managed to scrape together an elementary class, and young visitors finally started to appear at the library. All the maternal love Anatolia had accumulated rained down on them. She always kept a little dish of dried fruits and homemade cookies on the table next to the wooden tray with library cards. If the children asked for something to drink, she poured tea or juice for them and then entertained them with stories she had made up or had come across in her reading. Adults rarely dropped in because they had other things to do, but the children, who were funny, curious, and wide-eyed, could spend endless hours there. It was touching to see their caution as they wandered among the assorted flowerpots, striving to sniff every little bloom, observed the flight of the bees, added sugar water to saucers, read, did homework, and constantly gushed with numerous questions that kept them preoccupied. They unfailingly offered a cheek for a kiss when they left. Anatolia sincerely believed the children's love was nothing less than heaven's consolation for her own childlessness.

She resigned herself to her fate by making do with the small pleasures in her life.

After steadily falling apart over the course of eighteen long years, her agonizingly painful personal life ended in major tragedy. Embittered by everyone's universally affectionate treatment of Anatolia, one day her husband decided to taint her life for good by demanding she resign from her job. Anatolia usually kept silent, so she surprised even herself by firmly refusing. And when her husband put up his fist, as he usually did, she threatened to complain to Ovanes.

"Let him teach you a lesson," she blurted out in anger. "And if that doesn't do the trick, I'll divorce you. Mark my words, you will not raise a hand against me in my father's house!"

Her husband narrowed his eyes menacingly and kept quiet. He waited for her to leave for work and then he unleashed his anger on Anatolia's house: he knocked off the doors in all the rooms and smashed furniture with an axe, not even sparing Anatolia's most treasured and fiercely guarded possession, the trunk where her deceased sisters' little shoes, dresses, and toys were carefully interlaid with dried lavender and mint leaves.

Yasaman heard the ruckus but was fearful of going into the house herself, so she sent one of her grandsons to the library for Anatolia while she ran to the other end of the village to find her husband. When Ovanes arrived, panting, Anatolia was lying unconscious on the room floor, beaten nearly to death. Two deep scars from axe blows gaped in the smooth surface of the oval table. Her husband had turned brutal: he had laid her flat on the tabletop, chopped off her lovely honeyed braids at the roots and shouted, "You'll be done for without your hair," into her face with a triumphant, malicious pleasure. After that he had run from the house, taking her meager savings with him. Pursuing him yielded nothing since he had managed to escape down to the valley in a postal van, and from there he disappeared without a trace, never to be heard from again.

Yasaman nursed her friend with prayers and curative herbal infusions. The village was shaken by what had happened and also transfixed in alarmed expectation, since everyone remembered the curse that Tatevik had sent down on the family of Anatolia's parents, Voske Agulisants and Kapiton Sevoyants. To widespread relief, however, Anatolia was quickly on the mend and soon returned to work. Her body continued to ache for a long time, especially when the weather changed. The punch to the head had taken its toll on her vision, so she had to go to the valley to order glasses for herself, but she didn't complain. She even looked a little happier, since she had finally been freed from the oppressive fear that had haunted her during all her years of marriage.

Old man Minas, who had been waiting for her to recover, stopped by her house and groaned with shame as he apologized for his good-for-nothing assistant and offered to repair all the ruined furniture, but Anatolia refused to restore anything. She brought the debris out to the yard a little at a time and burned it to ashes so the only thing left was the oval table made from bog oak, with marks from the axe's blows. Ovanes hauled over a wardrobe for her, Valinka Eibogants let her have a bed and a daybed, and Magtakhine Yakulichants brought a wooden storage chest. Bit by bit, Minas fixed the interior doors and repainted the floorboards. Not a trace of the home's luxurious look remained but Anatolia had always been content with very little, so the sparse furnishings didn't dishearten her. She was indescribably joyful that her photograph album had miraculously escaped destruction – she had recently taken it to work to restore the spine and had saved it by forgetting it there on the table.

Five years remained until the war, which had been swirling over the valley like an unavoidable haze, and Anatolia lived those years in placid, blessed peace. She spent her days at the library, her evenings either at home or at Yasaman's, and on the weekends she called on relatives at the cemetery, where the weeping willow on her father's grave had grown, spreading its long thin branches over the stone crosses and rustling its silvery-green leaves in unending prayer. When the weather allowed, Anatolia would settle in among the gravestones until late, until the lilac sunset. Sometimes she fell asleep with her head leaning against the cool stone cross. Her mother and father lay to the left, her sisters and Babo Maneh to the right. And Anatolia would sit, embracing her knees and telling them happy stories: how, thank God, more and more children were being born each year, about tea roses whose aroma lured a whole hive of bees, and about ant paths that stretched out from under the floor, toward the library threshold, like tiny stitches.

And that was how she aged, slowly and steadily, alone but contented, surrounded by ghosts dear to her heart. Yasaman, who was disturbed by her friend's solitude, hinted several times that it wouldn't be so bad for her to marry again, but Anatolia always shook her head in disagreement, saying that it was too late and pointless anyway. "Was there anything good," she would say, "in my first husband that would lead me to expect anything good from a second?"

The war arrived the year she turned forty-two. First, vague news started coming from the valley about fire exchanged on the eastern borders, then Ovanes, who scrupulously read the press, sounded the alarm. Judging from urgent reports about battles, what was happening on the borders – first the eastern, then the southwestern – was unspeakably awful. News about the declaration of general mobilization arrived that winter. A month later, all Maran's men capable of holding a weapon in their hands were drafted for the front. And then war came to the valley. It swept in like a fanged whirlwind that pulled buildings and people into its horrendous maelstrom. The only road leading to Maran, which snaked along the slope of Manish-kar, was covered in ruts, the vestiges of mortar shelling. The village was plunged into pitch-black darkness, hunger, and cold for long years. Bombing broke off electrical power lines and knocked out windowpanes so people had to stretch plastic film over the frames because there was nowhere to buy new glass. And what was the point of putting it in anyway if the next shelling would inevitably turn it into a pile of shards? The bombing became particularly merciless during the sowing season, intentionally not allowing work in the fields; meager harvests from kitchen gardens didn't last long. The forest teemed with enemy scouts who spared nobody, not even women or the elderly, and there was nowhere to find firewood to heat the stove and at least shake off the excruciating cold. People first had to use wooden fence pickets as kindling, then attic roofs and sheds, and they later began taking apart verandas.

The first winter turned out to be especially agonizing: Anatolia had to move into the kitchen to live closer to the stove. Being in the other unheated rooms had become impossible, because the plastic-covered windows didn't protect from the damp or cold and a thick layer of frost coated the walls and ceilings, thawing a little when it warmed slightly, then flowing into little puddles on the furniture, blankets, and rugs, ruining them beyond repair. Scanty supplies of kerosene for lamps quickly ran dry, and candles were gone soon after. The school closed after the cold set in and the library was deserted too. Anatolia loaded a cart with books she was determined to reread over the winter, adding containers and flowerpots with plants to bring home into the warmth as well. She partitioned off a corner of the kitchen, covered the floor with straw, and relocated the pregnant goat there; the goat bore two kids toward the end of January. And so Anatolia spent the interminably long and cold winter by the stove, surrounded by plants, favorite books, and faintly bleating goat kids. She had to bathe in a wooden trough, washing one part of her body at a time: first her head, then the upper part of her torso, then the lower. Out of shyness, she turned her back to the goats when she washed. The winter was snowy, so there was no need to go to the spring for water. Anatolia scooped snow into pails, leaving some of it to stand overnight for drinking and cooking, and heating the rest on the stove for laundry and dishwashing. On Thursdays and Fridays she had to carry the used water out to the veranda, where it cooled so it could be poured out later. As they had through the ages, the Maranians faithfully heeded the superstition that hot water not be poured on the ground on Thursdays or Fridays, so as not to scald Christ's feet.

The winter days were as much alike as the translucent stones on Babo Maneh's rosary, something Anatolia never parted with. In the mornings she made her way out to the chicken coop to scatter grain for the birds and collect eggs, then she fed the goats, tidied up the kitchen, and cooked something quick; later she would read for the duration of a brief and overcast afternoon. When the hopelessly dark night fell, she would doze on the daybed wrapped in several blankets, or simply lie there, watching as the glow of the coals faded in the small opening of the woodstove door. The album with photographs of her loved ones was always at hand and she would page through it silently, wiping tears with the edge of her sleeve. There was nothing to tell them and she didn't want to annoy anyone by complaining.

Spring came a bit later than usual, so only toward the middle of March did Maran, haggard from the cold and darkness, finally breathe a sigh of relief, start unbolting squeaky doors and gates, and throw windows open to let sunlight into homes. Joy that the unrelentingly icy winter had finally passed was so great that it eclipsed the fear of death. The Maranians had long grown accustomed to the shelling and thus paid it no attention when they went about their endless lists of daily tasks. Nobody could have anticipated how much damage would be caused by the moisture and cold that had penetrated their homes. Houses that had grown damp over the winter needed to be well aired and dried in order to defeat the ubiquitous mildew that had contrived to slip into all the linen trunks and chiffoniers. Walls, floors, and furniture needed to be treated with a solution of alum and vitriol, and there was a whole month's worth of laundering to do because everything had to be rewashed, starting with bedding and clothing and ending with rugs and carpets. There was so much work that only toward the end of April, after the bombing had abated a little and classes resumed at the school, was Anatolia able to make her way to the library.

Anatolia started rubbing her cheek along the pillow and sighed bitterly, driving off the tears that had sprung up. Many years had passed since that day, but she had tremendous trouble coping with her deep heartache whenever she recalled the disastrous condition the library was in. The damp that had crept through the plastic on the windows had even reached the uppermost shelves, and there were horrendous mildew spots covering leather bindings and irreparably yellowed, warped pages.

"Oh Lord," Anatolia cried in dismay as she made the rounds of one shelf after another, all filled with book corpses. "What have I done? Why did I not protect them?"

When the school principal dropped by the library, she discovered Anatolia sitting on the threshold clutching her head in her hands and rocking back and forth in a rhythmic motion, choking on her sobs like an inconsolable child. The principal, a large elderly woman with a heavy masculine jaw and powerful shoulders, silently heard out Anatolia's rambling explanations then walked around the library, pulling out several books at random, leafing through them, and shaking her head. She returned them to their places, sniffed her fingers, and knitted her brow. Then she pulled out a handkerchief and fastidiously wiped her hands.

"What on earth could you have done, Anatolia? They would have been lost anyway."

"But how can that be? How can it? The old librarian protected them during the famine, but I couldn't keep them safe during the war."

"The windows were intact back then, but now... Who could have predicted that things would turn out like this!"

Anatolia launched a futile campaign to save the books. She brought in a length of clothesline and strung it up to make about ten rows in the yard. She hung it from end to end with books, in the hope that the sun and wind would pull out the moisture and then, just maybe, they could somehow be restored. From a distance it looked as if a flock of multicolored birds had soared up over the library yard only to become suspended in midair, cheerlessly lowering their useless wings. Anatolia walked between the rows, flipping the pages. She spent the night at the library, in case of rain. On the second day, the books withered and began shedding their pages like autumn leaves. Anatolia gathered them up, cast them in a heap behind the fence, locked the library, and never returned.

The war receded after another seven difficult years, taking the younger generation with it. Some perished, but others left for calmer, more prosperous places so that they could save their families. By the time Anatolia turned fifty-eight, the only villagers left in Maran were old people who didn't want to leave the land where their ancestors lay. Anatolia was the village's youngest resident. Although she was young enough to be Yasaman's daughter, she didn't look any different from her neighbor. She went around like all the other old women, wearing long woolen dresses, tying on a pinafore, and gathering her hair under a kerchief that she pulled into an intricate knot at the nape of her neck. At her tightly fastened collar she always wore the same cameo, the only remaining piece of jewelry from her mother. None of the Maranians entertained hope that life would ever change for the better. The village was meekly living out its last years as if condemned, Anatolia along with it.

A balmy, southern night had spread outside. It crossed the windowsill as shy moonbeams and it told of the world's dreams through the tender chirring of crickets. Anatolia lay on the pillows, clasping the album with photographs of her loved ones to her chest, and wept.

Chapter Two

Ovanes Shalvarants mercilessly clanked his fork as he whipped egg yolks and sugar into a fluffy froth. Every morning, no matter the season, circumstances, or even the state of his health, he breakfasted on his favorite treat and then brewed himself some strong tea with thyme, rolled a cigarette, and enjoyed smoking it while he watched aromatic hot steam curl over his heavy cup.

He had to economize with his cigarette paper. Before the war, there had always been plenty of asinine newspapers in the valley, so this was a new occurrence. Five days a week, the postal van had wheeled its way up the slope of Manish-kar with a strained snort, carrying whole stacks of newspapers smelling of damp printer's ink. Ovanes had made sure to glance at every page. Each and every headline was loud but the content was inane, reinforcing his opinion that most of these papers weren't worth the paper they were printed on.

"It's better to think a hundred times and then speak once than to circulate all this blather unthinkingly," Ovanes would grumble in annoyance as he rustled the pages.

"Maybe they thought a hundred times before printing?" Yasaman would argue.

"If they thought about each word a hundred times, the paper wouldn't come out more than once a month. Could anybody really think up so many smart things in one day?"

"I suppose not."

"Well, that's what I'm saying!"

A sheet of newspaper devoid of content didn't affect the flavor of the tobacco, though, so Ovanes faithfully continued subscribing to the papers. Unfortunately, the postal van came up the slope of Manish-kar ever less frequently after the war started, and eventually stopped completely because there were major disruptions in the valley's fuel supply, which was reserved for the most extreme and urgent needs.

The problem with paper began when the postal service was canceled. Villagers found ways around it as best they could. Old newspapers were put to use first, then people took the ruined books that the despairing Anatolia Sevoyants had once thrown in a heap behind the library fence. The old villagers silently peeled apart mildewed volumes of Shakespeare, Chekhov, Dostoyevsky, Faulkner, and Balzac that smelled of damp and dreary silence. The thickest book covers became trivets that they placed under hot dishes, and they used the ruined pages for day-to-day household tasks like starting fires. Cigarettes made with that paper tasted bitter, fumed, and kept going out. Ovanes Shalvarants squinted and cursed, relighting constantly using smoldering embers that he had to take out of the woodstove every time, burning himself – there weren't enough matches in the village either, so people rationed them out.

For eight long, unbearable years, the war reaped a harvest of restless souls around the world, but one day it sputtered out and retreated, howling and limping and licking its bloody paws. There still wasn't enough fuel, but little by little life began turning itself around and reverted to its normal course, albeit painfully slowly. Those changes didn't touch Maran, though, since for some reason nobody had any intention whatsoever of remembering the village. The only vehicle that came up the mountainside was the ambulance, but summoning it required sending an express telegram from the telegraph office because Maran had no other communication with the outside world. People in the valley had obviously already waved off the handful of stubborn old people who back in the day had refused to come down to the lowlands from the top of Manish-kar.

It was Mamikon, the postman, who now helped out with paper. Once every two weeks (even if there weren't letters, which were by now an extreme rarity), his shoulder bag contained stacks of unwanted advertising flyers that had flooded the valley. He left them at the post office, where telegraphist Satenik divided the flyers into twenty-three even portions, one for each inhabited home in the village, and set them on the counter by the window. People picked up the paper by evening.

Ovanes would study a flyer carefully before rolling a new portion of tobacco into the advertising. Judging from the content, intelligent thinking was not on the rise among the valley's residents. Quite the opposite, in fact. If these flyers were anything to go by, all they were doing now was consulting witches who would enchant people into falling in love, visiting banks to borrow money on credit – money they then used to buy unnecessary junk – and bringing pets to crazily expensive animal beauty salons for grooming.

"When God wants to punish mankind, the first thing He does is take away their intelligence," said Ovanes, shaking his head and taking a drag of bitter tobacco smoke.

He grew his own tobacco on an abandoned plot of land that had once belonged to his brother. This brother had died long ago and his children had dispersed around the world. His kitchen garden had quickly become overgrown with tall weeds and grass due to the lack of attention. Ovanes decided to plant the plot with tobacco because it was good for the land; plus, to Yasaman's joy, it freed up part of her kitchen garden for potatoes. Ovanes designated the veranda for drying: he pounded in slate nails at both ends, bending the heads to make them into hooks. He gathered the tobacco leaves as they matured – at night, of course, so there was as little moisture in the plants as possible. Using a steel needle, he strung the leaves on a cord that he stretched onto portable frames, which he then carried off to a dark corner of the house where the leaves could wilt for a while. Later he would bring the frames out to the sunny veranda, pull the cords with the yellowed leaves over the hooks, and leave them until they had dried out completely.

The tobacco turned out to be excellent: it was aromatic, mellow, and only moderately bitter. On Saturdays, when a small bazaar assembled on the village meidan, Ovanes would lay the dry tobacco leaves in a woven basket, take a backgammon set, and go to trade. Yasaman would stride primly alongside him, small and nimble, wearing her fancy kerchief and silk pinafore for going out and about. She always put on that pinafore for church, and each Saturday and Sunday. She wore it on Saturdays for the meidan, on Sundays for the chapel, plus for occasional (once a month) matins when the visiting priest, Father Azaria, officiated.

On Saturdays, weather permitting, the entire village gathered on the meidan. Everyone brought their own products: seasonal vegetables, fruits, and herbs; cheese, butter, quark, and sour cream; and ham, sun-dried meats with spices, and simple baked goods. They practiced barter, only rarely using money. You might receive a knife for ten hen's eggs; a pair of peasant shoes was exchanged for one *grvankan* (nearly half a kilo) of brined sheep's brynza or a smaller portion of goat's cheese; a pitcher of clarified butter went for two pitchers of flower honey; and four *grvankan*s of sheep brynza paid for the wool of one ewe.

In the past, when farms had been large and the number of residential households in the village numbered five hundred, you couldn't jostle your way through the meidan. The stands were weighed down with every possible kind of victual, the dairy row came after the fruit, and there was such a hubbub you practically had to cover your ears. Right behind the vegetable stalls, on the far side of the square, there stood a cattle yard where the Maranians' own strict barter rules, which their distant ancestors had instituted, reigned. There people gave a horse for a cow, traded a year-old steer for two ewes, and you could receive one ewe and ram for a pig, three goats for a heifer, or an ox for a calving cow.

When bazaar day was nearing, a long caravan of gypsy wagons would wend its way up Manish-kar's slope. The gypsies pitched their bright tents outside the village's limits and came to the meidan as a loud, colorful crowd, bargaining with reckless abandon and going out of their way to steal what they could, though if you were to catch them red-handed they would just laugh and pay what they owed in gold coins; later, they would disperse for home to read cards and beg for unwanted old items. After finishing their trading, the gypsies would depart by evening, leaving behind the smoky smell of campfires and a distant echo of strumming guitars.

A traveling circus came for big holidays: the summoning call of a zurna shattered the air, a cable was stretched over the meidan, and tightrope walkers were flung into the air to balance at such heights that it took your breath away. After tossing the poles aside, the acrobats would turn a somersault, never once slipping up as they landed the narrow soles of their feet on a wriggling rope that tried as hard as it could to slip out from underneath them.

Below, on faded little rugs spread across the dust, there sat conjurers with dark faces and yellow eyes who blew into reed pungi that elicited entrancing, drawn-out sounds. Charmed snakes swayed in a rhythmic dance that inspired pure horror in spectators. Saleswomen of Eastern sweets wandered among them, their long skirts sweeping up discarded husks as they offered to sell people dates and pastries with cashews or pistachios, which were quite a rarity for those latitudes.

These were just apocryphal tales from the old days, though: now, the village clung onto Manish-kar's shoulder like a burdensome weight, pointless and forgotten by everyone. The meidan had shrunk to the size of a thimble where there were several meager stalls, the regular clicking of dice, and days passed in leisurely conversations and reminiscences. Toward evening, the old people scattered for home without selling anything, each carrying away their goods because when all the items were identical, exchanging them wasn't much use to anyone. Only Vasily Kudamants and Ovanes Shalvarants turned a profit: Vasily, the village blacksmith, could sharpen dulled garden implements or exchange them, with an additional payment, for something new, and Ovanes could fill your tobacco pouch.

In addition to the Saturday bazaar, one could also make purchases at Mukuch Nemetsants's small shop. Mukuch harnessed his cart twice a week and headed to the valley, bringing back a little of everything: sugar, salt, rice, beans, matches, soap, tinned fish, a few pieces of clothing, and shoes to order, with an agreement to return them if the size wasn't right. He helped out in particular with drugstore goods like bandages, cotton wool, iodine, green antiseptic, and potassium permanganate.

Illnesses were treated in the village with remedies and decoctions prepared by Yasaman Shlapkants. The old people regarded ordinary medicines warily and with obvious disapproval.

Yasaman pottered around with her decoctions every day, strictly before sunrise or after sunset. While his wife brewed up medicinal herbs in the cellar early in the morning, Ovanes beat two egg yolks with a few tablespoons of sugar to create a thick froth, steeped some strong tea, and then smoked through the wide-open kitchen window, regarding pale shreds of transparent sky entangled in mulberry branches.

"Ahh!" he would exclaim in satisfaction along with each swallow of tea. Then, bent at the waist, he would lean out the window and call to his wife:

"Shlapkants! Hey, Shlapkants! You hear me talking to you? Yasaman Shlapkants!"

"What do you want, Ovanes Shalvarants?" Yasaman would say, irritated.

Ovanes would laugh.

They were the village's most amusing couple. Both Yasaman's and Ovanes's surnames were derived from nicknames, each rooted in words for different items of clothing. Every family in Maran had its own nickname. These were most often light-hearted and witty, sometimes ironic, but occasionally very hurtful. They would come from the distinguishing feature of some ancestor, and whether this quirk was an asset or a rather unfortunate trait, the nickname was passed on to their descendants as the family name.

During Yasaman's great-grandfather's youth, for example, he visited his cousin, a leading actor at a long-established theater in the valley. The cousin brought him to shows, introduced him to the high life, and taught him how to dress. One time the great-grandfather came home from the valley in headgear that was singular or even provocative. At least that was how other Maranians saw it. When answering questions about what he was wearing, the great-grandfather defiantly repeated, "Shlapka", mangling the Russian word *shlyapka*, a type of hat. For that they nicknamed him Shlapka, and his descendants became Shlapkants.

The story of the Shalvarants nickname was completely different. Ovanes's grandfather prepared himself for the world war as if it were a holiday: he curled his mustache, pulled his fluffy fur hat down over his forehead, crisscrossed a bandolier around himself, and put on very expensive new trousers. However, he came under fire before he even made it to his regiment, and took a shrapnel wound to his leg, below the knee. The injury turned out to be so serious that they had to amputate part of his foot and send him home, demobilized, after his treatment. For some reason, when Ovanes's grandfather grieved at the infirmary it had been for the new trousers he had needed to throw away, rather than for his mutilated foot. "Shalvars, shalvars," he would say, complaining to the sisters of mercy and the doctors about his trousers. And for this he was nicknamed Shalvar and all his descendants became Shalvarants.

People joked in the village that Yasaman and Ovanes were a perfect match: they both belonged in a wardrobe.

Ovanes loved gently poking fun at his wife and often simply called her Shlapkants instead of using her first name. Yasaman, of course, returned the favor by immediately reminding her husband of his good-for-nothing grandfather who had managed to come back from the war an invalid without having spent a single minute on the battlefield.

And so today, after exchanging their ritual pleasantries, Ovanes finished smoking his hand-rolled cigarette and was about to step away from the window when the gate suddenly slammed. Ovanes craned his neck and peered out at their early guest. Vasily, the blacksmith, a tall, sturdy man with thick bushy brows and big eyes the color of cooled ashes, was walking toward the house with a scythe hoisted on his shoulder. He looked much younger than his sixty-seven years: he was gray-haired and in good shape, with powerful shoulders and huge overpowering fists. One time, back in the days of his youth, he had even managed to kill Mukuch Nemetsants's bull on a dare. Mukuch later cursed when he had to put all the animal's meat to use for stew. He hadn't had the nerve to ask Vasily for money; and what was the point of asking anyway when he, a brainless fool frothing at the mouth, had brought it upon himself by asking Vasily to prove that he could fell the bull by punching it.

"Want me to show you?" Vasily had smirked.

"I do!"

Vasily took off his vest and rolled the sleeves of his short caftan above his elbows, then went below an overhang where the huge blue-black bull was firmly tied to a stake driven into the ground, snorting and shaking his large head and formidably prominent brow.

"You won't regret it?" fellow villagers started whispering behind Mukuch.

Mukuch groaned disdainfully instead of answering. Vasily smirked again, raised his fist over the bull and knocked him to the ground with a precise strike to the back of the head. After that incident, none of the village men dared pick a fight with Vasily, avoiding even the pettiest of squabbles. Vasily was a man of few words, someone who was always quiet until spoken to and who knew how to win people's unquestioning respect through his formidable appearance alone.

"Even his eyebrows drip with snake venom!" the Maranians would say about people like that, clicking their tongues in awed respect.

Vasily took the deferent attitude of his fellow villagers with a grain of salt; being a modest person by nature, though, he didn't show it. Although he was sullen, sometimes even rude and intractable, his lack of polish didn't scare off clients. He had a reputation for being an outstanding blacksmith and for having a conscience, too, so if a customer couldn't pay, Vasily agreed to wait as long as necessary. Despite the whole village being in debt to him, he didn't remind anyone about the money. His smithy had stood idle after the war and there was triflingly little work but he didn't grumble, answering his wife's endless complaints about their dwindling household funds by saying "We're in the same boat as everybody else," something that invariably drove her out of her mind. Magtakhine Yakulichants, with whom Vasily had lived for nearly half a century, had been an exacting, hardworking woman, though she was excessively talkative. Once she got going, she could spew words for all eternity, pausing only momentarily to come up for air. Vasily would withstand this torrent of words for as long as possible, but eventually he would take her by the elbow, lead her to a distant room, and bolt her in, with the words, "Let me know when you're all talked out!"

Incensed by her husband's brazen treatment, Magtakhine would take to complaining loudly (crucially, at a volume that Vasily would still be able to hear) about her wretched fate and her father and mother, who had given her in marriage to this uncouth oaf just to be rid of her, though they had placed the rest of their daughters in decent families, especially the youngest, their darling Shushanik – for whom, by the way, they had amassed the richest dowry, consisting of three rugs, two trunks of linens, a plot of fertile land, three cows, a sow, and twenty laying hens, plus so much gold that she would have broken her pathetic spine if she'd have put it all on at once. But Magtakhine had been allotted a dowry half the size, and had to make do with silver jewelry instead of gold, though time put everything in its proper place and the other children (obviously as punishment for their parents' unjust treatment of her) were the first to leave the earth: the older sisters didn't survive the famine, the only brother died from a lightning strike, and even their beloved Shushanik died from a severe attack of chest pains, choking on her own vomit; so the parents had to depend on Magtakhine until the end of her days. And she, of course, didn't let them down; she was always with them, devoted and loving, looking after and protecting them, taking out the chamber pot for her father when his legs gave way and applying hot vinegar compresses to the soles of her mother's feet to soothe the never-ending migraine attacks that had become more frequent after Shushanik left the mortal world. But then her parents died, with her father being the first to go, on his daughter's sixtieth birthday, meaning she now spent every birthday at the cemetery taking care of his grave. And then her mother passed away right after her father, wearing her daughter's remaining nerves thin by the end, because in her final days she had lost her mind for good and did her business wherever and whenever she pleased and then used the material to draw all over the walls and floors, meaning she had to be locked in a room so she wouldn't spread her artwork through the whole house, meaning that when she died, Magtakhine had to remove the plaster with her own hands so she could renovate the room where the murals on those unlucky four walls were numerous, because (unlike her brains) the deceased's bowels had been working perfectly, though of course defecating is not the same as thinking with your head. But now that all her loved ones were dead, Magtakhine was left on her own (if you didn't count her dolt of a husband, with whom she couldn't exchange so much as two words), and at least it had been possible before to talk with her mother through the locked door since even if she had lost her mind she could, after all, keep up a conversation: if you said one thing to her, she'd say another. And even if her mother's words hadn't made sense, at least there had been some kind of live communication and concern, so why had this bitter destiny befallen Magtakhine, to be underappreciated by everybody, and to die unloved like some old dog that no one can bring themselves to shoot but no one quite wants to take care of. Either way it's not long for this world.

After unburdening her soul like this for a while, Magtakhine would groan, crawl out the window, and spew curses as the soles of her worn-out shoes scrabbled for the next rung down on the wooden ladder she always kept under the windowsill of the room where her husband locked her. By this time, Vasily would be sitting at the smithy whiling away a leisurely day and puffing on his pipe, reminiscing about the years when there had been so much work he couldn't straighten his back and his wife was as quiet and meek as a snowy night, because she was kept so busy with domestic chores.

Magtakhine had been sure she would outlive her husband and always asked him what she would do after he died, but things worked out the opposite in the end: she got it into her head to go outside to weed the garden when the blazing sun was at its peak, and she fell down dead there and then, struck by a brain hemorrhage. Vasily mourned her and it took an agonizingly long time to grow accustomed to the stifling quiet that spread through the house like a boggy mire. Despite her abrasive character, Magtakhine had been a good wife, and even if you couldn't say she was affectionate (affection, as it happened, had been lacking for Vasily's whole life), she was devoted, caring, and always by his side, in grief and in joy, in wealth and in poverty.

The telegraph operator, Satenik, Vasily's second cousin, had been helping him with housekeeping. She had planted the seed of an idea in his head: what did he make of Anatolia Sevoyants? The question initially went in one ear and out the other, but his cousin wouldn't let it rest. She herself was almost eighty, meaning she was here today but could be gone tomorrow, and her cousin might be a good craftsman as a blacksmith but he was like a little child with housekeeping, unable to cook or do laundry. Solitude for a man is worse than the gravest illness, and, what's more, Anatolia was still young and pretty, not to mention single and taciturn, just as he liked, so why shouldn't they get along?

"And the main thing," Satenik said, advancing her most substantial argument, "is she's a smart one, she's read so many books!"

Of course, Satenik knew how to pressure her cousin. Vasily had nurtured a tremendous respect for educated people since childhood. As an illiterate peasant – there was no school in Maran during those years and his destitute mother couldn't pay for him to study in the valley – he had gone out of his way to give his sons a good education. And he hadn't lost hope of learning to read and write. At one time there had been plans to open a night school in Maran, something that made Vasily indescribably happy, but then the famine came, wiping out half the village's population, so, unfortunately, discussions about education ceased.

War took away his younger brother and sons. Vasily's sons were drafted to the front from an educational academy so Vasily and Magtakhine hadn't even had the chance to say goodbye to them. And his brother was drafted right from the smithy. Vasily still remembered his brother's distant, childlike gaze and the raised palm of his brother's left hand, where there was a deep scar in the spot where his crooked life line bent around his thumb and stretched off to the side. The scar came from when Vasily hadn't been able to keep his grip on a mold full of molten metal and dropped it on the ground. One of the spattering drops hit his brother's palm and nearly burned all the way through. The wound had festered and bled for a long, agonizing time, and Yasaman Shlapkants used up all her liniment supplies on it. By the time the burn finally scarred over and he could again take up a forge hammer, the war had arrived.

Vasily's palm went numb whenever he recalled his brother. He grew gloomy, groaned, rubbed his hand contemplatively and tensed his jaw, blinking frequently to drive away tears. He never reminisced about his sons; he had forbidden himself ever to do so and had barely recovered from the horrendous pain of receiving the news of their deaths. He had also forbidden his wife from mentioning the boys in her endless monologues: "That way, when we die and see them again, we'll all have plenty to talk about."

Magtakhine agreed unexpectedly easily and never uttered their names around her husband. Touched by her compliance, Vasily tolerated her unending blathering for some time. Until, that is, he came home earlier than usual one day and discovered his wife standing in front of a mirror with their sons' photographs in her hands, rhythmically rocking and shifting her gaze from one photograph to the other, lamenting her fate which had seen her sons' feeble grandfather confined to a rocking chair whose seat Vasily had altered so a trapdoor could be moved to the side and a chamber pot placed underneath without lifting the old man, whose pants Magtakhine had had to resew so he could do his business without taking them off. "There's no way around it," she complained. "I can't lift him and there's nobody to lend a hand, your father takes himself off to his smithy from sunrise until sunset, and there's no help from your grandmother, all she knows is how to hang around with the neighbors and gather gossip, she's grown kind of strange, you never know with her – I hate to say it but sometimes I think she's lost her mind, the other day I found her in the cellar sitting in the corner and her eyes were almost shining at me. 'I'm waiting for it to pass,' she says, 'the wind,' and I say, 'What wind, Mama?' and she answers, 'You wouldn't understand what wind,' and I ask, 'How am I, with my simple mind, supposed to understand you, it's another matter for your beloved Shushanik,' and Mama's the one who leaps up when she hears the name of your youngest aunt, starts squealing and racing around the cellar, almost broke all the clay jugs and I somehow quieted her down, brought her inside the house, gave her mint tea to drink, and rubbed her temples with mulberry brew. And she seemed to calm down and was quiet for a month but then yesterday she started acting strange again and she went to Valinka Eibogants's, stood at the threshold, and said, 'Call for your mother, I need to talk with her,' and so Mama was planning to have a talk with Katinka Eibogants, who gave up the ghost almost half a century ago. It's a good thing Valinka wasn't offended by what she said, she knew immediately that a person wouldn't get up to mischief like that on a clear head, so she took Mama inside, sat her on the daybed, and said, 'Hold on a little bit, I'll call for my mother now,' and then she came running to me, saying, 'Anyway, Magtakhine, it seems your mother's not herself,' so

I went to Valinka's house and your grandmother was sitting on the floor surrounded by sofa cushions like she's the shah's wife. 'Serve us some halva with sesame seeds and a *grvankan* of raisins,' she said, 'and do see that the raisins don't have seeds,' and then she turned to the bare wall and started talking with it, calling it Katinka."

The next morning, seizing a moment when his wife was out in the kitchen garden, Vasily wrapped the photographs of their sons in newspaper, brought them to Satenik, and asked her to hide them somewhere Magtakhine couldn't get to them. Satenik took the parcel from him, asking only why he was acting so harshly toward his wife.

Vasily cut her off. "I'm at my wits' end because of all her complaints, and now she's laying her hands on our sons. I won't let her disturb their peace!"

Satenik walked around the house for a long time in search of a hiding place and ended up tucking the photographs away in a tin for hard candies, then storing it at the very bottom of the linen trunk, under little calico sachets of dried lavender and mothballs. After Magtakhine discovered the loss, she was careful not to make a scene with Vasily but rushed over to see her husband's cousin. Satenik mustered all her will so as not to give herself away. After much persuasion, she managed to convince her sister-in-law not to raise the subject of the missing photographs with Vasily. Magtakhine heeded her advice but harbored a tremendous grievance toward her husband, and as payback supplemented her overflowing stream of endless lamentation with new hints that it was beyond the power of even this extraordinarily soulless blockhead to erase the images of those she loved from her heart because her heart was big and bottomless, no match for the pathetic hearts of those capable (without feeling even a pang of guilt) of removing from the house the dearest thing any selfless, loving, and unfortunate mother had, has, or will have, and maybe those callous-hearted people are capable of locking up their own grief with a key, but well, she was not in a position to do that because her strength was nearing its end and her soul was like a beast that had fallen into a trap and could neither free itself nor die but only wait, humiliated, for its inevitable and awful demise. Vasily always bore her complaints in silence, frowned and groaned, went off to the smithy, sat by the cold stove until late, smoked his pipe, and constantly rubbed his left hand in a vain attempt to soothe the aching pain.

Satenik had planned to return the photographs to Vasily after Magtakhine's death but then she decided to wait a little, to let him get a grip on himself after his initial grief had faded a little. Thanks to the hard candy tin, those photographs had now safely survived cold and the invasion of mildew, and they had migrated from the linen trunk to a wooden jewelry box, where they patiently awaited the moment they would once again rest under Vasily's fatherly wing.

Meanwhile, Satenik had taken it upon herself to assume charge of her cousin's personal life. She first had a word with Yasaman Shlapkants. Yasaman was happy to have an opportunity to put an end to her girlfriend's loneliness and promised to have a chat with Anatolia. After winning Yasaman's support, Satenik worked on persuading Vasily. He waved her off at first and didn't take what she said seriously, but then he reluctantly agreed since he himself knew perfectly well that there is little on this earth more agonizing than a lonely old age.

Vasily regarded Anatolia with great respect. Several times before the war he had intended to drop by the library to plead for books to use to teach himself how to read, but he was always too shy in the end and walked straight past, because he had once seen Anatolia wind a cloth around a broom, wet it generously in a weak vinegar solution, and wash the stone wall under the swallows' nests, carefully working around the bottom of each one so as not to catch it and knock it down inadvertently. He felt conscience-stricken when he remembered himself as young, empty-headed, and capable of killing a completely innocent bull on a dare. There it is, the difference between a literate person and an illiterate person, thought Vasily, hightailing it from the library to the hot smithy: the literate one's afraid of destroying an empty nest and the illiterate one's ready to knock the breath out of an innocent beast just to prove his own wicked strength.

"She's smart and well-read, so what would she want with an ignorant dunce like me?" he said, sharing his doubts with his second cousin.

"Was her husband smart and well-read?" snorted Satenik. "That callous tyrant beat her, it was like mortal combat, and she's so literate she just took it. Look at yourself, you're a decent, hardworking, reliable person. Not once did you raise a hand to Magtakhine, though, may she rest in heaven, many men would have been sorely tempted. Literacy, Vaso-dzhan, has no place here," said Satenik, tapping a finger on her cousin's forehead. "It's here, in the heart," she said, placing her palm against his chest.

Ceding to her persuasion, Vasily waited to run out of tobacco and then prepared to visit Ovanes. He brought some smoking material and asked about Anatolia too, stammering and clearing his throat sheepishly.

Ovanes didn't let him finish. "I'd be so happy if you two were to hit it off. Yasaman does say Anatolia's not intending to marry again, but you know women. Today there's one thing on their mind, tomorrow it's the opposite. Give her time to get her head around the idea gradually. Then we'll see what happens."

From that day on, Vasily dropped in on Ovanes and Yasaman often, talking a while about this and that and playing some backgammon. He did once run into Anatolia at their house and politely said hello, but for some reason she got upset, took some salt from Yasaman, and hurried off.

"My dear, haven't you just been complaining that your scythe has gone dull? Why don't you ask Vasily to sharpen it," said Ovanes, attempting to delay her.

"There's no need, thanks, I already sharpened it," Anatolia said gently, refusing Vasily's help and heading for the door.

"Stubborn as a mule. Just like her father," said Ovanes, throwing up his hands after she had gone.

"She's her father's daughter and I'm my father's son. We'll see who gets the better of who," snorted Vasily.

On that occasion, Ovanes had slapped himself on the knee and started laughing. And now, hiding his smile in his beard, he watched Vasily carry a brand-new scythe over his shoulder. The carefully sharpened blade and handle were polished to a shine, and they glinted in the sun.

"I see you came with a little gift," Ovanes said, grinning.

Vasily walked up the steps, catching the scythe blade on a grapevine that wound around the railing and the veranda's wooden posts.

"Maybe you could leave that implement down there?" said Ovanes, unable to bear the sight of it.

Flustered, Vasily took the scythe off his shoulder and leaned it against the railing so it wouldn't fall over.

"I'm...ah, that. I'm...planning to go to Anatolia's. I made her a new scythe because the old one's dull."

"So why'd you go to the wrong house?"

"Well, I... Yesterday I stopped by around sundown and all the lights were off. I came this morning but the birds hadn't been let out of the henhouse and the yard was dry, it's obvious nobody's sprinkled water or swept up. I knocked on the door and she didn't open it."

"Well, maybe she's still sleeping."

"Maybe she is. There's something I wanted to ask, Ovanes. Maybe Yasaman can go see her, find out how she's doing."

"She's brewing up some herbs. She'll go over when she's done. But basically" – Ovanes said this significantly – "if I were you, I'd see this through to the end, since you've finally made up your mind, thank goodness."

Vasily scratched the back of his head and hoisted the scythe back onto his shoulder.

"I'll go knock again."

"At least leave the scythe. You're walking around like it's attached to you. It won't go anywhere, you can take it over later."

"No, it's better like this."

"Well, yes, courting with a tool is more fitting."

"What's that?"

"Good luck is what I'm saying. Stop by later, tell us how it went for you."

Ovanes waited for Vasily to disappear beyond the garden gate then put on his peasant shoes, tucked the laces inside so they wouldn't get tangled underfoot, and hurried off to see his wife in the cellar. As it happened, Yasaman was straining a cooled decoction through gauze into a dark glass bottle. The room smelled strongly of dried herbs and the cornelian cherry home brew she invariably used for infusing her medicinal remedies.

"Listen to this, Yasaman." Ovanes closed the door behind him with care so as not to let in sunlight that could damage the mixture.

"Who were you talking to out there?"

"Vasily. He's saying Anatolia's not opening the door for him."

"What do you mean she's not opening it?"

"Just that. She's evidently afraid of the scythe."

Yasaman froze with the strainer in her hand.

"What scythe?"

"The scythe he showed up with to visit her. He's tired of waiting for her to appreciate him for his kindness, so he came to see her with a tool. It's like he's trying to tell her that if she refuses, she'll pay for it."

Yasaman snorted and looked askance at her husband. He held a bottle up to the light and examined it closely. Then he placed it back on the shelf and groaned.

"I was planning to go water the tobacco, but now I've got to wait for Vasily to come back. I want to see how this all ends."

"I do hope he can convince her," sighed Yasaman.

Chapter Three

Each time her father bends his left leg and mows a new row of grass with a sharp, broad swing of his right arm, Anatolia can see his muscles tense under his short caftan and the pants tucked into the top of his boots. It must be uncomfortable to work in such close-fitting clothes, she thinks. It's raining, a hard rain that's also surprisingly gentle, pouring as if it's just passing through. Anatolia holds out her palms and the rain's touch feels like Grusha's breath – as a child, she had brought carrots to the calf every morning. Grusha would eat the snack and then breathe affectionately on Anatolia's palms, gazing with large dewy eyes surrounded by downy white lashes.

"Gru-u-sha," Anatolia would say, feeling emotional. "Grusha."

"Moooo," the calf would answer, its big ears quivering. "Moooo."

Anatolia takes a deep breath of damp air. She's dizzy from the tangy scent of tiny, delicately blushing apples with dark raspberry-colored seeds and little pink splotches on the cut edge; her mother used to boil those apples with honey and cinnamon to make fragrant preserves. Anatolia's older sister would grab an apple out of the bowl by its long stem, put her palm under it so as not to drip juice on the floor, and hold it out to Anatolia to eat.

It's raining enough that it seems to be washing away all her troubles. It caresses her hair, embraces her shoulders, and tickles the back of her head. Anatolia puts her face under the rain but doesn't close her eyes, so she won't lose sight of her father. She's glad he's guessed the right time to work; it's easiest of all to mow grass in wet weather.

"A-ay-rik! Father!" she calls out in a singsong voice to her father. "A-ay-rik!"

Her father doesn't hear her. He's swinging the weighty scythe evenly, with no apparent exertion, as he advances toward the edge of the field. Only a man of gigantic height and strength, someone known in Maran as an *azhdaak* (a giant, in other words) works with such large tools, whose blades are nine hands long. Kapiton Sevoyants's lineage probably really did include such huge men since, at two meters tall, he's as powerful and unbending as a cliff and has such broad shoulders that he can sit his two eldest daughters on one and Voske and Anatolia on the other, then spin them around the yard to their breathless, happy squealing, accompanied by old Babo Maneh's fearful laments: "Just don't drop them, Kapiton-dzhan, just don't drop them."

"I won't drop them," Kapiton would laugh.

The rain cascaded in a curative flow, enveloping and lulling Anatolia and pulling her by the shoulder back to a place where things were loud and uncomfortable, to where she neither wanted to turn nor return. The streams of water were becoming thicker and denser, preventing Anatolia from discerning her father; she started worrying and attempted to take a step toward him but her legs didn't respond, and the noise behind her, which had at first been barely audible, intensified, swelled, and, finally, after overcoming whatever mysterious obstacles had kept it at a distance, reached her and spun her in the vortex of a persistent, drawn-out, desperate call:

"Anatolia! Hey, Anatolia! A-na-to-li-a!"

Anatolia opened her eyes. She immediately made out the thin strand of a spiderweb hanging from a wooden ceiling beam and swinging in a draft. Babo Maneh would have set to scolding her: a good housekeeper couldn't have a spiderweb under the ceiling, a good housekeeper should run a mop wrapped in dry fabric over the upper corners of the room at least every other day, otherwise she would get a reputation in the village as a slattern.

She buried her face in her hands and sighed heavily. She still hadn't died.

Anatolia threw off the blanket and sat up with the utmost caution. The oilcloth she'd had the foresight to put underneath herself was stained almost to the edges, and her wet nightgown had ridden up. Her ears were ringing and her mouth gave off a harshly unpleasant bitterness. She winced, poured some water into a glass, and drank. The dizziness abated a little, but her lower back ached so much it was as if she had spent all of yesterday in the kitchen garden instead of in her bed. Anatolia glanced at a sunbeam that had frozen at the edge of the windowsill and wondered how she had managed to sleep until almost noon. She was planning to get up when she suddenly heard footsteps in the next room. She had just enough time to lean back on the pillows and cover herself with the blanket when a quiet knock sounded at the door.

"Anatolia? It's Vasily."

Anatolia was scared; he had probably come with bad news.

"Did something happen?" she asked.

The door creaked and opened just a tiny crack.

"I knocked and knocked but wasn't getting anywhere. I walked around the house and saw an open window. I called to you but you didn't answer. I decided to come in since, well, you never know, just in case you needed help."

Anatolia sighed. So that was whose insistent call had brought her back to life. She sat up, pulled a jacket off the back of a chair, put it on and buttoned it up all the way, and then ran a hand through her hair to tidy it. She straightened the blanket so it covered the whole sheet.

"Well, you might as well come in since you're already here."

Something started thudding around outside the door. Then the door opened all the way, letting a nicely sharpened scythe blade into the room. Dumbfounded, Anatolia watched as Vasily turned the scythe blade-side down then leaned it against the wall, trying not to hook the linen cabinet. He turned to her and gave a quick nod. "Good morning."

She nodded cautiously in response, but her bewildered gaze remained on the scythe.

"Are you sick? Maybe I should go to Yasaman for a remedy?" Vasily asked.

Anatolia shook her head and slowly shifted her gaze to her guest's feet. He had taken off his shoes when he came into the house and was now standing before her in unmatched socks: one was brown and the other was multicolored, with dark blue, yellow, and green stripes. Vasily followed her gaze and became thoroughly bewildered. "I put on the first ones that came to hand," he muttered, then shifted from one foot to the other for a bit, confused. He attempted to put his massive hands in his pants pockets but failed so hid them behind his back instead. He scowled.

"Then I'll be on my way?"

"So why did you come over?" Anatolia finally regained the ability to speak.

"I brought you the scythe as a gift," Vasily grunted, flustered. Then, annoyed at his own indecisiveness, he added angrily, "Well that, and I wanted to ask you to marry me."

Anatolia rolled her eyes. Vasily had been walking around and around in circles, either looking in on Ovanes, allegedly to play backgammon, or to incite Yasaman to chat with Anatolia. And now he had shown up on his own, dragging over a new scythe for some inexplicable reason. He was standing as if somebody had sprinkled ash on his tail, eager to shake it off but not wanting to make a mess.

Every Maranian knew the ins and outs of their fellow villagers – they were in plain view, with all their misfortunes, hurts, illnesses, and rare, but very long-awaited, joys. Relationships between people in the village were sympathetic and congenial but implied nothing beyond neighborliness. Anatolia couldn't figure out why on earth Vasily had taken it into his head to ruin that measured way of life. His entire adult life – from the autumn morning she returned to her father's home as a nineteen-year-old (Vasily's firstborn had come into the world that same day) until the moment Magtakhine died, leaving him a lonely widower – had flowed past before her eyes. She had never expressed anything toward him beyond a friendly disposition, and had no intention of joining their lives together. But she also felt uneasy about upsetting him: there he was, glowering, gazing out from under his brow with big, slightly prominent eyes the color of cooled cinders, and he was ominously silent.

Anatolia's long silence made Vasily anxious and he didn't shift his tense gaze from her blank face, not even as he was thinking that if she refused him, he would leave right away, not delaying things, and go see his cousin at the telegraph office and pull out her spinal cord so she wouldn't egg him on to another folly such as this again. He had squeaked by these last three years as a widower and he would keep on squeaking by. People lived out their single years crippled and didn't complain. And what did he have to grumble about anyway? He still had both his arms and legs, and his brain wasn't in bad shape either; he still had his wits about him.

There was no point dragging out her answer. Vasily was turning as dark as a storm cloud before Anatolia's eyes, so she made up her mind. She wouldn't be around long anyway, so at least let him not hold a grudge against her for refusing him. Through sheer willpower, she smiled briefly and nodded.

"Meaning yes?" Vasily was stupefied.

"Yes," was Anatolia's simple response.

Vasily was confused. He had given careful thought to his various escape routes in the event of a rejection, but for some reason he hadn't considered how to react to a positive answer. Which was why he was now standing, gasping for air as if he had been struck by lightning.

"Looks like you've changed your mind?" Anatolia started laughing.

"Of course not!" Vasily said, finally coming back to life. He cleared his throat in embarrassment and hurried for the door. "I'm going to the telegraph office, I'll get Satenik."

"Why?"

"As a matchmaker. So everything's according to rank and tradition."

"You and I aren't twenty," Anatolia said. "Let's get by informally."

"Well, if it's informal, then why drag it out?" said Vasily, cheering up. "Pack your things, you'll move in with me."

"No. We'll live in my house. That's how I want it."

"Whatever you say. Then I'll go and pack my things. I'll bring them over this evening."

Anatolia raised her hand, beseeching. "At least give me two days."

"Why?"

"Well…to get used to it. And to get the house ready for you to move in."

"Fine, we'll do it your way." Vasily lifted the scythe and hoisted it onto his shoulder. "Where do you store your tools?"

"In the big cellar. Down the stairs and turn right."

"I'll put it there. And I'll tell Yasaman and Ovanes everything's okay with you. They're most likely fretting."

"And why are they fretting?"

"How should I know?"

"Tell them I'll stop by their place later."

"Then I'll stop by there too." And Vasily left the room, closing the door behind him.

Anatolia listened as his footsteps faded. Remorse tormented her but she couldn't have acted any differently, and the important thing had been to send her uninvited guest away one way or another. And so she had humored him. Fine, though, he wasn't a little boy, he would survive. She threw off the blanket and carefully got up. First she took off her stained clothes, wincing and barely able to stifle the urge to vomit. Never before, not even in the years when each new period had killed, little by little, her hopes of becoming pregnant, had she experienced such inexplicable disgust at her body as now. Menstruation had tortured her all her life and it hadn't stopped until she was almost fifty, turning her into a nervous wreck and always flowing with such horrendous pain that Anatolia wanted to die by her own hand every time, anything not to experience that again. The goose fat and pepper tincture that she meticulously applied to her lower belly didn't ease a thing and Yasaman's decoctions didn't help either, so Anatolia would wrap herself in a fluffy shawl and spend four long days hunched in a chair because the pain was slightly more tolerable when she was sitting down. She endured this monthly torture stoically, never grumbling. She only cried on Yasaman's shoulder every now and then, when she was driven to despair not so much by pain as by resentment. She didn't know what was happening to her now, eight years after her last period, nor was she concerned; since her remaining hours of life were numbered, there was no point in worrying.

She had to pull herself together; this wasn't the time for hesitation. Anatolia started breathing slowly and deeply, to settle the nausea. She closed her eyes to ease the dizziness and held onto the wall when she began walking. The first thing she did when she reached the kitchen was look for food. She found a little jar of leftover rose preserves on the shelf, long forgotten, and finished them without registering the flavor. The sweets gave her a bit of strength. She washed and put on clean clothes, then tied a kerchief over her wet hair and sat for a while, allowing herself a rest. She changed the bedsheets. Then she brought in some water from the rain barrel, dissolving a pinch of baking soda in it to wash out the spots, and soaked the stained linens. She let the birds out of the coop and picked a bunch of lemon balm before continuing down to the cellar for honey. The new scythe was hanging on a dowel and the dull old one had disappeared; Vasily had apparently taken it with him for repair. Remorse began stirring again in Anatolia's soul, but she brushed it aside. This was not a time for suffering. She took a small dish of honey and went into the house. She would make a drink with lemon balm and honey, have it with a little piece of bread, and that would be more than enough to hold on a little longer.

Yasaman stopped by when Anatolia was hanging her laundry in the yard.

"There didn't seem to be much point in waiting for you, so I came myself," she said in greeting.

"I got all caught up working around the house. I'm just finishing up," said Anatolia.

Yasaman tossed a concerned look at her. "You're looking a little pale today. You don't have a headache, do you?"

"I'm pale because I didn't get enough sleep."

"Shall I bring you a mint infusion?"

"No need, thanks, I already made some."

Ceasing with the ceremony, Yasaman stood with her hands on her hips and tilted her head toward one shoulder, as she always did when she was offering up complaints.

"Vasily dropped in. He said you came to an agreement. And here you are keeping quiet, not saying anything."

"Well!"

"Don't you 'well' me. Tell me!"

Anatolia untied her kerchief to let down her hastily braided hair so it would dry faster. She picked up the basin she had used to carry the laundry but didn't bother bringing it back to the closet. She left it leaning against the woodpile instead; she'd put the folded dry laundry in the basin later.

"There's nothing to tell, Yasaman. He asked me to marry him and I agreed. No matter what, you and Ovanes wouldn't leave me alone until I got together with him, am I right?"

"You're right," agreed Yasaman.

"So I gave in."

"And you did the right thing. Vasily's a good, worthy man. Why should you both live miserably, all alone?"

"Let's go inside, we're standing under the blazing sun," Anatolia offered, wanting to change the topic. Then she remembered that her pile of grave clothes was lying in the living room, in the most visible place. Unlike Vasily, Yasaman would figure out instantly why the outfit was on the table.

"Actually, let's sit on the veranda instead, it's stuffy inside," she said, quickly finding an excuse. "Want some lemon balm drink? I don't have anything else to serve you, I haven't had time to make lunch yet."

"Let's go to our house instead. I set the dough to rise, for baking a cheese pie. And I picked some beet greens and chickweed. You can help me make it, with garlic and matzoon. We'll have enough time before Ovanes comes back. And Vasily promised to come by, too." Here Yasaman fixed her gaze on her friend with a sly smile but then immediately grew serious. "I don't like your color today, you're looking awfully pale."

The laundry had taken the last of Anatolia's strength and all she wanted was to lie down for a while in peace and quiet, but she had no choice other than to follow her neighbor because refusing would have worried Yasaman even more. And so she headed toward the little gate without saying a thing. She would hold on somehow.

Yasaman first gave her an infusion of St. John's wort and made her eat a little honeycomb, sternly ordering her to swallow the wax instead of spitting it out. Anatolia felt much better after the infusion: the noise in her ears abated and she stopped feeling sick, but the thirst that had been bothering her since morning was stronger. She asked for some water but sipped it, afraid the flow of blood would pick up again.

Her neighbors' kitchen smelled deliciously of risen dough: Anatolia always loved that slightly sour aroma, which gave off a cool moistness. While Yasaman fussed with the cheese pie, Anatolia picked over the chickweed and beet greens, washed them delicately in cold water, and started cooking them. She braised a large bunch of scallions in clarified butter, added the chopped greens, and covered them with a lid. As soon as the greens released their juices and had almost started simmering, she took them off the flame and salted them to let them finish cooking away from the heat. She peeled a few cloves of garlic and tossed them into a stone mortar, added coarse salt and crushed them into mush, then put in the cold matzoon, beating it and setting that aside as well. While everything else was cooking, the matzoon would absorb the garlic's aroma and the garlic sauce could be poured on the braised greens.

The women spent the time on the veranda until the men's arrival. A grapevine clung to a heavy wooden beam, its thin tendrils stretching upward toward the slate roof. The pie, with its golden-brown cheese crust, was cooling in the kitchen and a lone cricket who had confused evening with night was broadcasting a doleful song in the garden as the sun slowly rolled beyond the horizon, hiding behind sparse clouds as if it were trying them on and refusing one cloudy outfit after another. Anatolia was sitting with her back resting against a cool stone wall and Yasaman was singing a nasal plowman's song.

"I dreamt of my father," confessed Anatolia.

Yasaman stopped singing and folded her arms across her chest; she didn't turn her head.

"Did he say anything?" she asked after a moment's silence.

"No. He didn't even look my way."

Yasaman unfolded her arms with visible relief.

"What day of the week is it?" she asked.

"Thursday."

"Thursday's a kind day."

The Maranians placed special meanings on dreams. They shared them with one another, trying to guess the secret meaning carried within. They made certain to clarify the day of the week. There was no reason to worry if it was Sunday because a Sunday dream is idle, neither offering nor promising anything. But you had to remember everything in a dream on Tuesday night because it was on Wednesday mornings, between the rooster's first and second crows, that dreams were prophetic.

"If only I could know how he's doing," Anatolia sighed.

"If you dreamt about him, that means he's fine."

"You think so?"

"Well, that's certainly what I've always thought."

"That means you're sparing my feelings."

"Would I really just be sparing yours? I'm sparing my own, too."

The evening sky that May was low and sticky, with a bilberry tint. If you were to run a finger across it, it would part like waves, scared, baring its soft, velvety, and live interior.

"We won't find out until we die how they're doing there without us," Anatolia whispered, to somewhere above.

Yasaman nodded guardedly. She pulled a folded lap blanket off the armrest of the daybed and ran a gnarled finger along the worn stitching of its hem. It would need to be mended or it wouldn't survive another laundering.

Chapter Four

"Human memory is selective. You might be horribly humiliated but you'll immediately forget how your mother thrashed
you mercilessly with a wool-beating stick because you stole a
wheel from the neighbor's shed. The cart had met its maker
long ago but the wheel remained and it was big, round, and
strong. I released it down a pocked village road then flew
after it, jumping in excitement over puddles clouded with
yellow clay, my heart beating fast. I forgave my mother and
forgot, but I'll never forget and never forgive my neighbor
Unan, a huge man with shaggy eyebrows and a fierce jaw.
Instead of cuffing me on the back of the head like a man
and taking away the wheel, he dragged me home and turned
me over to my mother. And what was she supposed to do?
She'd owed him three *grvankan*s of clarified butter for two
years. She couldn't repay the debt because for some reason
Unan wouldn't take it in installments and it just didn't work
for her to accumulate half a jugful of clarified butter, tearing
it from the mouths of hungry children. And so she took it

out on my back and for three days I could only sleep on my stomach.

"My mother was from the other side of the valley and didn't understand the local dialect very well. She'd miraculously saved herself and us four children from the massacre, escaped to Maran, and settled in at Arshak-bek's estate. Arshak-bek, may he rest in peace, was a generous and conscientious person, so he sheltered our unfortunate family and helped with materials for building a house. He promised money to get us started but didn't have time to give it because he went south to escape the Bolsheviks and from there went west, across the sea, or so they said. The estate was looted after the tsar was overthrown and there was nothing left for us to do but move into our unfinished house on the western slope of Manish-kar with neither household goods nor food. My mother had to go to the neighbor, Unan, and humbly ask a favor. She took half the clarified butter she'd pleaded for and then borrowed from him and brought it to the meidan, where she exchanged it for a *grvankan* of wheat and a bucket of potatoes; we then held out until spring with the remaining butter. The plants started coming up in March and we sowed a kitchen garden. We settled in, bit by bit.

"Each time Unan reminded my mother that it was time to return the butter, she meekly replied '*Ku dam*' in her dialect. Unan teased her at first but later started calling her Kudam. Even after she'd returned the butter, he stubbornly continued using that nickname. That's why we, sonny, are known as Kudamants, from *ku dam*, 'I'll give it back.'"

Vasily Kudamants first removed the scythe blade from its handle by lightly knocking the cutting edge with a hammer, then he began sharpening it with an abrasive whetstone. He was laboring with the spare, precise motions he had developed over the years. It was dark and cool in the smithy, and the tools had gathered a fair bit of dust because they had gone unused for a long time. Sometimes Vasily grabbed something from the bench without looking and then cursed angrily, brushing off a clump of dust that had stuck to his hands.

In the past, when there had been so many customers he could barely straighten his back and the forge's hot breath made the air sting so unbearably that it scorched on the exhale as well as the inhale, the only rubbish to be found at the smithy was waste from metalwork. Now, though, the place was forgotten and useless, cocooned in dust, strewn with shards of tiles, and covered in cracks. It was aging and dying, and nobody needed it.

"There's nothing more destructive than idleness," his father had loved repeating. "Idleness and leisure deprive life of purpose."

Vasily now understood the truth of his father's words. Life does, indeed, lose its purpose at the very instant a person ceases bringing benefit to those around him. And how could he bring that benefit? Only through his labor.

More than half a century had passed since the day Vasily's father had brought him, as an eight-year-old boy, to the smithy for a little training in the trade. He turned out to be a sharp and industrious assistant who grasped everything very quickly, so before long he took a portion of the work on his own shoulders. His father died just after Vasily turned fifteen, and his memories of that day stayed with him his entire life. It had been morning, very early, but the village wasn't sleeping: garden gates were opening wide and slamming shut with a squeak; dogs howled to one another and roosters crowed; a herd walked along with yellowish, round-sided cows at the front, drawing out their lowing and raising reddish road dust. Goats and sheep followed the cows, and the procession concluded with a shepherd and his two sons, a year apart in age, one carrying a little bundle with food, the other helping out with a stick and the shout of "tsoh-tsoh" reverberating every now and then as he ineptly urged on the herd when it spread out too much. Vasily and his father stepped back, waiting on the side of the road for the flow of animals to ebb, breathing in the smell of damp straw and bitter manure, and Vasily's father ran his palm along the damp side of a stockade fence, brushing off the dew and wanting to say something, but then abruptly leaned his shoulder against the fence, slipping downward and gasping for air.

Vasily's mother was in her second month of pregnancy and took to her bed immediately after the funeral, ailing for a long time and not recovering for six months. Vasily didn't let anyone in to see her and cared for her himself with devotion and humility, feeding her with a spoon, giving her decoctions to drink, and helping her bathe by filling a washtub with warm water, putting in a pinch of ashes with soap flakes, undressing her to her nightgown, washing her hair and feet, rubbing her skinny back (her pointy vertebrae and ribs showed helplessly through the wet fabric), and then leaving her by herself while he stood at the door, listening with rapt attention as she took off her nightgown, moaning, then finished washing and pulled on a fresh change of clothes. He would carry her over to the daybed, wrap her in a blanket, give her tea, and sit next to her until she fell asleep. When the weather allowed, he carried her out to the garden in his arms for some fresh air; his mother weighed about as much as a lark, though her belly stuck out, large and round. Vasily would sit her on the bench under a pear tree so her back rested against the rough tree trunk while she observed him working the land, breaking it up, watering, and weeding.

He would go to the smithy in the afternoons, leaving his mother in the care of his aunt or Satenik, who by then had married and given birth to her second son.

Miraculously, his mother carried the child to term, when he was born weak and sickly but alive, the eighth baby after Vasily and the only one who managed to survive. The other seven children had died before they were even born; Vasily's mother and father had bitterly mourned each one but had not abandoned hopes of having at least one more child. Families in patriarchal Maran were usually large, with many children, and their family seemed to be the only one not destined to experience that happiness.

Giving birth to the child returned his mother to life and the house finally awakened and began breathing with familiar childhood aromas that Vasily had missed so very much: smoky, spicy raw-cured ham, nut preserves, and mature brynza with dried mountain herbs. Their dwelling now greeted him not with deathly silence but with the sated knock of the butter churn, the stony whoosh of a hand-operated mill, and the heat of a clay oven, where his mother baked lavash and then stewed lamb with spices.

The boy, named Akop in honor of his father, was the second Akop Kudamants in the Arusyak lineage (that of Vasily's grandmother, whose insolent neighbor had given her the offensive nickname Kudam), and the boy grew to be bright but surprisingly quiet and pensive. Vasily loved him so much it made his heart ache, but he didn't spoil him and didn't let his mother either; his brother certainly needed to learn to read and write, so he was glad that a school was being built in Maran. The smithy brought a small but steady income and Vasily gave almost all his earnings to his mother, setting aside a small amount for a good education later because he was planning to send Akop to the valley. In the spring, Vasily turned nineteen, so it was time to marry. His mother had hinted a few times that he should take note of Magtakhine Yakulichants – a girl as good as gold, modest, and hardworking, why not ask for her hand? – but Vasily took his time because he doubted Petros Yakulichants would agree to give his eldest daughter in marriage to an unrefined blacksmith. Without asking Vasily's permission, his mother gathered her meager gold jewelry (earrings, two rings, and a bracelet) into a bundle and went to Petros's house. They greeted her warily but hospitably, setting a table with a rich assortment of refreshments: sugared rose petals, nut *pastila*, and airy hazelnut cookies. Vasily's mother grew timid but forced herself to follow through with the plan she had envisioned. She pushed her plate aside, untied the bundle, and emptied the contents onto the tablecloth, saying, "This is all I can give to your Magtakhine."

"She never once shifted her gaze, and that was all she said," Petros told Vasily years later. "She sat up straight, hands folded on her knees, and spoke to me as an equal. That's why I agreed to marry off my daughter to you."

They decided to hold the wedding in the autumn after gathering the harvest, as was traditional, but they had to wait five whole years. First there was a mourning period for

Magtakhine's younger brother, who died after being struck by lightning, then there was the famine that circled over Manish-kar and set in during the first dry summer: it had been inevitable and seemed it would last forever. Only later, with the passage of years, did the Maranians bitterly recall that the famine, which seemed to be playing cat and mouse, had been sending advance messengers and warning signs, or perhaps mocking them. Unfortunately, though, people immersed in their day-to-day cares didn't recognize the hidden meaning of those signs.

Everything began the night the village was roused out of bed by an unusual din. People stayed close by their windows observing, horrified, as thin trickles of rats and mice flowed together into a huge rustling stream moving toward the meidan. Out front, taciturn, threatening, and mottled with scars sustained in numerous battles, walked the males, with their confused offspring jostling behind them; the smallest hung on to tails and went out of their way to climb on the adults' backs, but even they got painfully bitten all over and so fell back, squeaking from the offense, only to be trampled by those behind them. The females brought up the rear of the procession and were strangely indifferent to the deaths of their children, taking tiny steps in disorderly rows, dispassionately skirting bloodied little bodies writhing in their death throes.

The moon hung in the sky like a huge millstone and for some reason the yard dogs, enormous bowlegged curs that normally responded to even the most insignificant noise with a threatening snarl, had gone silent, while people froze with horror, wary of going out on their verandas and instead silently observing this inexplicable, sinister exodus from their windows. The herd of mice that reached the meidan huddled in a seething horde that surged toward the edge of the village in a broad wave before waning and dissolving into the pale moonlight, leaving behind them a rough village road strewn with stiffening little corpses and the smell of rotting flesh. Maran greeted the morning without the usual bustling around in cellars and basements, but housewives wary of the rats' return continued sprinkling strips of hound's-tongue seeds on the ground around grain bins, stuffing empty burrows with broken glass and arsenic, and moving shelves of provisions away from the walls so that the rodents couldn't reach them. People in the valley said the mice had gone east, where the boundless ocean-sea brimmed with dark waves, and they said people who lived by the seashore saw the distraught rodents flinging themselves into iridescent waves at sunset and that the mice were paddling with little paws that had been scraped raw, swimming until the bitter end, when they finally lost all strength, mournfully squeaking and gasping for breath before departing in whole flocks to be covered in stifling silt at the deadly bottom of the sea.

People would probably have discussed this unusual occurrence for much longer if not for the disaster that took place afterwards, at noon on a quiet, sunny early spring day, on the eve of the Annunciation. The dawn sky was calm and cloudless, promising a day of bright sunshine, but then an impenetrable veil of blackness suddenly covered it from one edge of the horizon to the other and started screeching with a clanking, ominous cricket-like chirping. Hurriedly fumbling with their clothespins, the women didn't have enough time to tear dried laundry off the lines or drive chickens into coops before threatening clouds suddenly turned into swarms of heavy, sharp-winged insects that descended on the village, striving to cling like a grotesque, teeming blob to everything in their path: flower gardens, kitchen gardens, fences, houses, and outbuildings. There were so many of them that it seemed as if God had been angered by some misdeed and sent down a plague of insects as punishment. They swirled through the air in nettlesome throngs, getting into mouths, sticking to eyes, gnawing at young plant shoots, laying waste to feeders for barnyard birds, and even attempting to steal livestock feed. They penetrated houses through chimneys and crawled away along corners and crevices, leaving indelible dark spots on walls and furniture. They were huge and frightening, each the length of a pinkie finger, with transparent yellow-green wings, five stripes all along their backs, and another five stripes across their heavy grayish abdomens. They reproduced with such horrendous speed it was as if they intended to take over everyone and everything. When the males courted the females, their wings made a loud grating chirr that filled the ears. They mated in the air, falling like rocks and madly spinning along their axes, with the females groaning and squealing but unable to get away because the males had immobilized them by spraying some toxic liquid out of their salivary glands. The larvae that hatched several hours later were insatiable and omnivorous, and before anyone knew it they had already grown into massive, loathsome, jelly-like worms the size of the palm of a hand. They devoured not only plants but also small creatures like ants, beetles, and bees.

The Maranians held the line as well as they could, boarding up chimneys, locking farm birds and dogs in cellars, not allowing livestock out to pasture, keeping windows closed, and hanging sheets in doorways that led out of the house. When outside, they had to wear heavy clothing that covered the whole body, winding their necks with scarves and their heads with kerchiefs, leaving a narrow opening for their eyes. In order to exterminate all the insects that had flown into residences, they wielded carpet beaters but soon started catching the bugs and throwing them outside because when the insects died, they released caustic little puddles of poison that ate away at the skin of anyone who wiped it up. Those ulcers were difficult to heal and festered for a long time. Everyday poisons did not affect the bugs, which even turned out to be immune to undiluted vinegar and arsenic. Yasaman Shlapkants boiled up a vat of an infusion with castor bean, false hellebore, and belladonna, which she set out in the yard, but it had no effect on them whatsoever.

The couriers Maran sent to the valley returned empty-handed because the chemical poisons that used to destroy the insects didn't help and many people had suffered from their excessive and incautious use. It turned out that things were more complicated in the valley than in the village sheltered at the top of Manish-kar: the vast majority of the insects preferred quiet, fertile lowlands to a mountain peak where the wind blew. When they returned, the Maranians said panic broke out in the valley on the third day of the insect invasion. Someone started a rumor that food would soon run out because supplies were waning and there was nowhere to get anything new because production was at a standstill. The panic did its dirty deed: first the food shops were emptied and then all the warehouses were looted. There was nothing more to save by the time the government brought in troops and announced a curfew, because the supplies had been pilfered and hidden away in houses where people were now ready to guard them with their lives. The Maranians didn't know what happened in the lowlands after that and didn't even speculate about it. Knowing what mankind was capable of, what was the point in guessing?

The insects didn't leave until late May. They soared upward in massive chirring flocks, swirling for a time over the valley and Manish-kar, then they flew off to the north, leaving behind poisoned water, denuded forests, and pastures devoured to the last blade of grass. Nature attempted to take the upper hand by unfurling new leaves, allowing boundless fields to start turning green, and, after the insects went away, bringing an entire week of rain to wash off all the filthy remnants of the invasion: toxic feces, larvae shells, little bird corpses picked to the bone, and husks of other small dead insects. But then a drought set in just after the rains. An utterly scorching sun, enormous, merciless, and blindingly white, hung over the valley like a fiery sphere, steaming away all the moisture and even burning up the greenery that had barely revived itself. Its fiery hand covered the world, making it impossible to pause for even a moment to catch your breath. The dried-out land broke into dusty cracks, became covered in powdery sediment, and then started hissing like cast iron that had been heated red-hot on the stove: *phshshshsh, shshshshssh*. Rivers grew shallow and then disappeared completely, springs fell silent, shadows lost their curative coolness, and trees dried up, protruding from the ground like teeth, looking as sharp as masts broken off in a gale.

The drought was the final advance messenger that the famine sent before descending shortly thereafter, riding on a carriage of blisteringly hot wind. The famine was putrid and foul, devoid of mercy or empathy, and it was more frightening even than life's greatest mystery: death itself. Whenever Vasily recalled that horrible time, he would choke with a cough that irritated his lungs. Even drinking cup after cup of water wouldn't quench his thirst, and then he would cry his helpless heart out, able only to hunch over and gasp for breath from the torment of the scratchy cough. He would remember butchering the last sheep. The drought scorched all the meager remainders of grass, there was no feed at all, and the cattle were dropping like flies, so they buried the dead animals and hastily slaughtered those on the brink of death, dressing them and drying the meat in the breeze after it had soaked for a while in strong brine.

Back in his day, Vasily's father had paid a small fortune for a huge pedigree ram, who was bred for meat and wool. Even back in the winter he weighed about five hundred *grvankans,* but by the fourth month of the drought he was thin, starved down to skin and bone, had lost his teeth, and had nearly gone blind. Vasily laid the animal on his side and pressed with his knee; though in the past he had needed help from a few strong men to restrain the ram, now the animal allowed himself to be caught and just mooed dolefully like a cow, as if sensing that the end was near. Vasily looked away, slit his defenseless throat with a sharp knife, and waited for the spasms to abate before lifting the limp carcass with one hand and hanging it on a metal hook by a tendon to let the blood drain. Five-year-old Akop stood close by, holding his breath and silently observing as his older brother removed the sheepskin with short, precise knife strokes. In the unfortunate animal's stomach were scraps of polyethylene, a clothespin, and Akop's leather sandal that had disappeared the day before. Their mother scrubbed the sandal with ashes (they had to be mercilessly thrifty in their use of water) and then rubbed it with a rag moistened in vodka, but the child flat-out refused to put it on.

The famine years gaped like a dark chasm in Vasily's memory – he didn't allow himself to look back, for fear of remembering something he might never be able to recover from later. He couldn't completely close himself off from his memories, though, since it was inevitable that they would occasionally surface out of the maelstrom of the past, tormenting him for long hours with details that pained his soul. Even decades later, Vasily could recall the bitter aftertaste of the watery stew that his mother became adept at boiling from roots, spruce cones, and tree bark. There were no vegetables or grains to be found, no matter the price, so they stretched out the dwindling supplies of dried meat from the slaughtered livestock, but then that ran out too, and eventually there was nothing left to eat at all. The drought didn't recede until late autumn, offering an opportunity for nature, which was able to wait for the November rains, to begin tentatively casting its green shadow over the landscape in the tiny segment of time allotted before the snows began.

And so the village held out until March on meager portions of grass, roots, spruce cones, and tree bark, losing half its population by the end of winter. February turned into a month of burials. Vasily and the other men made the rounds of houses each morning to gather up the dead, whom they buried in common graves because they lacked the strength to dig individual trenches. The elderly and children were the first to go; the women followed, and the men held on longer than anyone. It was an overwhelming and inhuman curse, seeing off to the great beyond the people who are dearer to you than life, one after another after another.

The only young man who departed in the first year of the famine was Anatolia's father, Kapiton Sevoyants. After burying his elder daughters, he brought Anatolia to the valley, turned her over to distant kin, and then, in a moment of unbearable despair after the death of old Babo Maneh, he completely refused to take any drink or scrap of food. He still helped gather up corpses in the village for the next two days while he had enough energy, but he weakened severely on the third day and took to his bed, never to rise again.

Only Ovanes knew that Kapiton had decided to end his own life voluntarily. He had repeatedly attempted to convince his friend not to bring the sin of suicide upon his soul, reminding him of Anatolia, but Kapiton responded to all of Ovanes's admonitions with cold silence. Only once, right before the very end, did he begin speaking, asking to be placed alongside his wife and daughters rather than buried in a common grave. Ovanes asked for Vasily's help, and they overcame their tremendous weakness to dig up Voske's grave and lower Kapiton's body, wrapped in a blanket, onto her half-decayed casket. There were so many deceased that nobody gave coffins a thought; it was most important to commit the bodies of the dead to the earth as quickly as possible. Afterward, the two of them smoked in silence for a long time, seemingly oblivious to the cold or the stinging snow that was getting under their collars. Vasily had vaguely guessed the reason for Kapiton's death but didn't consider asking anything. He faithfully came with Ovanes to his friend's grave every February, though.

They would stand in silence, leaning their elbows against the chilly fence.

Only once, after long years, did Ovanes allow himself a small bit of candor. "Who are we to judge someone's actions?" he sighed, unwrapping a bundle of incense.

"Some decisions and actions are not subject to judgment," Vasily told him shortly.

Ovanes gave no answer, but when they parted he shook Vasily's hand firmly. They never went to Kapiton's grave again. Apparently what Vasily said had convinced Ovanes, either through its correctness or, if nothing else, the inevitability of the step Kapiton had decided to take, and Ovanes let Kapiton go in peace.

That first February of the famine stayed in Vasily's memory not just for its endless funerals but also for his younger brother's inexplicable behavior. Akop was only skin and bones, but he was surprisingly full of energy and healthy thanks to a jug of honey Magtakhine's family had given them: his mother dissolved a spoonful of the honey in a pitcher of warm water, added pine cones, and fed that tisane to her son morning, noon, and night, which is why he remained a cheerful and happy child despite being so thin that you could practically see through him. Although his good physical condition gladdened those around him, something about his state of mind upset them. He was noisy and restless throughout the afternoon but he wilted by evening, refused to go to bed, and spent half the night by an iced-up window covered in frosty squiggles. He would sit, wrapped in a woolen blanket, tensely gazing into the darkness, and when asked what he was looking at, he would say "Dark blue poles." His mother would look out into the darkness as well, but seeing nothing herself she would take fright and cry. Akop would pretend he did not notice her tears and then ignore her requests that he go to bed.

Once, when Vasily attempted to carry him to bed, the boy burst into such bitter tears that they had to sit him back by the window. After that, the adults had to spend the night in a vigil; his mother was sure an evil spirit, a *dev*, had stolen her youngest son's soul, so she recited prayers and stealthily wiped her tears while Vasily talked with his brother to distract him. Akop responded willingly but didn't look away from the window, and he sometimes fell silent during conversations, soundlessly moving his lips, bending his fingers, craning his neck, and moving his eyes up and down while pressing his forehead to the windowpane. An hour or two later, he would get up with a sigh as if he felt assured he wouldn't discern anything else in the dark, then announce that there had been five and four poles today (he only knew how to count to five) and go to bed. For some reason, one day Vasily compared the number of townspeople who had died overnight with the number of "blue poles" that Akop spoke of and was horrified to discover that the figures coincided. He didn't think of telling his mother, so as not to scare her even more, but he spent the next night keeping close track of his brother. Akop showed no fear, though he sometimes flinched as if he had been caught unawares, and then he would freeze, breathing very, very shallowly, sit without stirring, and just look up at something.

"Tell me what you see," Vasily asked him once.

"Well," Akop's voice faltered, "first a light comes on in the sky, like a star. Then a pole comes down from there. It's like water but it's dark blue. And a little bit violet."

"What do you mean it's like water? It flows down like a river?"

"No, it's see-through like water. That's why you can see what's inside it."

"And what's inside it?"

"There's two people inside. No, first there's one person. Coming down from up there. The person has wings hanging on their back but doesn't fly with them. That person with wings comes down and then goes up leading a boy or a girl or a grandmother or a grandfather."

"Where's he leading them?"

"Up."

"And what's up there?"

"Dark blue light."

Vasily turned to their mother. She was sitting with her hands on her knees, bitter tears running down her pale, emaciated face. Vasily was scared and pained for her because she was so helpless and lost.

"He's seeing angels of death," he smiled to her, then hastily covered his mouth with his hand, his lips quivering and betraying his confusion and fear.

That night Akop counted "five, five, and three dark blue poles". The next day thirteen people were buried in the village. The night after that, Vasily wrapped his brother in a woolen blanket and carried him to the outskirts of the village – fortunately it wasn't far to walk, only five households away from where the edge of Manish-kar that had collapsed in the earthquake now bared its sharp notches. He stood on the very brink of the bluff and turned so Akop saw the pitch darkness that had swallowed the valley.

"What do you see there?"

"It's as bright as daytime there," the boy said without turning his head.

"Because the sun's shining?"

"No, Vaso-dzhan. There's a lot of blue poles there, it's light because of them."

It was impossible to come to terms with the boy seeing messengers flying in for dead people, but their mother attempted to at least get used to the idea. It was unbearably difficult for her to reach that point. She kept crying and quietly reciting prayers, and there was nothing Vasily could do but doze on the daybed while he waited for Akop to ask to go to bed after having counted the last human souls flying up into the sky. They now only put Akop to bed with Vasily because their mother was afraid the angels of death would guess that he was seeing them and show up for the child. The angels had no time for that, though: they were run off their feet accepting and escorting ever more souls to heaven after they had finished suffering.

"*Enbashti* is a scary time," their mother once said to her eldest son in a whisper. "Your grandmother, the late Arusyak, told of how most people die just when the roosters are sleeping soundly. And they sleep deepest at *enbashti*, from midnight until daybreak."

"What do sleeping roosters have to do with it?" Vasily asked, looking around at his younger brother, who was frozen in place by the window.

"Their crowing scares away death. If someone dies during the day, that's because the rooster can't crow in time."

Vasily shook his head and sighed deeply. "It'll be spring soon, the famine will finally end, and people will stop dying. Akop will calm down, you'll see."

Everything happened exactly as he predicted. A week or two later, after the first spring greenery appeared – nettles, shepherd's purse, and marsh mallow – the village that had been reduced by half revived itself little by little as people started working in their kitchen and flower gardens and took out their most precious vegetable seeds. Akop fell asleep for the first time at a usual hour for a child of his age, rather than long after midnight, and from that day on he slept calmly and deeply, right up until lunch. He was apparently making up for the sleepless nights he had spent by the window.

Toward April, people in the valley finally remembered Maran, and one day a truck of wheat grain and potatoes arrived, guarded by soldiers who distributed three *grvankans* of grain and four of potatoes to each family, all to be used as seed. The grain was ordinary and local, so apparently not all the government storehouses had been looted by people who had been driven out of their minds by hunger, but the potatoes turned out to be some sort of new freckled tubers that were oblong, smooth, and lacking a single defect or wrinkle; each one was like a shiny hard candy. The soldiers explained that this assistance had come from somewhere overseas, and that there were no great hopes for this kind of potato to survive in our part of the world, but that they absolutely had to be planted because no food at all was left and people had to somehow tough things out until harvest time. New aid arrived a week later, in the form of a few dozen loads of livestock. This time it came from the other side of the northern pass, where an enclosed semicircle of mountains divided the valley from the outside world. After painstaking allocation, Maran received a cow, a ewe, two goats, and a pig that particularly astounded the

Maranians because it was as clean and neat as a round turnip that had been thoroughly washed under running water. The villagers oohed and aahed, clicked their tongues, and walked around it, inspecting it from every angle, surprised by its small ears and smooth skin because the local pigs were renowned throughout the region for their huge, almost elephant-sized ears and extreme hairiness, but here was a gentle, milky-pink creature with a snout like a heart and tiny little hooves.

After lavishly admiring the remarkable pig, the Maranians finally came to their senses and started asking themselves how to handle the aid. They made a decision to keep the animals in the cleanest and most spacious shed, which belonged to Vano Melikants, and to share the milk strictly among the families who still had children. And when the descendant animals would come, they would be distributed to various homes so everyone would, little by little, have their own beast and the village would have a new herd. Although what kind of descendants could they be talking about, people suddenly realized, if they had only received females? How would they be fertilized? They waited, but received no answer to the express telegram that telegraph clerk Satenik sent to the valley. But then a second batch of animals arrived a week later with the long-awaited male component and an entire flock of farm birds: turkeys, ducks, guinea hens, and geese. The birds were delivered in eighteen nailed-up wooden crates so the animals wouldn't trample them, and after the final crate was opened there was tremendous amazement among everyone present when a frothy-white peacock stepped out. Once freed, the peacock began shrieking huffily before walking away, limping slightly and catching its broken feathers in mud on the road that had swelled after the spring rains. The vehicle had unloaded the animals and birds and set off for home long ago, so there was nobody to ask where the peacock had come from or what to do with it. At the request of Vano, who now answered for the Noah's ark flock that had arrived from the north, Satenik composed a new telegram. They didn't have to wait long for an answer: the valley responded with a brief but irate rebuke along the lines of "We're not interested in your uncalled-for jokes."

They lodged the peacock along with the other birds, but it cried and refused to eat from the common feeder. Vano's wife, Valinka Eibogants, brought the peacock into the house, washed it in a trough, carefully pouring water from a dipper, and then the bird spent more than an hour on her knees drying off, wrapped in an old sheet. Valinka marveled that such a beautiful bird smelled like any other wet hen. Once he was dry, the peacock fluttered to the floor heavily, began taking small steps toward the door, and shrieked wistfully, demanding to be set free. Valinka let him out and he wandered the yard aimlessly for a while, walking past a loud gaggle of chickens, guinea hens, and geese without turning his head before returning to the veranda, where he took shelter under a wooden bench and went silent. It didn't seem possible to pull the peacock out because he cried and shrieked each time anyone attempted to come within two steps of him. Valinka left him a bowl of water, chopped some nettles and sorrel, and forbade members of the household to linger on the veranda lest they scare the bird. Once the peacock calmed down, he crawled out from under the bench, nibbled a little at the nettles, and spent an entire day on the veranda strolling from corner to corner. Toward evening, he fluttered up to the railing and went to sleep, his luxuriant tail hanging to the floor.

With time, he got used to his new place and even ventured beyond the gate, where he would walk along the road, look around, and then stand motionless for a long time after reaching the edge of the bluff. He was handsome and majestic in his snow-white crown and feathers that took on a rusty sheen from the road dust, sometimes shrieking with a call that tore your heart out. He lived on the veranda year-round and Vano threw together a large crate that he filled with hay, but the peacock stubbornly ignored it. Only after the weather turned exceptionally frosty did he climb in, burrowing under an old woolen blanket that Valinka had tenderly used to cover it; the peacock would then go morosely silent, his vacant gaze watching occasional snowflakes that floated under the awning. Sometimes he went out to the wintry yard, where he instantly turned nearly invisible on the snow cover as he observed a snowstorm for a little while, looking sumptuously out of place amid the realities of the village surrounding him. Then he would heavily flap his sodden wings and fly back up to the veranda, where he would perch, motionless, on the railing for a second before dipping back into his box with the hay.

The rest of the animals that had been delivered from the valley quickly adjusted to their new home. The cow, goats, and sheep yielded so much milk that some was even used occasionally for butter and cheese, though the output of food-stuffs turned out to be so small that there was only enough for families with children. Things improved in the village by summer: kitchen and flower gardens were green, and currant and raspberry bushes were colorful with berries, though the joy from the life that had arisen was clouded by fears that drought could return. And although it wasn't as lengthy as in the previous year, it did return. It was wicked, blazing with intense, fiery heat, and the only thing that saved people was that it descended late, toward the end of July, so they managed to save part of the harvest. The trucked-in potato didn't germinate, though a few tubers of old potato in Vasily's garden sprouted unexpectedly, thanks to a fortunate confluence of events. A number of potatoes had been forgotten in the soil after the previous harvest and his mother dug up some of the new harvest later and hid the potatoes until the next spring, for new seed crop. People survived for a second year on brined cucumbers and tomatoes, berries, mushrooms, and nuts (walnuts, hazelnuts, and beechnuts) – and honey as well; thank God the beehives made it through the drought and had time before the intense heat set in to generate enough reserves to catch up again in October when the heat finally abated.

Vasily and Akop's mother died during the second winter of the famine; she held on until the end of winter, when one day at noon she lay down for her midday nap and simply didn't wake up again. Her sons were at the smithy; Vasily had brought Akop with him to distract him from his night vigils, which had resumed with the onset of another winter, and the boy, who had been observing his brother pouring molten metal into a mold, abruptly straightened up and elbowed him. It was a miracle the metal didn't spill on Vasily. Vasily wanted to shout at Akop but stopped short because Akop was deathly white, gasping for air, and trying hard to say something. Vasily was afraid his brother couldn't get enough air in the hot building so carried him out of the smithy, where the boy had trouble catching his breath then let out a sob and began crying, "Vaso-dzhan, the angel came for Mama."

Vasily set off at a run without watching where he was going and got tangled up in his long blacksmith's apron; he was hold-ing Akop close, trying to cover him with his arms because it was cold outside and they weren't wearing coats. An ominous silence filled the house and their mother was lying with her hands tucked under her cheek like a child. Vasily set his brother on the edge of the daybed, crawled toward their mother on his knees, pressed his lips to her temple, and began weeping when he felt the deathly coolness of her skin.

That was the first winter night Akop did not spend by the window. He sobbed the whole day by their mother's body and was utterly weakened by evening, when his temperature spiked. They summoned Yasaman for help and she wanted to take Akop with her to care for him at her house, but he wouldn't allow it, saying, "I'll be here, I want to be here." Yasaman stripped Akop naked, rubbed him with mulberry home brew, wrapped him in a woolen blanket, gave him an herbal tisane made with cornelian cherry pits, and let him sweat things out before rubbing him with mulberry brew again; she went home once she was sure his temperature had dropped a little, promising to return in the morning. During the night, Akop pressed his hot forehead to Vasily's shoulder and admitted he had known their mother would die that winter.

"That's why I sat by the window, to see where they were flying. If I'd been at home... If I hadn't gone with you to the smithy..."

"What would you have done then?"

"I would have asked them not to take her away."

"The angel wouldn't have obeyed you."

"He would have."

From that day on, Akop stopped keeping watch by the window and he answered Vasily's cautious questions by saying that there was no longer anything to worry about, that nobody from their house would die now.

The second winter was not as terrible as the first, but even so, many people departed for the great beyond. They didn't die so much from hunger as from undernourishment that damaged their health. The same winter that Vasily and Akop lost their mother, Yasaman and Ovanes lost a son and two grandchildren and Magtakhine's parents lost three daughters. Only two girls from Petros Yakulichants's family survived: eighteen-year-old Magtakhine and ten-year-old Shushanik, who miraculously recovered from severe pneumonia toward spring. Crushed by grief, Petros nobly offered to take in Akop, explaining it by saying a six-year-old child needs female care and affection, but Vasily politely thanked him and declined. They would somehow cope on their own. He didn't consider hinting about a wedding because what kind of wedding could there be when the whole village was in mourning? His future father-in-law raised the subject himself, though, saying, "Let's wait another year. If we survive the winter, you'll marry next spring."

By that time, Magtakhine had grown into a real beauty: she was transparently fragile, dark-eyed, dark-haired, and so tall she gave Vasily little advantage in height, but she had been carefully fashioned, with a high forehead, neat nose, long, thin neck, and slender hands and feet. She wasn't shy around her fiancé and didn't avert her gaze. She and her mother stopped by once a week to help with the housekeeping and cooking, and one time when she was left alone with Vasily for a short while she permitted him to take her hand and kiss her cheek. This was the only liberty she allowed before marriage since customs were strict in Maran, where young women went to their weddings chaste and unkissed. It was extremely rare to tie additional bonds of marriage after being widowed, meaning they mourned their husbands their whole lives.

Vasily and Akop went to Magtakhine's on Sundays for reciprocal visits. They always brought a gift, either strawberries or a few mushrooms or maybe five young apples. Magtakhine's mother accepted those modest tributes with great reluctance, making excuses as her eyes brimmed over with tears since every grain of food counted in the village. Hunger had erased the distinction between rich and poor, lining everybody up as if it were Judgment Day, all of them in one humiliating row at the edge of the grave, mocking them with grand, undisguised pleasure: either the famine's intense heat singed the seedlings or its endless rains turned the fields into impassable swamps, or it drove in clouds of hail the size of hens' eggs that damaged fragile fruit tree blossoms. Everyone ate in the same meager way, and nobody had seen meat in ages. There was only a small amount of wildlife left in the woods because the animals that survived the drought had been hunted down during the previous winter and the few that had escaped the hunters had taken refuge very deep in the woods, trying to stay out of harm's way. Life, though, had unquestionably prevailed, taking the village back from the famine one millimeter at a time. Noah's herd increased during the winter, almost doubling in size, and by spring there were already half-year-old chicks and ducklings running around Valinka Eibogants's yard, ready to fledge into adult birds by autumn. The sow offered unexpected descendants in twelve large-eared piglets covered with thick fur – those who came to the shed to admire them oohed and aahed and clicked their tongues, wondering how it could be that the smooth, white-sided pigs brought from the north had given birth to little piglets who looked nothing like them.

The famine receded three years later, leaving behind a cemetery containing as many dead as there were still living in Maran, and a village petrified with grief.

These days, when Vasily wanted to sense the long-forgotten feeling of happiness, he would cautiously, without breathing, back away from everything that had wounded him and left him with a perpetual aching in his heart: his father's death, his mother's death, his brother's death, Magtakhine's death, and the death of three sons born one year apart from each other. Then he would look far back, to when summer had been boundless and the trees had grown so tall that their tops held up the sky. He recalled himself as a little five-year-old sitting on his grandmother Arusyak's knees as she stroked his hair with a withered hand and told stories. He also remembered his mother as young, pretty, and walking back from the spring with a copper pitcher on her shoulder, striding carefully, watching her step for fear of stumbling, her wary expression melting into a heartwarming smile when she saw her son. He remembered his father, who'd gone gray early but had been young and strong, with eyelashes and brows singed from the forge's breath, a man who would sometimes come out of the smithy for a little while to rest toward nightfall, when an evening chill was filling the yard: he would lean his back against the masonry wall and tell stories about their kin, about how his mother had been saved from the massacre by a miracle, escaping here with four children, and about the noble behavior of Arshak-bek, who had disappeared into oblivion after sheltering their unfortunate family, about the neighbor Unan, a lowlife who had refused to take the clarified butter in installments and then thought up an offensive nickname, Kudam, for Arusyak.

"That's why we, sonny, are Kudamants," his father would invariably say when he finished his story. "From *ku dam*, 'I'll give it back.'"

Chapter Five

Anatolia didn't die the next day or the day after, either. The bleeding abated completely by the fourth day, but the ringing in her ears hadn't quieted and the excruciating affliction that was wearing her out came in waves, sometimes becoming so intense that she had to cling to the wall, slide to the floor slowly, and sit with her eyes closed so it was easier to bear the dizziness. In addition to the aching in her body and the nagging pain at the pit of her belly, her hands were numb. When she took a glass of tea from the table, she was surprised it had cooled so quickly but after drinking just a sip, she realized that the tea was in fact hot; it was her fingers that had lost their sensitivity. She had no intention of being afraid, let alone of turning her condition into a tragedy, so she continued to run the house as usual. When answering inquiries from the anxious Yasaman (who had caught Anatolia sitting on the bare ground in the middle of the yard) Anatolia lied, saying she had picked up food poisoning from eating some of last year's overfermented salted cabbage that she hadn't had the heart to throw away. Yasaman got to work feeding her decoctions for upset stomachs and then, after she had taken Anatolia's pulse and checked her heart rate, fresh compotes made from cherry plums and dried cornelian cherries. Anatolia felt a little better the next day, but the weakness and aching never quite receded and the dizziness didn't abate.

It wasn't her poor overall state that disturbed her so much as Vasily's impending move. She lacked the strength to go to his house to apologize and turn him down, so she asked Ovanes to do it for her. He reluctantly agreed, but (to Ovanes's undisguised joy) he was too late because the groom himself showed up that same evening, accompanied by his second cousin and bringing a change of clothes, the sharpened scythe, a stack of freshly made corn flatbreads, and a bowl of garden strawberries that Satenik was grandly holding out before her. Behind them, urged on by his dog, a huge snow-white Armenian Gampr, were a nanny goat with two grown kids and two phlegmatic sheep who scampered along, bleating and baaing tunelessly now and then. Rounding out the procession was an old ram which had certainly seen better days: he had a cataract and one of his horns was broken.

As it happened, Anatolia was just returning from a trip to the cellar for clarified butter. She retreated a step when she saw the unexpected guests, fumbled for the banister, and cautiously bent without turning to set the dish of butter on the bottom stair.

"Good evening to you, dear bride," Satenik welcomed her.

"Hadn't we agreed on tomorrow?" Anatolia blurted out in surprise.

"Hold the gate so we can bring the animals into the yard," said Vasily, who hadn't heard what she said.

Anatolia headed toward the fence, feverishly pondering how to wriggle out of an awkward situation. Feeling ill at ease after not coming up with anything, she opened the gate and waited as the animals pushed their way into the yard. Vasily left a bundle of his things by the fence, handed Anatolia the tray with the flatbreads that hadn't yet cooled, and confidently drove the animals into the cowshed, which had already been empty for six months. Anatolia's goats had been sick and then died during the winter and she had been intending to get new livestock toward autumn – she had already agreed to take a female kid from Yasaman when she was strong enough to live away from her mother. The dog led the animals to the shed then ran back, touched the hem of Anatolia's dress with his damp nose, sniffed her, and raised his big, large-eared head before letting out a sharp bark.

"He acknowledged you," laughed Satenik. "Patro-dzhan, that's your new mistress."

Anatolia mechanically patted the dog's head and scratched him behind the ears.

"Hadn't we agreed on tomorrow?" she repeated, watching as Vasily shut the animals in the shed and headed toward the cellar to put the repaired scythe there.

"Really?" Satenik asked in surprise. "My cousin said you'd told him to come the day after tomorrow."

"I said in two days."

"He must not have understood right. So, dear bride, am I supposed to stand by the fence or are you going to invite me in?"

"Come in, of course," Anatolia said, remembering herself.

"Leave the things there, Vasily will bring them in himself," said Satenik, heading toward the stairs. "Don't forget to take

the butter or Patro will eat it up in a second. Right, Patro-
dzhan?"

Patro barked eagerly and wagged his tail.

"Where's he going to sleep? In the shed?" asked Anatolia.

"In his doghouse. My cousin will bring it over later."

Vasily came out of the cellar and closed the door tightly
behind him. He jabbed a threatening finger at the dog.

"You're not allowed in there, is that clear?"

Patro started whimpering and taking slow, downcast steps
toward his master, lumbering comically on his large paws.

"I left a wheel of lightly brined cheese for a second yesterday
and when I came back he had already stolen it and polished
it off," Vasily explained when he caught Anatolia's surprised
glance. "Tomorrow I'll put a latch on the outside of the cellar
door so he can't get in there. I'll have to put one on the front
door, too."

Anatolia silently walked up the stairs, pressing the tray with
the flatbreads to her chest. Her head was spinning and her
legs were buckling treacherously. She had no thoughts, none
whatsoever, and the only question on the tip of her tongue –
why? – was addressed more to herself than to Satenik and
Vasily. She had cooked up this mess herself, so what did they
have to do with it? She decided to serve them tea, apologize,
and send them back.

Satenik picked up the clarified butter Anatolia had left on
the step and came into the kitchen. She wiped the bottom of
the dish with the edge of an apron, put it on the table, and sat
down, propping up a wrinkled cheek with her hand. Vasily,
who had slammed the door in front of Patro's nose ("Go
on, out in the yard, you pesky mutt") brought his things into

the hallway and lingered for a second, apparently wanting to ask where to put them, but then seemed to think better of it and threw them on the armrest of the daybed. He would work out the finer details later. While the guests were getting settled in, Anatolia opened the stove door, reached up to the kitchen shelf for matches, and was overcome by a sudden dizzy spell. Although the stove's broad back kept her from falling, she collapsed onto it facedown and hit her side hard, losing consciousness.

She came to in her bed, brought around by the strong smell of the ointment Yasaman was rubbing into her temples; Satenik was sitting on the edge of the bed, diligently massaging the balls of her feet; Ovanes and Vasily were talking in the next room, and when Anatolia listened in, she could make out snatches of what they were saying: *sick for the fourth day in a row, my wife just can't figure out what's going on with her, my timing was bad getting this thing going with the move, you're wrong, now there's someone to look in on her at night.*

"If she's not better by morning, I'll send a telegram to the valley so they can dispatch an ambulance," Satenik said in an undertone.

Leave me alone, Anatolia wanted to demand, but a long moan emerged from her throat instead of words.

"What?" said Yasaman, leaning toward her.

Anatolia attempted to catch Yasaman's gaze but her eyelids felt leaden; she closed her eyes, waved her hand vaguely in the air, and caught her friend's fingers, which she squeezed weakly.

"No," she whispered. "No."

Patro burst into a loud, demanding howl and Satenik delicately placed Anatolia's feet on the sheet, stood up, took little steps toward the window, and shook a threatening finger at the yard as if saying, *Stop your yapping or you'll be chained up.* Patro darted toward her without watching where he was going and ran full tilt into a barrel, knocking it over before freezing on the spot, drenched from head to paw in slightly rancid rainwater. The barrel rolled along the ground with a deafening, drumming racket and hit its side against the wooden fence, sending the frightened birds into an alarmed uproar and scaring the sheep and goats in the shed. Then they heard quick footsteps in the next room: it was Vasily, who had leapt to his feet at the noise and was now hurrying off to the yard to see what had happened.

It's impossible even to die in peace with all these people around, Anatolia thought just before she was overcome by an abrupt feeling of relief that caused her to fall into a deep, heaven-sent sleep. She didn't open her eyes until noon the next day, awakened by Patro's barking and the clomping of his heavy paws crumpling the grass as he rushed along the wall, yelping away at the dandelion fluff that, unusually for May, was threatening to bury the village like a veritable snow-fall by the following month, when the poplar grove would also bloom.

Anatolia's neatly folded dress was hanging on the back of a chair. She put it on, buttoned it up all the way, and looked for her indoor shoes but couldn't find them. She stood up carefully and her body seemed unusually light, almost weightless; the aching had abated and it was considerably easier to breathe, even very deeply, and she felt only a tiny bit dizzy when she cautiously exhaled. Dishes were clinking in the kitchen, which meant Yasaman was pottering around and cooking. Anatolia went into the living room, where the daybed had been taken apart for use; someone had spent the night in the next room, protecting her sleep. The hallway, which was long, with a creaky floor and sunlight beating in through the windows, led straight and then to the left, toward the kitchen door. She walked slowly, her feet absorbing the warmth of the planks, but she winced from the grit underfoot – this was the fifth day without cleaning, so she would at least have to summon up the strength tomorrow to sweep the floors and do a wet clean. The kitchen door was wide open and a light breeze was swelling the cotton curtains in the window. Vasily was sitting at the table, squinting crookedly, chewing the end of his extinguished pipe, and clumsily wielding a knife, scraping pliant skin off little new potatoes.

He stood up instantly to help Anatolia into a chair, but she brushed him away with her hand as if to say she would do it herself.

"I'll get your shoes now. Yasaman knocked a bottle of tincture over them yesterday and they had to be rinsed and set out to dry. They're probably already dry."

He went out to the veranda and came back with the shoes, bending with a grunt and setting them on the floor. "I'll help you put them on."

"That's the last thing I need," said Anatolia, indignant.

"Whatever you say," said Vasily, not wanting to argue. He picked up the knife again. "Yasaman dropped in first thing this morning, listened to your heart, and said you sound better. She ordered me to peel potatoes and get the stove fired up. So I'm peeling as best I can."

"And who spent the night in the next room?"

"I did. I looked in on you a few times, to listen to your breathing. You breathe so faintly I practically had to put my ear right against your lips."

Anatolia ran her hand along the soles of her feet to brush off the debris stuck to them, then put on her shoes. Under other circumstances, she would have been embarrassed about having a man she wasn't related to spending the night on the other side of the wall and looking into her room, but now, thrown off-kilter by her affliction, she was only feeling slightly indifferent to the idea of him living in her house. Even if she didn't particularly mind the idea later, though, she had to put an immediate end to this silly scheme of Vasily's. Attempting to regain control of the situation, she turned to him:

"You need to go back to your own house."

Vasily tossed a peeled potato into a bowl. "Why?"

"I've had enough of this silly scheme of ours."

"Well, maybe it is silly. So why make it even sillier?"

Anatolia caught his mocking glance. She was angry. "What do you mean, make it sillier?"

"It's unwise to scurry around at our age. We've moved in together, so why move back out? What will people think of us?"

"At our age, someone else's opinion shouldn't worry us one bit," said Anatolia, mocking him.

Vasily grunted, moved the pipe from one corner of his mouth to the other, and stood up. His knife clattered when he set it down in front of Anatolia.

"Go ahead and work if you're so smart. And I'll start a fire while you do."

Anatolia jerked her shoulder but picked up the knife.

When Yasaman and Ovanes dropped by, they found a

vision of domesticity that was a pleasure to behold: Anatolia, her mouth stubbornly drawn, was scraping at the potatoes and Vasily was on his knees, blowing at a fire in the stove. He slammed the stove door shut at the sight of the neighbors, rose, and extended a hand to Ovanes: "Good afternoon."

"And a good afternoon to you, neighbor."

Yasaman put a pot of cold soup made from wheat and matzoon on the table, and went over to Anatolia.

"Let's see how you're doing. Sit up straight. Look at the end of my finger."

Anatolia obeyed compliantly. Yasaman drew a finger from Anatolia's right temple to her left, then back again, carefully following Anatolia's gaze. She sighed with relief. "Your pupils aren't jumping, so the dizziness seems to have let up."

"Yes, it's a little better," Anatolia agreed.

"I brewed up some rose hips with mint for you and left the mixture to cool. I'll bring it over later. You should drink it throughout the day. Vano Melikants was planning to slaughter a lamb today and promised to give me the liver and heart. I'll roast them with onions and you'll eat that, too. Don't make a face – you're ill, so you need treatment."

Anatolia sighed. "I'm perfectly fine. My blood pressure obviously dropped, but that happens to everybody. I have something else to worry about now. I've been trying to send Vasily back to his own home but he won't agree to go. He says we'll disgrace ourselves in our old age by trudging back and forth with our things."

Looking as serene as if they were talking about some other man, Vasily opened the stove door wide, stirring the logs around with a poker to help the fire catch from all sides.

"What do you mean, send him home? We decided to celebrate your, hmm, holiday," croaked Ovanes. "We'll set a table in our yard and we can all sit for a while. Satenik's already got the word out to the whole village and started on some wedding paklava."

"What are you talking about, paklava?!" said Anatolia, startled. "Why are you making us into a laughingstock?"

"The usual wedding paklava, with honey and walnuts and a coin for happiness. Whoever gets it will be the next to marry," chuckled Ovanes.

Anatolia was dumbfounded. "What are you talking about? Have you lost your minds or something?"

"Watch your tongue, would you?"

"Well?"

"Without insults!"

While Anatolia and Ovanes bickered, Yasaman rinsed the peeled potatoes, placed a large skillet on the stove, and spooned in some clarified butter. She waited for it to heat up before tossing in the little potatoes and immediately covering them tightly with a lid.

"Ovanes, get some herbs from the garden. And bring some cheese. We'll sit down to lunch when the potatoes are roasted," Yasaman told her husband.

"The kitchen garden hasn't been watered since yesterday," Anatolia remembered.

"I already watered it this morning," Vasily replied and headed for the door. Ovanes followed, grumbling indignantly.

After the men left the house, Yasaman moved a chair toward Anatolia and sat down across from her.

"Why are you being so cross?"

"I don't want to live with him, that's why I'm cross."

"You actually *want* to grow old alone?"

"What's the difference, alone or not? I'll grow old either way."

"If it's the same either way, then why be so stubborn?"

Anatolia drummed her hand on the tabletop. "But I'm not being stubborn. It's just that none of this is to my liking," she said, starting to count on her fingers in annoyance, "neither his moving in so fast nor the yapping dog in the yard nor the animals in the shed that he brought without asking if I needed them. He's behaving like he's the master of my house."

"And how's he supposed to behave?"

"I don't know. But he could at least ask if he's allowed or not."

"Since when do the men in our village ask permission?"

Anatolia leaned against the back of the chair and rubbed her eyes wearily. "I should have turned him down from the start."

"You didn't, though, so what's the point of getting indignant now?"

"Can I take back my word or not?"

"Come on, what kind of promise can be made one instant, only to be taken back the next?"

Anatolia couldn't find any sort of answer. Yasaman stood, poured soup into the bowls, and sliced the bread. She stirred the potatoes with a wooden spatula and salted them. Anatolia watched, her lips pursed in offense. She didn't understand why her friend was persuading her to resign herself to what had happened rather than supporting her.

Yasaman caught her distressed gaze. "If only you knew, my dear, how awful it is to grow old alone," she sighed, bitterly.

"Oh, I do know," said Anatolia, weakening.

"Well then, if you know... You see how we're living here. Waiting for death, from one funeral to the next. What lies ahead for us? Not a ray of light, not a shred of hope. So why are you refusing an opportunity to make someone at least a tiny bit happier? If you're not going to think of yourself, then at least think of him."

The veranda's plank floor started creaking as Ovanes and Vasily returned from the garden. Patro plodded behind them, whining plaintively.

Yasaman peered out the window. "What's he crying over?"

"He's asking for some cheese. I broke off a little piece but it wasn't enough. Something made me take in a dog in my old age. Satenik kept telling me, get one, get one," Vasily said, hilariously mimicking his cousin's squeaky voice. "'It's not so lonely with a dog,' she'd say."

"Your cousin doesn't stop. She's either matchmaking you with a dog or a wife."

Vasily gave an embarrassed laugh, breaking off another little piece of cheese and tossing it to Patro.

"That's it, no more."

The dog swallowed the treat in a flash and wanted to start singing another plaintive song to beg for more, but when his eyes met his master's stern look he realized there would be nothing more to catch. He conquered the stairs in two leaps and darted off to the yard to chase chickens.

They ate lunch in silence and tranquility. They spoke little and only of distant things, and there was so much that was offhand and ordinary in the clinking of spoons, the request to pass the salt and slice a piece of cheese, or in a swallow of water and the slightly dry heel of the homemade bread, that Anatolia sensed for the first time that life was a gift, not something to take for granted. She shifted her gaze subtly from Yasaman to Ovanes and then to Vasily, catching his measured, unhurried gestures and mentally agreeing with them, feeling surprised that she had never noticed this unconditional connection between herself and everything around her, be they people, birds, or the reddish stones at the old cemetery. Anatolia suddenly grasped that there was no heaven and no hell; happiness was heaven and grief was hell. And their God was everywhere, all over, not just because He was all-powerful but also because He was the unseen threads that connected them with each other.

After lunch she let Yasaman feed her rose hip tisane and put her to bed. She slept until evening and woke up just as the herd was returning to the village, smelling of the setting sun and May fields. The herd wandered the crooked street, thinning out at each gate.

Anatolia went outside just as Vasily was gathering up his goats and sheep. They exchanged the usual few words with the shepherd and Vasily drove the animals into the shed. When he noticed Anatolia on the veranda, he slowed his pace and smiled with the very edge of his lips. Only then did Anatolia discern the unusual steel-gray tint of his eyes. She leaned against the railing and nodded sedately.

"I'll milk the animals. The main thing is for you to bring water to the shed, so they can be washed before they're milked."

"Oh, I'll manage on my own. Satenik taught me."

"She taught you how to milk?"

"Well, yes."

"And how's that going for you? Can you do it?"

"The sheep haven't complained yet."

Anatolia buried her face in her hands and burst out laughing.

"Fine, get the water. Today you'll milk them yourself. And I'll just be there with you."

PART II

*For the One
Who Told the Story*

Chapter One

Vano Melikants's house stood on the very edge of the section of Manish-kar that had cascaded into the void after the earthquake. The cliff had split in two and then collapsed into the chasm, leaving behind a lone notch on which there towered a two-story house with a huge fruit garden, a kitchen garden, and several sound outbuildings, all enclosed by a solid fence. The Maranians marveled that something like this could happen: the neighboring households had fallen into the depths, yet Vano's family had not only survived but were left with all of their property intact, right down to the logs heaped outside the fence, waiting for someone to split them for firewood.

Valinka was certain that Providence had spared them not through mercy but because of a chance oversight. Apparently, when Providence's deathly hand had drawn the line that was supposed to separate the living part of the village from the dead, it had somehow grown distracted and passed over their household. Unlike his wife, though, Vano saw nothing supernatural in their survival. On the contrary, he got terribly annoyed when she set about sighing and lamenting, imagining what might have happened if their home had been washed into the chasm by the deluge of loose earth.

"We'd have been done for, it's as simple as that!" he would say, angrily cutting her off.

Valinka would gasp and clutch her heart in offense, then Vano would slam the door and go off to the far end of the garden where there was a stubby bench under a crooked old cherry tree. It was far too small to fit two adults: it could barely seat one person comfortably now that one of its legs had rotted away and you had to perch at the very end to avoid tumbling over.

Vano could sit under the old cherry tree until the stars came out, riffling through memories of those dear to him who had passed into nonexistence. His mother was a sister of Arshak-bek, who had been forced to flee the new regime that overthrew the tsar at the beginning of the last century. Her grandfather, Levon-bek, descended from the eastern branch of the noble line of the Lusignans, and was always proud to bring up his distant ancestor, Levon the Sixth Lusignan, who was the last king of Cilicia, a knight of the Order of the Sword, and the seneschal of Jerusalem. Given his lineage, Levon-bek had opposed his granddaughter marrying a commoner. But during her years of study at an institute for noblewomen, Vano's mother, a stubborn young woman, had picked up enough ideas about equality and brotherhood (not to mention various suffragette inclinations) that she went against the old man's will, binding her life to the son of a peasant – a prosperous one, but through and through a peasant's peasant. She knew perfectly well that her kin would not agree of their own volition to the unequal match, so she she ran off to the valley with her beloved and returned only after she was certain she was pregnant.

Infuriated by his granddaughter's obstinacy, Levon-bek vowed to remove her from his life once and for all. He held to his vow but in a very peculiar way. Vano's mother told of how she would come to the ancestral home and head straight to her grandfather's study, where he spent the greater part of his time reading and taking notes. She would settle on the floor and lay her head on his knees. Her grandfather silently stroked her hair and each touch of the old man's weightless hand seemed like a blessing. By then, Vano's mother was near her time and suffering terribly from bouts of nausea that had resumed toward the last month of her pregnancy, but she calmed in an astonishing way when she was alone with her grandfather; she was even able to indulge in eating a little, though most of the time she vomited at the mere smell of food. Her grandfather upped and left without exchanging a word with his granddaughter, but it was to her that he left an amateurishly painted portrait of Levon the Sixth in Crusader's armor, standing in front of a fluttering flag decorated with the blue-and-white seal of the Lusignan clan. Maybe the gift was for edification, maybe for reproach. As a granddaughter worthy of her grandfather, Vano's mother hung the portrait in the most visible spot in her living room without so much as raising an eyebrow and made sure there were always fresh flowers in the vase below.

She suffered tremendously from being separated from her brother, who was forced to escape the new regime; she apparently sensed in her heart that they would not meet again in this life. She wasn't persecuted but she was cautious, never again appearing at the family's estate, which by that time had been looted and nationalized, and she took the portrait of her crowned ancestor from the wall and stored it away in the attic, irately rejecting her husband's proposal of burning it in a bonfire to be safe.

"I'm not going to destroy my only memory of my grand-father," she said, cutting off her husband and hiding the por-trait behind a big wooden chest full of assorted unnecessary odds and ends, which is where the painting lay, befouled by the fly invasion, covered in a dusty cocoon of spiderwebs, and hopelessly dampening and fading during the hundred years of solitude to which it was consigned by the ambivalence of their distant progeny.

Vano's mother took her husband's surname in order to cover her tracks definitively and not let her noble origins make the new regime nervous. This was an unprecedented occurrence in Maran since local young women did not change their surnames when they married, remaining an integral part of their own kin rather than renouncing them. The villagers piously kept Vano's mother's real surname a secret but among themselves they called her husband "Melikants-son-in-law", since *melik* means "prince". Which is why Vano's family became known as Melikants. Princely.

Tigran Melikants, Vano's oldest and only grandchild, came into the world the year Noah's herd arrived in the village; he turned out to be the only baby born during the famine who survived. Vano remembered in the minutest of details the morning his daughter-in-law was delivered of a little boy toward daybreak after the torment of never-ending hours of contractions; his body was so tiny and gaunt that it fit completely on his grandfather's palm. Vano's daughter-in-law died the next night, worn out and lifeless, not so much from giving birth as from the exhaustion of hunger. Her death placed all care for the newborn on the shoulders of Valinka, who by this time had buried her two younger daughters.

On the very same morning Tigran was born, the white peacock came out to the edge of the chasm for the first time and stood, motionless and unwavering, as if keeping watch; he didn't return until nearly evening, weakened and with bald spots on his back and wings. He then molted for a month. Valinka swept an entire heap of feathers out of the corners of the veranda each day, gathering them into a sack so she could sort through them later and sew a feather bed for the baby. The newborn's life hung in the balance that whole long month, but he somehow pulled through and started turning a corner when the peacock, now liberated of his old plumage, slowly began growing a silvery down as light and weightless as the baby's breath. Nobody paid those strange coincidences any attention until Valinka finally found some time to untie the top of the sack and discovered there weren't feathers inside but debris that very much resembled wood ash. She scooped up a handful and held it closer to her eyes to examine it more carefully. The ash was lighter in weight than dust. It sparkled like snow in the sun and smelled of cinnamon and almond. Vano ordered his wife not to tell anyone about it, not so much out of fear that they would be regarded as insane as that he was unable to find an explanation for what had happened. He buried the sack of ashes under the fence, then for some reason hastily tied together dead sticks to make a cross which he drove into the ground; the lifeless little pieces of wood revived, growing into a cherry laurel that, though lopsided, bore fruit. Whenever he attempted to straighten the cherry tree's trunk, it stubbornly extended its branches sideways to where Manish-kar's left shoulder had collapsed during the earthquake. Its blood-red berries dropped into the void during the summer months, and by autumn it was adorned with crimson leaves.

Tigran grew into a sickly and nervous child who slept fitfully at night and cried constantly. He only gained strength after turning five, the age at which he also started talking, expressing himself for a long time with only simple words: "something to drink", "want bread." After losing all their children to famine over the years, his grandmother and grandfather doted on him. Valinka never left him by himself, even bringing him with her when she went to visit the women next door. Tigran played with wooden soldiers or pebbles while the women focused on their handiwork: some embroidered, some knitted wool socks using four needles, others mended clothes. Never taking their eyes off what they were doing, they discussed their business in a whisper. In the evenings, Valinka would hand him over to her husband so she could take care of household chores while grandfather and grandson weeded the kitchen garden, brought the birds into the henhouse, and then sat on the bench under the young cherry laurel tree, which remained gaunt and long-limbed. Vano told stories, both invented and true, while Tigran listened, propping up his cheek with a weak, transparent little fist; if you stroked his back, you could count his sharp protruding vertebrae. When the little boy ran uncertainly around the yard, catching the toes of his shoes on even the tiniest of stones and doing his best to fall and bloody his nose, his grandmother and grandfather froze, tracking him with alarmed gazes, but if

Valinka felt the impulse to dart off to her grandson whenever he stumbled, then Vano was the opposite, standing still and angrily holding his wife back by the elbow as if to say: *Don't you dare. Let him fall, that's why he's a boy, he needs to fall and get back up*. In those moments, the peacock, who was indifferent to everything around him and unsociable too, would abruptly take wing onto the railing, anxiously call with a crane-like rattle, spin his handsome head that bore a regal snow-white crown, and not shift his gaze from the child. Tigran was the only being that the peacock displayed any interest in: he simply ignored the rest of the world.

Vano didn't believe the peacock had just appeared out of the blue, even suspecting it had some sort of important goal, perhaps even a mission. One day, he rewound time, comparing dates and recalling that the truck with the birds had arrived in the village on the exact same day his daughter-in-law had told them she was pregnant. Being a sensible person who regarded anything that seemed inexplicable with skepticism, Vano attempted right then and there to find some sort of rational interpretation for what had happened. After meeting defeat, though, he waved it off and gave in, coming to terms with the fact that there are things that ordinary words cannot explain and the human mind cannot comprehend. He supposed the peacock's arrival was somehow connected to Tigran but he didn't want to speak with his wife about that lest she start gasping again, grasping at her heart, and speculating – all of which would have scared the neighbors too, since the Maranians were a rational people who nevertheless believed in dreams and signs. They would doubtless have resumed the habit of coming to gawk at the bird, who would become nervous from their attention, just as he had been in those first days, when the village was so taken aback by his haughty beauty that people swarmed the yard, clicking their tongues and making an effort to pat his splendid feathers whenever he let his guard down and allowed anyone to come within two paces of him.

Out of deference to the peacock, Vano decided to display his gratitude using all the resources he had available: he spread a rug on the veranda, attached a three-step perch to the fence so it was easier for the bird to climb onto the railing, and ordered his wife to add only select wheat with raisins to the feeder and personally change his drinking water several times a day. The peacock, however, didn't notice these attentive gestures and ate very reluctantly, picking at the grain in his dish with distaste; he ignored the perch and flew up to the railing by energetically flapping his wings; and he sat motionless on the edge of the railing, gazing blankly at the barnyard birds milling around below.

Vano then went to the valley and came back with a peahen that he had procured at great expense. Yes, she was mostly brown instead of white, since white peacocks were not bred in the valley. He carefully let the female out on the veranda, but the male wouldn't even turn his head to look at her. She walked along the patterned rug, pecked at something from the food dish, drank some water, and then went down to the yard to mingle with the chickens and turkeys. Vano observed the peacocks attentively for about six months and when he was convinced the male had no interest in her, he prepared for another trip to the valley to return the female to her former owner. The owner moaned and groaned but eventually agreed to take the peahen back, though he only refunded half Vano's money.

The money, however, hardly worried Vano; he was just bothered that he might not have done everything he could to thank his grandson's savior. Vano had no doubt that Tigran had survived thanks to the peacock. The peacock responded to Vano's care with absolute disinterest and paid no attention to anyone but Tigran; the bird was usually quiet and indifferent, but sometimes he would make his way to the precipice and shriek into the sky with a despairing, heartrending call, as if he were asking to go to the place from which he had been unjustly banished. When his shout didn't reach the heavens, he would return home, his snow-white feathers sweeping the reddish road dust, and then take refuge in a corner and keep to himself for a long time.

Unlike Vano, Tigran had been accustomed to the white peacock since early childhood and took his continual presence on the veranda of the house for granted, treating him like any other backyard bird. Only once did he ask why the chickens, guinea hens, and turkeys slept in the coop but the peacock slept on the veranda.

Vano thought quickly: "It's so the peacock's long feathers don't bother them."

"Okay then," Tigran agreed easily. He believed his grandmother and grandfather unconditionally and had grown into a considerate, hardworking, and very inquisitive child who was tremendously eager to attend the school where he was the only student. When he was starting first grade, the other children born after the famine had barely learned to talk. He went to classes twice a week, studying diligently, and even if he wasn't reaching for the stars, he read a lot, and so Anatolia (who had begun her librarian duties by that time) doted on him and allowed him to borrow books for longer than the usual loan period. He was always in demand for household tasks, either helping his grandfather dig up the kitchen garden, lugging water, running to the neighbors' house on an errand, or grinding wheat with the manual mill in no time at all, something his grandmother might have taken half the day to do.

By the time he turned fourteen, Tigran had grown into a bright, industrious adolescent who was completely satisfied with his life. The only thing that weighed on him was solitude. There was nobody for him to be friends with since the only other young man in Maran, Vasily the blacksmith's younger brother, had already turned twenty-two, and he hardly socialized with anyone because of his health problems. Seven-year-old children, meanwhile, were boring and uninteresting for Tigran, a youth with a bass voice and fluff over his lip. And so when he finished eighth grade, his grandmother and grandfather reluctantly gave in to persuasion from the school director and Anatolia and sent him to the valley to continue his education.

Being separated from their grandson was like lopping off one of their limbs with a knife. Vano suffered from insomnia for a long time and Valinka fell ill with an attack of nerves, but, fortunately, that all passed without grave consequence: she cried for a week and then rose, alive, despite having aged and thinned severely. Tigran was living with distant relatives of the school director and paid for his accommodation with groceries that Valinka gathered up once a week, sending two sacks to the valley in the postal van. There was food in one sack: cheese, clarified butter, cured raw meat, honey, dried fruits, brined vegetables, and a large stack of lavash. She sent the other sack with Tigran's laundered and carefully ironed clothing; the next van returned clothes for washing. Tigran came to see the old people twice a year, for Christmas and summer vacations. By the time he graduated from high school, he had shot up in height and matured dramatically, and his deep, affectionate voice boomed out to his grandmother and grandfather from under the ceiling. Since he didn't let them work around the house, he did the weeding, harvesting, roof patching, and splitting of firewood for autumn. What's more, he wasn't lazy about it and stacked the logs so the previous year's dry wood was on the top and the unseasoned wood was on the bottom.

Tigran went to a military academy after high school and rose to a senior rank by the age of twenty-five. He had been planning to marry, but the war started so he didn't get around to it and then the regiment he commanded was surrounded and there was no news at all from Tigran for eight long years. Valinka cried her eyes out and prayed every hour of every day, wearing down the threshold at the old chapel; Vano had serious problems with his veins, and his feet ached and burned, but the old man endured without saying anything. By this time, the peacock was frail but still alive and surprisingly well, giving Vano strength because that undoubtedly had to mean his grandson was alive. Valinka brought the peacock inside when the time came to take apart the veranda's plank floor so there would be something to feed the fire. The bird gave in without complaining and started living in the kitchen; he watched the fiery faces that the woodstove painted on the wall and lost his feathers, which Vano gathered up and carefully put in a pillowcase. Valinka knitted sweaters and patterned socks to send to the front, placing in each anonymous package a peacock feather and a tiny figure of the Holy Mother of God that Vano had carved. The packages had no return addresses, so they went off and didn't return the way other correspondence came back to Maran homes in lieu of death notices.

Vano remembered right down to the last detail the spring of the year the war ended, just as clearly and completely as he recalled the day Tigran was born. For some reason, he had taken it upon himself to do some calculations the night before and discovered that exactly thirty-three years had passed since the day the peacock had appeared in his home. The next morning, he and Valinka woke up to the peacock's husky shrieking. By some wonder, despite not walking at all and barely being able to hold up his head during his last winter, the peacock had made his way to the kitchen, where he was scratching his beak at the door in an attempt to open it, and calling for help. Vano picked him up and went out on the veranda at the very same moment the gate opened, letting his grandson, who was skinny and scar-riddled but very much alive, into the yard. The peacock died that same evening, in Tigran's arms, during his story of how he had been surrounded, how he had miraculously escaped from captivity and spent that entire time as a partisan in the woods, and how his leg had been wounded and his thigh had had to be cauterized without anesthesia so an infection wouldn't spread, and how there was a deep, ugly scar that had frozen a muscle and didn't allow him to bend his leg fully. In the middle of his grandson's story, Vano distinctly sensed light breathing from up on high and then the heavens themselves descended down below the mountains, opened the windows wide, swept into the house, intertwined their hands to form a cradle, and placed the tsar bird's sparkling soul inside before soaring upward, leaving behind the light aroma of cinnamon and almond, and something else elusive and incomprehensible but eternally beautiful.

They buried the peacock by the precipice. Tigran ordered a low openwork fence from Vasily and planted white mountain lilies on the burial mound. After deciding he intended to live out his days in the village, Tigran went to the valley to renounce his military rank and honors, but then yielded to his grandmother and grandfather's entreaties a year later and packed his things to go beyond the northern passage for a new life in a place where another war wouldn't catch up with him. He became both the only man from Maran to return from the war alive and the last of the young to leave the village of old people. Living up north was difficult, but he neither complained nor became downhearted. He found work and shortly thereafter married a local woman with a one-year-old daughter; his wife had a beautiful, melodious name, Nastasya, which Vano and Valinka pronounced syllable by syllable, *Nazz-stas-ya*. They knew her solely from photographs: she was pretty, with high cheekbones and full lips, and had light, wavy hair and big eyes that they imagined were probably blue, or perhaps green. Six years after their grandson left, he had not visited Maran once. But then he gladdened his grandmother and grandfather with the joyous news that his wife had given birth to a son in December and they had named him Kirakos in honor of Vano's grandfather, who had died in the massacre.

From that place beyond the mountain pass that skirted the valley like a wide horseshoe, they received letters with a promise of coming to visit before too long. Valinka stored the envelopes in the bureau with lavender and often went to

Anatolia to ask her to reread them, even though she knew each letter's contents by heart. And Vano would sit under the old cherry laurel tree, riffling through memories of kin who had passed into the river of oblivion, never taking his gaze from the edge of the bluff. It was bathed in sunbeams on clear days, swathed in snow during the winter, and on overcast days it was despondent and restless, smelling of damp stones. Sometimes a rippling luminescence would appear over the peacock's grave and when Vano spotted that light, he would rise slowly from the bench and approach the stockade fence without going through the gate, because he lacked the nerve. He would shield his eyes with his hand, squinting, and scrutinize a lonely silver silhouette, a head that was proudly thrown back and wearing an ethereal crown, a dome-like fan of feathers, and a lost gaze that was striving upward into silent heavens that held no answers.

Chapter Two

Vano died shortly before Pentecost. He ate lunch, lay down to rest, and didn't wake up. It was as if Valinka had known something was going to happen to her husband. She hadn't left his side since morning, when they had pottered around in the kitchen garden together, headed down to the edge of town to pick sorrel for a pie, then dropped by the meidan to say hello to fellow villagers and have a look at who had brought what to barter, and then, finally, stopped in at Mukuch Nemetsants's shop on the way home to pick up shoes they had ordered for Vano.

The shoes turned out to be just what he needed: high quality, leather, with a solid sole, capable of withstanding the mercilessly beat-up village roads, and they were slip-ons, which significantly eased the process of putting them on because he didn't have to bend, grunting and squinting half-blindly while his disobedient fingers dug around for laces. The shoes were a bit large but even that gladdened Vano, given that the problems with his veins meant any pinching caused unbearable agony;

Valinka even knitted his patterned socks without elastic so they wouldn't press on the sensitive skin at his ankles.

Vano tried on the shoes, walked from one corner of the shop to another, and caught his reflection in a shard of mirror covered with rusty spots. He sighed with relief. He wanted to keep the shoes on, but Valinka wouldn't let him.

"You'll put them on for Pentecost," she said, handing the old worn shoes to her husband. "That's what a holiday's for, after all, flaunting new things."

Vano silently paid and went outside. Though he hadn't considered arguing, he left the bundle with the sorrel and new shoes on the counter for effect. Valinka shook her head and took the things, said goodbye to Mukuch, and followed her husband. He was walking without turning around, and his large, work-weary hands were clasped behind his back.

"At least take the sorrel," his wife shouted after him.

"I won't," Vano growled without looking back.

"So what was it I said that got you so offended? Pentecost's in two days. What, you don't have enough patience or something?"

Vano said nothing. Valinka picked up the pace, caught up to her husband, and shoved the shoebox at him. He took it but didn't turn to look at her.

"You've become grumpier with age. You get offended over the littlest things," sighed Valinka.

"If you don't create those little things, I won't get grumpy."

"And what was it I said?"

"Nothing."

"Exactly, it was nothing. I'm only looking after you. Have I ever, in all our life together, done anything that's caused you harm?"

She opened the gate and stood aside to let her husband in but he made a point of walking past and heading to the far end of the fence, where a section was lying on its side and had crushed a currant bush that hadn't borne fruit in a long time. Valinka folded her arms across her chest, pursed her thin lips, and watched as her husband turned sideways, raised the box with the shoes and the little bundle of sorrel over his head, and pushed his way through the narrow gap in the fence. She threw her arms up and went inside to heat up some lunch, thinking he would be more amenable on a full stomach.

Vano caught his pant leg on a knot sticking out of the wooden fence, jerked his leg to free himself, and cursed when he heard the sound of ripping fabric. He freed his leg and looked at his pants. The material had been slit and hung hopelessly, exposing part of his calf. He stepped on a shred of material, tore it off, and left it to lie on the grass.

"That's where you belong!" he said angrily, although it was unclear whether he was speaking to the fabric or himself. Then he set off through the fruit garden, all scattered with light pink and snow-white blossoms.

Once he reached the veranda, he sat on the top step, rolled and lit a cigarette, and spat out little bits of tobacco in irritation. Of course Valinka was right. He had turned into a grumpy old man over the years. But she hadn't grown any sweeter either! She was quarrelsome and uncompromising. All she did was nag at him from morning until night. He'd hung up his towel wrong, he had splashed water everywhere, he hadn't opened the window wide enough, he had looked at her the wrong way, or he had thought the wrong thing. At breakfast this morning, she had really given him what for because he had spilled his tea. He should put the sugar in the cup first, she said, not the hot water, then he wouldn't overfill it with water or splash it when stirring.

"Why'd you sit down on the stairs? You'll get a draft on your back and won't be able to straighten up!" said Valinka. She was leaning out the door as if she had read his mind.

"Maybe that's exactly what I want!" snapped Vano.

"What do you mean, that's what you want?"

"To get a draft on my back."

"Vano!"

"What?"

Valinka wanted to shoot off a caustic remark, like usual, but checked herself.

"Nothing. Let's go eat, lunch is hot."

"I'll finish smoking and come in." Vano didn't let on that he felt lost because the usual rebukes he was so sick and tired of hadn't come.

Valinka went inside, leaving the door ajar. Vano could hear her through the kitchen window scraping the bottom of the pot as she poured the rest of yesterday's soup into bowls. The main course would be boiled potatoes with turkey pieces, and then there was peach compote: the last two jars were left in the cellar and she had wanted to set them aside for Pentecost, but she gave up on that and opened a jar to make her husband happy. Peach slices were his favorite treat, and he ate them like a child who had fallen upon some forbidden sweetness, almost choking in his hurry, licking his fingers and rolling his eyes in pleasure.

After lunch, Vano lay down for a rest, as was his habit, and Valinka took up her work stitching woolen quilts. She had to do that on the floor, otherwise the wool batting, which was evenly dispersed inside the fabric, clumped up. Sitting side on, she moved along the quilt's perimeter, basting large stitches, and when she reached the center she quilted a round sun, following the habit of her mother Katinka, who had been renowned throughout the area for her skilled hands and love of order. Katinka had taught her children needlework and neatness, too, and so her daughters had been the most coveted brides in Maran. The eldest, Sarui, had lived on the very edge of the gorge. The only thing farther from the village at that time was the church of Grigor Lusavorich, so Valinka used to look in on her every Saturday after matins because Sarui very rarely went to services, instead caring for her gravely ill father-in-law, who suffered from respiratory troubles. Valinka would take it upon herself to do Sarui's household chores for the whole day, cooking, tidying up, taking care of the children, and sitting at the bedside of her sister's father-in-law when he had uncontrollable coughing fits, all so Sarui had the chance to catch up on her sleep and rest a little. Valinka often brought Sarui's children back to her house and then shared their care with her mother, who had come to live with Valinka after she had married.

Then the earthquake carried away Sarui and her entire family, including her husband, father-in-law, and three children – a girl and two boys. Valinka went numb inside whenever she recalled how her mother, who lost her wits from the unbearable grief, used to dart along the precipice, calling to her daughter and dead grandchildren. After that ill-fated event, Katinka would wake up with her face covered in tears and cry all day without sobbing or moaning; she cooked, laundered, tidied, went shopping and poured, poured, poured out tears.

Valinka wound her mother's wrists with handkerchiefs each morning so she could wipe her face with them, and she changed the soaked ones for dry ones hourly. In eternal pietà for her unfortunate daughter, Katinka departed too, in rainy weather, during the strongest of downpours, which continued for exactly seven days after she died. The storm took only a small respite to allow the funeral procession to reach the cemetery and commit Katinka's coffin to the earth.

Once every two or three years, Valinka washed the woolen quilts and restitched the inevitable round sun in the middle, in memory of her mother, sister, brothers, and the children who had slipped, like sand through her fingers, into nonexistence, to the other edge of the universe, to the edge that is locked away from mortals by seven seals, each the size of the eye of a needle and the weight of an entire mountain, making it impossible to discern how to open them up or how to move them in order to go through.

Over time, a barely noticeable crack that had appeared on the day of the earthquake began growing along the wall of the marital bedroom and rising toward the ceiling. After reaching the very top, it moved sideways, painstakingly carving out a narrow space in the stone through which a lone ray of sun pushed its way during the day and a dim patch of moonlight at night. Vano had reinforced that side of the house with wooden beams and filled in the crevice with mortar, but it felt as if their residence were breathing and walking, creaking its shutters and sides, so the mortar didn't hold well and began crumbling with time, baring the wall's torn wound again. Irritated, Vano again neatly filled it with cement, but in vain. The cement disintegrated a year or two later and the sections of the crack that had opened gradually became covered in sickly grass that grew, against all odds, right out of the stone. By the time the exasperated Vano again set to filling in the crack, spiders had spun their ethereal webs in the blades of grass and a thin, jagged strip burned by the sun's persistent heat had blossomed on the wooden floor, which was painted dark blue.

"There's life everywhere," marveled Valinka, scrutinizing cobwebs chock-full of dried insect corpses and stunted stalks of grass making their way into the room. "There's death everywhere, and life too."

They had last filled in the wall two summers ago, but that had been enough time for it to crumble and become overgrown, so Vano had been planning to tackle the matter once again, though not until autumn, after the heat abated. Valinka shuddered as she waited for yet more repair work. It didn't seem like much of anything, but it was a whole day of fuss and then cleanup for a week. She was ready just to bolt the bedroom door and move into the guest room, leaving the entire room for the crack to take over, but her husband was against that. "The earthquake didn't manage to drive me out, but that'll do it?" he said, gesturing angrily at the cracked wall. Valinka argued with him about it sometimes but later resigned herself: fine, let him. He hadn't tired of battling the crack all these years, so why try to stop him now? We all have our own purpose in life, our own battles to fight.

After she finished stitching the quilts, she brought them out to the yard and hung them on the clothesline so they could breathe in plenty of warmth and air during the afternoon. In the evening, she would need to put them away in the linen chest with lavender until the cold hit. Valinka brought some matzoon, bread, and cheese up from the cellar for a snack and then went to wake her oversleeping husband. The whole way to the bedroom – through a small entryway and two rooms, and past the guest bedroom furnished with old furniture and which they looked into only twice a year, at Christmas and Easter, the only holidays that meant having guests to set a large table for – not one string of her soul quivered or moaned in warning. But when she opened the door, Valinka realized instantly what had happened and kept walking a few more steps out of inertia before stopping, unable to take her gaze from her husband. Vano was lying with his head cast back lifelessly, his left arm tangled up in the bars of the headboard and a blanket clumped up by his legs. The sun was not shining in directly, but a dazzling light was pouring through the crack in the wall, flowing powerfully and endlessly, and filling the room. It was unrestrained and blinding, and its reflection gave her husband's eyes a glassy shine.

"Vano-dzhan?" Valinka called in a whisper.

As an ambulance hurtled along the hardened and pot-holed village road, scaring all the livestock in the vicinity with its siren's heartrending wail, Valinka was hanging sheets over the mirrors in the house and filling the bedroom with incense smoke. By the time the doctor arrived, the yard had already been swept clean and sprayed with water, and the chickens and turkeys had been herded into the coop so their idle, bewildered look wouldn't irritate anyone. Dressed in black from head to toe, Valinka sat silently and sternly at the headboard by Vano, her hands clasped on her knees as she examined the crack in the wall. "Who's going to fill it in now?" she asked the air.

The doctor, an impossibly thin, hawk-nosed man whose eyes were red-rimmed from lack of sleep, reluctantly turned toward the broad, three-centimeter crack that snaked from the plank floor to the ceiling. He shrugged uncertainly and kept silent. Then he asked anyway: "A bomb?"

"The earthquake."

The doctor wouldn't have dreamt of asking how someone could live half a century with a wall cracked through like that. He wrote up a death certificate and left for the valley, escorted by the backyard birds' squabbling din, their commentary on the siren's penetrating howl.

Valinka buried her husband in his old tweed suit and worn-out shoes. She would try to return the new ones, unworn, to Mukuch Nemetsants.

The story took a further, completely sudden new direction, like the wag of a tail. The night after his funeral, Valinka dreamt of Vano, gloomy in his suit and socks, gazing at her reproachfully:

"You pinched my new shoes!"

She woke up in a cold sweat, then tossed and turned for a long time. She ran off to the chapel in the morning and lit a candle for Vano's repose. Then she stopped at Mukuch's shop and asked if she could return the shoes. He said that was possible.

She dreamt of Vano again that night. Now naked, he was standing up to his knees in a swamp, silent and disapproving.

"Why are you being like this, anyway?" asked Valinka, upset. "Shoes can be returned. We're not made of money, you know!"

Vano turned away and waded through the swamp, working hard to pick up his emaciated, veiny feet.

Valinka's heart broke.

"Be patient a while. Someone will die and I'll pass them along then," she shouted.

Vano nodded, but still he didn't turn around and continued to walk, quickening his pace. Valinka looked closely and saw he was no longer limping.

Nobody in Maran died for a month. Then an opportunity finally came when Mariam Bekhlvants's mother-in-law passed away. Valinka wrapped her husband's new shoes in a clean kitchen towel and went to see Mariam. She asked for the shoes to be put in the coffin with the deceased.

"Where am I supposed to squeeze them in?!" Mariam threw up her hands helplessly. "You know what a fatty she was." Here Mariam stopped short, looked all around her, and continued in a whisper, "We had to order the widest coffin so my mother-in-law would somehow fit!"

Valinka burst into tears. She told of how she hadn't let Vano put on his new shoes. How he had been lying with his arm tangled up in the daybed's headboard, how he had been trudging naked through the swamp on his sickly feet, blue with protruding veins. Mariam chewed at her lips and gave a little sigh. She took the shoes.

"I'll put them on my mother-in-law. I daresay there's no difference for her what shoes she's wearing when she crosses the threshold into the great beyond."

And that was how they settled things.

Chapter Three

The envelope was large, very wrinkled, and covered in numerous colorful stamps that had been slapped on. The postman, a skinny, wiry man in a tattered peaked cap and pants that were stretched and worn thin at the knees, pulled the envelope from his shoulder bag, turned it over in his hands, and for some reason reread the address, though he remembered it by heart: village of Maran, last house on Manish-kar's western slope.

"Hope it's good news," he muttered. "I wouldn't want to drag myself all this way for something bad."

"If it is God's will," Father Azaria answered phlegmatically.

The postman put the envelope back in his bag and carefully pulled the zipper. He chewed at his lips.

"Father Azaria, may I ask one more question?"

"Don't start in again, Mamikon!" The priest cut him off impatiently, putting his hand over the heavy cross he wore on his chest so it wouldn't swing as he walked. He quickened his pace.

Mamikon watched Father Azaria stride along the rutted mountain road, the sleeves and hem of his robe fluttering in the dusty, dry wind. The day was hot, and the scent of scorching rocks, freshly mown grass, and dry St. John's wort hung in the air. A flock of village swallows soared up out of the gorge, chattering furiously and circling overhead before flying east, toward the sun.

Mamikon stood and shifted from one foot to the other, inhaling deeply and then slowly exhaling. He straightened the shoulder strap of his bag, took off his hat, and carefully dusted it off. He adjusted his pants. He accomplished all this without taking his eye off the priest's receding back.

Father Azaria seemed to feel Mamikon's gaze upon him. He took sweeping steps at an unhurried pace and didn't turn. Only when he reached the brink of the road, which veered off to the right after that and disappeared beyond a steep cliff, did he stop and reluctantly glance back.

"Are you coming or what?"

"Where else would I go, Holy Father? Of course I'm coming!" Mamikon instantly set off, satisfied that he had proven more stubborn than his companion.

"As stubborn as a mule," said Father Azaria, unable to hold back.

"Might be something to that," the postman answered with dignity.

The conversation with Father Azaria had gone astray at the very foot of Manish-kar, right when Mamikon had dared doubt the rationality of the assertion that one needs to turn the right cheek if struck on the left. Offended to the depths of his soul by this disrespect, the priest had burst into an entire sermon, attempting to drive home to his opponent the groundlessness of his doubts. After listening attentively to Father Azaria's lecture, Mamikon clicked his tongue, shifted his cap toward the back of his head, and scratched his forehead, then grunted:

"Holy Father, and now imagine it's not Jesus but a landowner who says the words *Turn your other cheek to him that strikes your right.* And he says that to his servant, who has no right to speak up. Could those words really summon anything in the servant but hatred?"

"What are you trying to say?"

"That the meaning should not change depending on who utters it. Otherwise what's the sense?"

Father Azaria was planning to object, but then waved it off. He knew Mamikon very well. If Mamikon was out to prove a point, there would be no moving him, so it was better not to try. They exchanged meaningless phrases for the rest of the trip. Father Azaria nipped in the bud any attempt to return to the theological argument.

Mamikon walked to within a few steps of the priest and lowered his rather lean, large-nosed head in a joking half-bow.

"So why do you think pronouncements that only apply to one person are senseless?" he asked, pressing his point.

"Once a fool, always a fool," Father Azaria said, cutting him off.

"Holy Father, you could explain what you mean without calling me names."

"Why bother explaining anything to you? Nothing will change your mind anyway."

"Right you are."

Father Azaria pulled a rosary out of his pocket and went on his way, fingering the worn stones. Mamikon set off, following him and humming quietly.

They didn't have much farther to walk, only three kilometers, but it was uphill. Awaiting them there, at the very top of Manish-kar's head, was a rocky old village drowning in fruit gardens. Father Azaria was on his way to a funeral service, Mamikon to deliver a letter.

It was Wednesday, the sun had risen before the roosters, and the morning dew had fallen so you could scoop it up by the fistful. It was finally summer.

∽

A coffin that was unexpectedly wide but not especially long stood on the table, just as it should, with the feet toward the door. Several elderly women were sitting around the coffin, their dark sweaters buttoned tight all the way to the top and their gray hair pulled into severe buns.

Most of them weren't crying, or even showing signs of being upset. Only the pointy-nosed woman sitting at the end sobbed and trumpeted as she blew her nose into a handkerchief when she saw the priest. The others silently rose, bowed, and dispersed to the corners of the room.

Father Azaria walked around the table and stood at the head. He glanced at the deceased. The coffin was obviously too small for her. She was lying in it, dissatisfied and sullen, the wooden edges pressing hard into her sides and pulling her large shoulders up toward her ears. Her hands rested on her big round belly so her left hand covered the right; a worn wedding band gleamed dimly on her ring finger. Peering out from under the piece of silky lilac fabric that shrouded her body from head to toe were the tips of large male shoes, roughly size forty-five.

Father Azaria became flustered when his gaze slid over the shoes, but he tried not to let that show. He opened his prayer book, breathed deeply, and began to read a prayer without moving his gaze from the lines, but, to his even greater horror, he kept losing his place and repeating his words, faltering stupidly. In order to concentrate, he cleared his throat, frowned, shifted from one foot to the other, and tugged painfully at his beard, but he underestimated his strength and pulled so hard he choked on his saliva and had a coughing fit.

They brought him some water. He drank, squeezing his eyes tightly shut so as not to catch sight of the ridiculous shoes sticking out from under the fancy piece of fabric. But that was in vain: his eyes latched onto them again after he had returned the glass. They beckoned to him like a magnet, not allowing him to focus or set the tone for repose of the soul. The old women, arms folded across their chests, were standing along the wall and keeping silent, waiting. Only the pointy-nosed one scurried around among them, either to bring something to drink or take someone's kerchief, neatly fold it, and toss it on the back of a sagging chair that stood in a corner.

I have to keep myself together, Father Azaria reprimanded himself, sighing inaudibly and reopening his prayer book.

Several feeble old men were sitting in a row on a wooden beam in the yard, smoking and talking in hushed voices. A table set for a wake stood under a sprawling nut tree and the edges of the tablecloth fluttered. There was nothing on it now but empty dishes and salt cellars; food would be brought out immediately after the funeral. One of the old women would stand by the gate, toss a towel over her shoulder, place a bucket of water next to herself, and wait patiently. Each person returning from the cemetery would approach her and cup their hands. She would scoop out a mugful of water and pour it into their outstretched hands, washing away the cemetery's sorrow. After rinsing, they would wipe their hands on the towel hanging from her shoulder, and only then would they go into the yard, where the wake table awaited, set according to all the rules.

As was customary, Father Azaria tormented himself until noon with the prayer for the deceased. Then the men came into the house to carry out the coffin, but they had a hard time dragging it away: five old men and Mamikon, who had arrived just in time, could barely lift the heavy casket. It didn't fit through the doorway because of its unnatural width so they had to tilt it a little to the side, holding in the departed so, God forbid, she wouldn't topple to the floor. Outside the gate there awaited a squeaky wooden cart harnessed to a donkey; this was the cart Mukuch drove to the valley twice a week for goods. Relieved, the men hoisted the coffin onto the cart and the procession moved uphill along a narrow rocky road, toward an old cemetery overgrown with tall weeds.

"Tsoh! Tsoh!" clicked Mukuch, urging on the donkey in the mournful whisper the situation required.

Remaining behind were the pointy-nosed woman and a second woman who was tall and very thin, gray-haired, and with dazzlingly blue eyes. This was Valinka Eibogants, granddaughter of the Onik who had fought in the tsar's army. After demobilization, Onik had started to repeat the Russian phrase

Ei-bogu every other word. The language was incomprehensible to the other Maranians, but the words meant "really and truly." It was how he had earned the nickname Eibog and why his descendants had become Eibogants. The women bustled around the kitchen, cutting large pieces of slightly sour village bread and arranging slices of homemade ham, cold boiled beef, and bunches of washed greens and radishes on platters. They started carrying the food out to the yard just before people returned, so it wouldn't dry out in the breeze or attract flies.

"Father Azaria almost forgot all his words when he saw her," grunted the pointy-nosed woman as she rinsed a small head of creamy, fatty brynza.

"Maybe he should have been warned right away that she was wearing my husband's shoes?" wondered Valinka.

"Maybe he should have. It's just that we didn't realize it at first, and then it was awkward later on."

Father Azaria hadn't known the mysterious story of the shoes, so now, after tossing aside all attempts to at least present something resembling a composed facial expression, he shuddered as he observed three old men using the brute force of their body weight to firmly and forcefully nail down the lid of the casket, which was edged by a ludicrous raspberry-colored ruffle. The lid was resisting, though, and it slid along the top of the coffin, not wanting to stay in place because either the footwear or the deceased's huge belly was in the way. The old women gasped quietly and rolled their eyes in horror but didn't meddle by offering suggestions; what could they suggest, anyway, if they themselves didn't know what could be done?

The awkward fuss that ensued seemed to drag on for an eternity. Eventually, they somehow managed to nail the lid closed and the men lowered the coffin into the pit, hurriedly tossed soil onto it, and stepped away from the grave.

Father Azaria came to his senses and mumbled a burial prayer that the old people listened to with lowered eyes. One of them began coughing and stepped aside so as not to disturb the priest, then finally took himself outside the gate, because his cough just wouldn't subside. After finishing the prayer, Father Azaria made the sign of the cross to the funeral procession and headed for the gate.

They brought him back in the same cart they had used to deliver the coffin to the cemetery. Father Azaria rode with his hand grasping the splintery side of the cart, which shook a fair bit, despite the slow speed. Of course it would have been possible to ask Mukuch to stop so he could walk, but that would have been a mortal affront to the other man. And so Father Azaria endured, gritting his teeth, looking sternly ahead, and just counting the number of turns that remained until they reached the departed's house. Only once did he turn to look for Mamikon, calming down a little after catching sight of his familiar cap. It was two o'clock in the afternoon, so there wasn't much time left. The wake came next, and then he would go back to the valley. Ten kilometers down the slope of Manishkar was not, of course, the same as ten kilometers up. But a long trip lay ahead, and they wouldn't finish everything until nearly sunset.

Chapter Four

The sun had been rising for a long time, as reluctantly as if it were playing cat and mouse with a cloud: one side would roll out, then the other, then a cloud would cover it and the sun would peek out the other side again. When it had finally finished playing, it abruptly pushed away from the horizon and rose to its full height, flooding the sky with fiery rays.

Valinka managed to accomplish almost all her chores before morning came. When she let the birds out of the coop, they quickly dispersed through the yard, clucking, gobbling, and peering under every blade of grass in search of a reckless beetle or earthworm that had let its guard down; then she milked the animals and led them out to pasture. After hastily weeding the kitchen garden, she lugged some water from the rain barrel to soak parts of it more thoroughly than usual because the hot weather was crueler to the cress leaves and cilantro than the other herbs.

Once the yard chores had been taken care of, she went inside to cook. Before closing the door behind her, she paused on the threshold and glanced with satisfaction at the neat, tidied yard. Logs that were perfectly uniform in size lay in the woodpile; laundry that had been moderately blued and washed with care now hung in order, flapping in the morning wind; and copper kettles that were drying under the wooden fence caught their breath after having been mercilessly scrubbed with sand. They shone so much they nearly overshadowed the sun.

The kitchen sparkled with cleanliness and there was not a speck of dust to be found on the diligently scoured floor no matter how hard you looked; the dishes in the little cabinets were piled in low, even stacks, and the cups were turned with their handles to the right so you could take one without knocking into the rest and ruining their harmonious order.

Valinka lit the woodstove, put a chicken she had plucked and gutted the night before on to boil, and got ready to go to the cellar for flour – it was time to get to work on the dough for her sweet puff pastries. The letter that Mamikon delivered had brought the joyful news that Tigran would finally visit, and that he would be traveling with his family: his wife, adopted daughter, and six-month-old son Kirakos, whom they had called Kirill, using the strange northern version of his name.

"Ki-rill." Valinka tried saying it in different ways, listening to the unusual sound of her great-grandson's name. "Kir-ill."

Mamikon hadn't found the lady of the house at home, so he had left the envelope lying on the floor of the veranda, weighted down by a rock so the wind wouldn't carry it away. He threw up his hands in apology when he ran into Valinka at Mariam Bekhlvants's house: "I wanted to bring it to the funeral, but then I thought again, since you never know – what if I didn't see you? So I left it on the doorstep."

"Do you know what's written in it?" she interrupted him impatiently.

"How should I know?" said Mamikon, taking offense. "I don't read other people's letters."

Valinka found an opportune moment to make a quick trip home as fast as her considerable age allowed, so she could pick up the letter. The envelope turned out to contain a piece of notebook paper covered in small handwriting, plus three photographs. She examined her chubby, rosy-cheeked great-grandson for a long time, her heart sinking. There he was, sleeping in his little bed, with his head turned to the side and his little fists sticking out from under a blanket; Valinka clicked her tongue, upset, wondering why he wasn't swaddled, since babies should be tightly wrapped until eight months so they sleep more soundly. There he was, his toothless mouth smiling crookedly. His great-great-great-grandfather Kirakos had smiled just as crookedly and toothlessly; it seemed he was living up to his namesake after all. The whole family was in the third photograph and Tigran, who had grayed noticeably and put on weight, had his arm around his seven-year-old adopted daughter's shoulders and his laughing wife was standing next to them, clutching a frowning baby to her chest. Well, look, Valinka thought proudly, admiring her great-grandson's grouchy little face. Just a little bedbug, but already showing his strong personality!

Anatolia still hadn't regained her strength after the illness so had stayed at home rather than coming to the wake. Valinka tried pestering Satenik a little, but she couldn't figure out a single line without her reading glasses so Valinka had to wait patiently for the end of the funeral ceremony. If it had been up to her, she would have dropped everything and rushed off to Anatolia's, but she would have felt guilty leaving Mariam on her own after she had helped out with the delicate issue of handing over the shoes to the great beyond. Valinka waited calmly for people to head for home, then she lent a hand clearing the table and washing the dishes. It was nearly dusk by the time she got away to see Anatolia – a little later and a balmy southern night would slide over Manish-kar.

Valinka found Anatolia in the yard, arms folded across her chest and watching Patro, who was rolling his eyes and yelping with irrepressible happiness as he picked a large marrowbone clean.

"Sometimes a soup bone is enough to bring happiness," Anatolia said, greeting her guest.

"And sometimes a letter from a grandson is enough," Valinka said, waving the envelope joyfully.

Anatolia pulled out the photographs but set them aside to look at later because she first had to find out what was in the letter. She quickly scanned the lines, something she always did in case of unforeseen news, to give her a chance to choose the right words and warn the addressee. Valinka was waiting, fidgeting impatiently.

"Tigran's coming!" Anatolia said, throwing up her hands. "With his family!"

Valinka caught her breath.

"Wh-when's he coming?" She could barely utter it.

"June third."

"What's the date today?"

Anatolia looked up at the sky, attempting to recall at least the day of the week, if not the date, but then gave up and rushed into the house. Valinka followed her, fingering the empty envelope.

"Vaso, oh Vaso," Anatolia called out after throwing open the front door.

"Yuh, Nahto, my heart," Vasily answered from somewhere in the depths of the house.

Shy and flustered by her husband's affectionate greeting, Anatolia glanced sideways at Valinka, who was so caught up in the joyful news about her grandson's visit that she either didn't notice anything or at least pretended not to.

"Vaso," Anatolia asked, "what's today's date?"

"The first!"

"The first!" Valinka went as still as if she had been struck by lightning, then she came to, slapped herself on the knees, and rushed down the steps. "What does that work out to? That works out to them coming the day after tomorrow?!"

"The letter!" Anatolia shouted after her.

"The letter!" said Valinka, turning around without stopping.

She was long gone by the time Vasily showed up at the doorway.

"What happened?" he asked Anatolia.

"Tigran Melikants is coming the day after tomorrow. With his family."

"Ah…" At first Vasily was glad, then he wilted when he remembered his own sons. His big, silvery-gray eyes instantly went dim, and the corners of his lips quavered and sank.

Anatolia embraced him, pressing him to her chest: "Sh-sh-sh-sh."

He gave a long sigh and stroked her head. "Everything's fine, Nahto, my heart. Everything's fine."

Out by the garden fence, happy Patro was burying the large marrowbone he hadn't finished gnawing, his paws tangling goofily in his haste as he growled, threatening unseen enemies.

∾

Valinka had to go to the cellar for flour. The stone walls maintained their coolness even at noon on the hottest summer day, and they were hung with bunches of dried herbs and ears of red corn. Empty jars stood on the wooden shelves, their mouths turned down; last year's provisions had run out during the winter and the time had not yet come for laying in new ones. There was a cardboard box stuffed full of little white packets on the highest shelf. Valinka stood on her tiptoes, reached for the box, pulled out one little packet, and went over to the window, where she tried to make out the expiration date. Happy at what she had seen, she took the box and hurried out to the yard.

Three years ago, Tigran had opened a bakehouse in his northern city. A little later, just before Christmas, as it happened, he had sent a very heavy package that Mamikon spent half an entire day dragging all the way up Manish-kar, cursing. Mamikon arrived, chilled to the bone, his face blue from the cold and his mustache frozen into ice. Valinka ladled him some hot bean soup and set out a bottle of mulberry brew, too, so he would grumble less. He ate the soup with marinated Solomon's seal and half a round of homemade bread, drank two shots of the home brew, then made Valinka give him a goat-hair scarf, which he wrapped up to his eyes as he began preparing for the return trip. Before he left, though, he helped Vano open the package. In the box with the indelible blue northern postal service labels there lay several containers of potted meat, canned fish, vacuum-packed sausage, three containers of large-leaf black tea, and a box with fifty envelopes of dry yeast.

"What's this?" Valinka had asked, turning over one of the little packets in her hand.

"Shit, that's what it is," snorted Mamikon.

"Shit in what sense?"

"Yeast. My sister-in-law puts it in dough instead of sponge. It makes the dough rise fast but the bread comes out with no flavor. It's like you're eating cotton wool."

And so, worked up and clicking his tongue, Mamikon had buried his nose in the fluffy scarf, waved a hand in parting, and fearlessly stridden off into the storm.

Valinka had cleared the table and washed the dishes. She sat for a bit, thinking. She wasted no time before starting to knead up a little yeast dough as a test and baking a few rounds in the woodstove. She cut off a heel, pensively chewed some with cheese, then with honey, then with butter. Vano pinched off a piece, tried it, and made a face:

"I'm not going to eat that!"

Valinka had thrown a heavy knitted jacket over her shoulders, wrapped half a bread round in a napkin, and gone to see her next-door neighbor.

"Rubbish," was the neighbor's merciless verdict as she spat out the bread.

"I think you might be right," Valinka agreed with a sigh.

She hadn't been able to bring herself to throw away the yeast Tigran had sent, so she put the remaining packets away in the cellar, promising herself she would get rid of them as soon as the expiration date had passed.

Now that day had come, coinciding in some astonishing way with the eve of Tigran's arrival. Valinka ceremoniously carried the yeast out to the yard, where the silvery-white packets gleamed ostentatiously in the sun. She turned them over in her hands, thinking a little, then went inside for the scissors, neatly cut each little packet, and poured the contents into a bowl. She threw the yeast into the cesspit and stacked the little packets, which she tied up with coarse thread and put away in the uppermost kitchen cabinet. They would come in handy for something.

Then, finally, with the sense of having accomplished her duty, she got down to making *sali*. She mixed a dough made of water, salt, and flour, layered it with several doses of nutty-tasting browned butter, and put it away in the cold cellar until tomorrow. *Sali* had to be eaten hot, so she would bake it after her dear guests arrived. The chicken was boiling away when she finished up with the dough. Valinka strained the fatty broth, salted it, rinsed some excellent wheat (each grain was better than the last) and added it to the broth, then stirred and left it to finish cooking on a low heat. She sat down to pick the chicken meat off the bones.

A photograph of Vano stood on the upper shelf of the dish cabinet. Valinka had handcrafted a frame for it, using the lid from that very same shoebox. He was forty-one in the photograph, exactly the same age as their grandson Tigran now.

"Vano-dzhan," Valinka said, looking up at her smiling husband, "I won't cause trouble and dishonor your name. I'll welcome them as I should: feed them well and make clean beds. And I'll be affectionate and patient. So don't you worry. Nazz-stas-ya will be pleased."

Chapter Five

The stars had not yet had a chance to dissolve into the sky but early bees were already buzzing away and flying to greet awakening plants, as lovestruck little birds chirped a song for the new day. The world was wonderful, placid, and joyful, singing like a child who had been washed and fed after a long sleep. The air was as clear as a bell, streaming and flowing like a spring thaw; the air hovered, spread, fluttered, splashed, breathed, and...smelled. It smelled so much that the village had assembled, at full strength, by Valinka Eibogants's home: only Mukuch Nemetsants, who had gone to the valley, and old Anes, who had been laid up that same day with an attack of the gout, were missing. Even Anatolia came, arm in arm with Vasily, her first public appearance accompanied by her husband. She was trying not to make herself obvious and attract excessive interest, but there was no need to worry about that since everyone's attention was riveted not on her but on frightened Valinka, who had wrapped her face in a headscarf and was stamping desperately at the contents of the cesspit, which had spilled over and flooded part of her yard during the night.

The yard, which was always very neat and tidily swept, presented such a sorry spectacle that each new arrival looked at the gate and recoiled, then cursed or raised a gaze to the sky, as if appealing for compassion, before stepping aside.

"How could that have happened?" people kept asking.

"We'd like to know too!" said those who had arrived earlier.

"It's yeast," sighed Valinka. She pushed through the gate with her hip, pulled off her kerchief, and ran a hand along her hair, smoothing locks that had come out of a bun, then buried her face in her hands and burst out sobbing.

"What yeast?" people asked, worried.

"Tigran sent it to me three years ago. It expired, so I threw it away. But I guess it hadn't lost its strength. It's summer now, so it rose overnight from the heat and, well..." Valinka was overwhelmed by tears and stammered as she began telling the story.

A deafening silence reigned all around. The Maranians exchanged incredulous glances and stared at her again, apparently expecting some sort of coda, or at least a little more detail about what had happened. But Valinka just sobbed and threw up her hands, giving them to understand that was all, there was nothing more to explain.

"What did she say?!" rasped Suren Petinants, a hard-of-hearing, moth-eaten old man of ninety. "Who heaped all that shit up at her place during the night?"

Ovanes burst out laughing. The other men started roaring with laughter as well. Suren's perplexed gaze shifted from one fellow villager to another, then he waved it all off and started laughing as well.

"Help me clean it up. My grandson's coming today. It'd be one thing if he were alone, but he's with his family!" pleaded Valinka.

"Uh-huh, meaning that if he were coming alone, then it wouldn't need to be cleaned up, right?" said Ovanes, poking fun.

"Come on, why are you mocking her?" Yasaman scolded. The women didn't share in the men's merriment and were waiting, arms crossed over their chests and lips pursed in dissatisfaction, for them to stop laughing. "If Tigran were coming alone, he would clean it all up himself. You couldn't surprise him with, uh, village things. But his northern wife's another matter!"

"Well, yes. Up north they probably poop flowers! Not like us!"

Yasaman clicked her tongue and stepped aside angrily. The old men enjoyed themselves a little while longer, teasing Valinka, who had tossed the yeast into the cesspit without thinking. Then they calmed down and started deliberating on how to deal with the disaster that had splashed into her yard.

After a little squabbling, they decided to dig up the pit, remove the waste and tamp down the soil, then cover the hole in the privy with boards and seal it off with concrete.

"Otherwise it'll ferment and smell right up until winter," said Ovanes.

"And where do we go to the bathroom?" Valinka spoke up.

Ovanes wanted to joke again but caught his wife's stern gaze and reconsidered.

"You'll go to the neighbor's for now. When Tigran comes, we'll put up a new privy. But that'll do for now. Who has cement?"

They found cement at Satenik's. Lumpy but usable.

They spent the greater part of the day cleaning. Only toward evening, tired out and weak, did the old people head for home. Valinka offered to set a table for them, but they politely declined. They had to wash and change their clothes and after all the bother with the...*basically, the last thing we want to do now is eat, Valinka...*

"I wanted to greet my grandson like a normal human being, but now look at all this!" said Valinka, casting a glance at her destroyed yard and wiping away her tears.

"Let's look on the bright side," said Vasily, who was the last to leave. "Everything balances out, so now something good is on the way."

Valinka nodded at his words but was not consoled. After seeing everybody off, she lit the stove and tried to return order to the yard as much as she could while the water was heating. She swept, shook out and folded the paper sack from the cement (she would return it to Satenik later because it might come in handy), and then went to the shed, dragging a bucket that held concrete-gobbed spades soaking in water. The unpleasant smell that had roused the whole village early in the morning had dissipated a little and only the damp, gloomy scent of drying concrete remained, but that didn't bother Valinka. After taking care of the cleaning, she quickly washed, mercilessly rubbing herself with a prickly sponge. She tied the clothing she had been wearing into a bundle and put it out of sight in her room to launder later.

She combed her damp hair and made it into two braids that she secured at the nape of her neck with hairpins. She put on a clean dress and tied on a silk pinafore. The stove was crackling peacefully as it slowly but surely began giving off heat. Valinka went to the cellar for wheat kasha with meat and put it on to reheat. Then she went out to the veranda and sat on the bench that they had used to partition off the peacock's living space; she folded her hands on her knees and began waiting patiently. By the time Mukuch Nemetsants's cart stopped at her gate, she was sleeping peacefully, worn out from long anticipation and a thoroughly hectic day.

Chapter Six

The village turned out to be exactly as Nastasya had imagined it from her husband's stories: built of stone, with crumbling tiled roofs, decrepit crooked fences, and woodstove chimneys that clung to the hem of the sky. On her second day, she walked around the village in about an hour. Kiryusha was sleeping, rolled up like a round loaf of bread in a sling that Valinka had crafted instantly from a large checkered kerchief. Alisa was all in a whirl, either racing over with yet another fluffy yellow mallow flower – "Here, Ma, sniff this, it smells so funny" – or running ahead to wait, impatiently jumping on one foot – "And this house is already completely broken, see how the roof's all holey and the front door's wide open, can we go closer – can we?"

"We can," said Nastasya but she didn't go inside the houses because anything could happen – what if a wall or ceiling were to collapse? She would stand in the yard, carefully studying wooden supports for a veranda that had been eaten away by beetles; if you looked closely enough in some places, you could still discern simple patterns with chalices, crosses, and a round sun. The houses' facades were entwined by grapevines run wild; intricate latches on fences were completely rusted and squeaked distressingly, sending uninvited visitors back to a road that was uncomfortable to walk on because it was rough and coarse-stoned; and fruit trees that were bent from illness and had long not borne fruit sighed when they walked past. On the veranda of one abandoned home there hung several rows of dried tobacco leaves – apparently one of the remaining villagers had decided to use the veranda to prepare certain indispensable items. Alisa spotted this and turned her freckled face toward her mother to ask what it was, so Nastasya explained that it was tobacco.

"Who would have thought they make cigarettes out of grass!" said Alisa, perplexed, shaking her head.

Nastasya laughed with restraint so she wouldn't awaken her sleeping son. Although her daughter's curiosity amused her, it also kept her from focusing.

"You won't be offended if I go for a walk without you next time?" she asked.

"Am I bothering you?" Alisa pouted.

"No, but I need to concentrate, can you understand that?"

"Do you need to think again?"

"Yes."

"Fine. You can go tomorrow without me. I'll stay with Papa."

"Thank you, my dear," said Nastasya, touched.

"You. Are. Wel. Come!" And Alisa skipped ahead, nimbly jumping from one crumbling pothole to another.

Valinka greeted them at the gate, standing so her hand shielded her eyes from the sun. Nastasya was amazed yet again at the simple beauty of her long straight nose, stubbornly pursed thin lips, and blindingly dark blue eyes in a tanned face. She was glad that Tigran had taught her and Alisa to express themselves a little in Maran's language, otherwise how would she have communicated with her grandmother-in-law?

"Are you tired?" Valinka asked, taking the sleepy baby from Nastasya.

"No!" Alisa shouted loudly, before scurrying past and rushing off to Tigran, who was working in the woodshed Valinka had designated as the privy.

"What's the point in taking on something substantial?" she had said, waving him off when he offered to build a stone structure. "I live here by myself and haven't used the shed in ages anyway, you can see all the firewood's stacked under an awning so I don't have to lug it very far. You just dig a pit in the corner, cover it with boards, and put up a partition. We'll get by."

"I'll deal with the privy, then I'll get to the wall in the bedroom," Tigran promised.

"Don't touch the wall. Your grandfather's soul flew out through that crack. And soon it'll be my turn to fly off."

"That's probably why he fought with that wall his whole life. It's almost like he knew things would end that way," said Tigran. Tigran's conscience troubled him, making it unbearably difficult to speak about his grandfather's death. He had kept putting off coming – first one thing would prevent it, then another – and when he finally got around to planning his visit, he didn't make it to see his grandfather alive. And he wasn't in time for the funeral either, though that wasn't his fault: by a stroke of bad luck, a telegram got lost in the post and when it

finally reached Tigran, he was a week late in finding out that
his grandfather had passed on. He'd only managed to make
it to Maran about a month later and he had wanted to go by
himself because this visit wasn't just for pleasure. He wanted
to bring his grandmother back north with him, but his wife
had insisted the whole family go.

"When else will I be able to see the place you were born?"

Tigran had asked her not to reveal the true purpose of the
trip until later.

"She'll refuse," he'd said. "She won't want to leave her relatives' graves unattended. Let her get used to you first. When
she gets used to us, it'll be harder to part with us. Then we'll
propose that she come with us."

"And what if she doesn't agree?"

"We'll convince her."

The first thing he and Nastasya did was leave Valinka in
charge of the children and go to Vano's grave. The cemetery
hadn't changed much since the day Tigran left, except that
about a dozen wooden crosses had been added because wooden
crosses had replaced traditional gravestones after the mason
died several years back. Nastasya left her husband on his own
to allow him to mourn his anguish while she went to wander
the churchyard, which was overgrown with colorful fescue and
snakeweed. Although it was hard to make her way through
the dense thickets to the old gravestones, she didn't give up,
because it was important for her to get as close as possible to
them so that she could examine the stone patterns coated in
spots of lichen and draw her hand along delicate crosses chisel-
ed into the heart of the stone slabs, marveling at their humble
beauty and trying to retain the subtle sense of consolation she

felt when her hand meekly touched their warm sides. The gravestones gave off a whiff of centuries and a hint of doom.

Nastasya didn't figure out right away that the stones stood at the feet of the deceased rather than at their heads, or that they were turned to face west. To check that she hadn't imagined this, she returned to the newer graves and saw that was the case: the wooden crosses stood by their heads, unlike the stone ones. She didn't think of bothering her husband with questions since Tigran was sullen and taciturn after returning from the cemetery and had gone off to the far end of the garden, where he spent a long time chain-smoking and staring toward the edge of the precipice.

"They're doors," Valinka explained to Nastasya in a whisper because she was sitting next to the children, guarding their slumber on the daybed where they lay, surrounded by pillows and overcome by the rarefied mountain air. "So when Judgment Day arrives, the deceased will rise, throw the door open, and enter heaven. That's why they put the stone markers with crosses at the feet."

"And what about the ones with the ordinary wooden crosses?"

"The other deceased will take them away."

"How about that," was all Nastasya could say.

Kiryusha started fidgeting, smacked his lips, and sighed loudly. Nastasya stretched toward him but Valinka beat her to it, helping the baby turn on his side, rubbing his back, and straightening the collar on his little shirt so it wouldn't chafe his tender skin.

Valinka stood and let Nastasya have her spot. "You lie down for a bit while the children sleep. Have a rest and I'll go work on lunch."

"I'll help."

"You'll help tomorrow. You're still a guest today. You won't be a guest anymore on the third day. Then you'll help."

"And who will I be tomorrow?" smiled Nastasya.

Valinka tightened the ends of the kerchief on the back of her head and brushed off her pinafore. "You'll be the lady of the house, Nazz-stas-ya-dzhan."

"Call me Stasya."

"What?"

"Stasya."

"Fine, you'll be Stasya. You go rest up, my dear, because there'll be a lot to do later. Tomorrow we'll go gather horse sorrel early in the morning. And you'll meet the old ladies from the village then, too. And Tigran will see the old men, they'll have things to talk about. On Sunday we'll set a table and invite everyone to visit. So people in the village will finally get to know you."

Nastasya felt an urge to ask what all the ceremony was for, but she held back. "Good," she said.

After Valinka left the room, Nastasya took off her shoes, carefully lay down at the children's feet, and put a well-filled pillow under her head. Her breasts tingled and pulled as if it were time for Kiryusha to feed, which worried Nastasya a lot because her milk had stopped coming in a month ago, over-night, when she had been very sick with the flu. Nastasya didn't know why on earth her breasts were aching now, as if filling with milk after the long break. She promised herself that she would see a specialist as soon as she got home. Feeling calmer, she closed her eyes. She remembered the last week of all the long preparations for the road, how Alisa had suddenly caught a cold and a runny nose just before leaving, how Kiryusha had fussed the whole way because he was teething, how her husband's blood pressure had gone up and there weren't any pills handy, how she had managed a hundred times to curse the day and hour she'd begged that she and the children could come along on the trip, but nothing could be changed by that time. After suffering the whole way, Nastasya expected no joy whatsoever from her visit to Maran, so she could barely hold back tears when they were greeted in the valley by Mukuch Nemetsants, who was to drive them to the top of Manish-kar in his cart. Mukuch Nemetsants, a gray-haired, brown-eyed old man of gigantic height, embraced Tigran and then extended a hand to her.

"Hello, my dear," he said.

"Why do they call you Nemetsants?" Nastasya asked, squeezing his withered hand.

"Because my grandfather came back from the world war with a German bride, and we call Germans *nemets* here, like they do in Russia, and so, well, they started calling us Nemetsants in my grandmother's memory," answered Mukuch, making funny goat horns at Kiryusha, who smiled and reached for the gray-bearded stranger. "He's the spitting image of Kirakos," laughed the old man, glancing questioningly at Nastasya to check that she was happy for him to pick up the baby.

Nastasya gave him her son right away and smiled. "My great-grandfather fought in that war too, you know, and he also came back with a German wife," she said.

"Well, how about that, how nice is that," said the old man, amusing Kiryusha sweetly. "It's a small world, but we're big, though we're silly and naïve and think the opposite our whole lives."

"Stasya-dzhan, the main thing's to not pull out the root, otherwise the plant will take offense and won't grow next year," Yasaman explained, showing the right way to cut a horse sorrel stem with a knife, so a tiny stub was left sticking out of the ground.

Nastasya nodded, struggling to follow Yasaman's difficult speech that sometimes sounded rough, sometimes chirring. "Could you just...hmm...speak softly, so I understand you?" she asked.

"Am I really shouting?" said Yasaman, throwing up her hands.

Valinka started laughing. "She wants to say you should speak slower. You're chattering away like a machine gun and she doesn't understand your fast talking."

"I'll go slower," Yasaman promised.

Nastasya turned toward the huge oak tree, the sprawling canopy of which was sheltering Kiryusha as he lay on a home-woven blanket folded in two. Anatolia was sitting beside him, making a calming hand gesture to Nastasya, indicating that everything was fine. Because of her weak health, she wasn't able to pick horse sorrel in earnest; she was dizzy after just a half-hour and could feel nausea in her throat. They had put her in charge of the child while the other women, bent double and slowly progressing up the gently rising slope, cut the wavy-edged horse sorrel with knives and placed it in a sack, trying to preserve the entire stalks.

"The stalks are edible too?" asked Nastasya, curious.

"No, we'll throw them away later," said Valinka.

Nastasya thought her grandmother-in-law was teasing her, but Valinka wasn't even smiling.

"After we've gathered the sorrel, you'll understand why we need the stalks."

Alisa picked and ate an unripe wild strawberry, grimacing at the bitterness.

"Why are you ruining them? Leave them so they can ripen," Nastasya reprimanded her.

"It's so delicious!"

"It'll be more delicious when it ripens."

"Fine, I'll eat two more and that's all!"

The sun had risen long ago but the day was mercifully cloudy, and the wind had blown in a foggy mist that stretched from one edge of the sky to the other; the air was golden and damp, and it smelled sharply of spicy herbs Nastasya didn't know the names of. She breathed deeply and freely, adjusting herself to the measured pace of existence here that was so new to her. Everything around her was permeated with it, beginning with the ancient forest surrounding Manish-kar's crown, where each tree seemed to speak its own language, and ending with the people.

The old women were in no hurry as they worked, and they had tucked up their aprons so they could pile the sorrel in the pouches that formed. After picking enough, they would take cautious steps to the sack and pile the damp bunches of greens there. They had given Nastasya an apron too, but she held it up with her hand because she wasn't able to tuck it in so the edge didn't come out.

"Maybe you'd like to take a rest, my dear?" suggested Valinka.

"What do you mean?" Nastasya was disconcerted. "You mean you'll do the work and I should rest?"

"We've been doing this our whole lives. We're already used to it."

"I'm enjoying it."

"Well, if you're enjoying it..."

Nastasya neatly cut off a stalk, piled it with the bunch, reached for the next clump, and suddenly went still. Her breast smarted with tenacious pain but then suddenly went numb and damp. She straightened up sharply, stuck her hand into the opening of her dress, and felt one swollen nipple, then the other. She folded back the cup of her bra – it had almost soaked through.

"I'll be right back," she whispered to Valinka and hurried over to the century oak. Kiryusha, who was babbling and blowing bubbles, crawled along the edge of the blanket, enthusiastically pulling up blades of grass that Anatolia immediately plucked out of his chubby little fists.

"I'll be right back," Nastasya repeated. She fished a handkerchief out of her bag and ducked behind the broad tree trunk, where she undid her dress, freed her breasts, and gasped. Her nipples were streaming with milk. She dashed off to feed the baby but then checked herself because she was afraid the milk that had returned so suddenly would harm him. Without a second thought, she bent and began hurriedly expressing the milk, pressing her hands at the base of her breasts, moving them toward the nipples. The milk streamed over forget-me-nots that grew abundantly under the oak, then flowed down along petals and blades of grass, disappearing into the earth.

"Is everything all right?" Anatolia called out.

"Oh yes," Nastasya answered quickly.

After she had finished with the milk, she tidied herself up, tore her handkerchief in half, and put the pieces in the cups of her bra to protect her nipples from the wet fabric. Kiryusha started fussing when he saw his mother, and wanted to be picked up. Nastasya lifted him and held him to herself, smothering his chubby cheeks with kisses, burying her nose in the folds on his neck, and inhaling the unbearably dear aroma of delicate baby skin.

"My sweet little son."

Anatolia glanced at Nastasya and smiled. Then she sighed heavily and lowered her gaze. "I never managed to have a child."

Nastasya put Kiryusha on the blanket and he started whimpering with dissatisfaction; "Now, now, hold on a little," she told him. She fumbled around in her bag for a bottle of formula and held it out for Anatolia. "Will you feed him?"

"Of course I'll feed him," said Anatolia. She turned the baby on his side so it would be easier for him to drink, then tucked a cloth under his cheek. "And I don't want you to worry, Stasya-dzhan! I do know how to handle children. Just ask Yasaman. I spent so much time with her grandchildren back in the day!"

"And where are Yasaman's grandchildren now?"

"They died in the war."

"And her children?"

"Some died from the famine, others in the war."

"Maybe… Of course I won't go too far with this," Nastasya began, hesitantly, "but I had a thought… Maybe you don't have children because God wanted to protect you from overwhelming grief?"

Anatolia's eyes were unusually dark, their color such a deep brown that the black of her pupils was barely visible. She looked up at Nastasya.

"Maybe so, my dear."

Nastasya went for a walk around Maran that evening. Alisa dashed ahead, chirping joyfully and flashing the heels of feet covered in road dust; Kiryusha slept, curled up like a ball in his sling. After conferring with Valinka, Nastasya had decided to feed him after all, and he had taken her breast reluctantly, having apparently grown used to sweet artificial formula, but then he'd got carried away and fell asleep like that, whimpering at an attempt to move him to the daybed and clinging to her nipple with his aching gums. Clasping him to herself, Nastasya wandered through the village, from one abandoned house to another, stopping near each gate and peering into darkened windows, at crumbling walls where birds had built nests in crannies long ago, rusty drainpipes stuffed with wind-blown detritus, and dried-out wooden fence posts that stuck out of the ground like a prehistoric dragon's rotten teeth. Sometimes, after she'd had her fill of looking at yet another building, she would draw her fingers through the air as if to somehow grasp the vanishing essence of crushing solitude that seemed to flow out of each house, whether occupied or not. Nastasya asked herself how this could be but found no explanation. The village kept silent, cherishing the boundless sorrow it held within its stony embraces.

Nastasya's fingers smelled of bitter juice and she remembered clumsily braiding horse sorrel bunches earlier, adding one leaf at a time to each new plait and leaving the stem to stick out, making the braid look like a spike of wheat – a very large one of about a meter and a half long. Later they neatly cut off thin tendrils with scissors.

"Now you can understand why we needed the stems – so it's easier to braid the leaves into a bundle," explained Valinka.

"And what will you do with them next?"

"We'll save the tails for the animals and we'll hang the bundles on the clothesline, let them dry out thoroughly. Then we'll put them in canvas sacks and leave them for the winter."

"How do you cook it?"

"It's easy. You boil it well, pour out the water, braise it with fried onion, pour garlic matzoon over it, then eat it with bread and brynza. If it's a holiday, you sprinkle it with pomegranate seeds and grated walnuts. It's fancier that way."

"Is it tasty?"

"You wouldn't like it," laughed Valinka.

"Why?"

"No food seems tasty if you're not used to it."

"I'll get used to it," Nastasya promised her for some reason.

Valinka bound the end of a sorrel bunch with coarse thread, which she wound around each clump before setting it aside and taking up the next.

"There's a little left from last winter. I'll make some. Maybe you really will like it."

When Nastasya left, there were eighteen fat horse sorrel braids on the clothesline, swaying slightly in the breeze. Tigran walked her to the end of the street and returned to his work in the woodshed, relenting after her assurances that there was no need whatsoever to accompany her on the walk.

And Nastasya was left face-to-face with Maran.

She returned two hours later, focused and pensive.

"Do you know what I regret?" she asked after she had bathed the children and put them to bed, when she and her husband were on the veranda drinking the tea with thyme that Valinka had brewed. "That I don't have a pencil and paper handy."

"We could ask Mukuch Nemetsants, he'll bring it from the valley."

"Please ask him. I haven't thought about drawing in years so I'm not sure it will come out well, but for some reason I feel like trying now."

Tigran embraced her shoulders and kissed her on the temple. "Good."

Chapter Seven

By the end of the second week, a fairly large stack of pencil sketches had risen on the windowsill. Valinka went through the rough sheets of paper covered in dark pencil lead, examining them long and hard, sighing, and clicking her tongue. She hadn't been able to have a real talk with Nastasya because caring for the children took a lot of time and energy, plus Nastasya's mastery of Maran's language was pretty weak and she often grew frustrated that she couldn't formulate her thoughts well enough to get them across to Valinka. Tigran would disappear for days at a time, going around to the old people's houses, repairing everything he could: he reinforced fences, cut down dried-up trees, split wood, hurriedly patched up roofs, cleaned stove pipes, carried away and burned unnecessary odds and ends on the outskirts, and beat worn, faded rugs in the sun. He helped as much as possible.

Alisa often tagged along with him, hanging around nearby, eagerly interacting with the old people and telling them stories of her own – her prattle made them radiant and they grew more talkative and smiled. They crafted lopsided toys for her, gave her knickknacks, and taught her how to make flower dolls: you turn a poppy bud inside out, neatly tear out the core, thread it on the stem, and spread out the cocoon of petals, ending up with a black-haired gypsy woman in crimson poppy skirts. Alisa followed along, holding her breath. Her little face was freckled and sunny, her eyes were green and feline, and her straw-colored hair was as light as dandelion fluff. She ran to Tigran with each flower doll: "See, Pa, what a beauty came out?" When Valinka asked, he reluctantly referred in passing to a difficult divorce and Alisa's real father's unwillingness to communicate with his daughter and participate in her upbringing in any way. Valinka shook her head and sighed, then the next day she went to the neighbor women to round up ingredients she lacked for baking a big cinnamon cake that was exceptionally labor-intensive to make, with five layers soaked in syrup made from toasted almonds, walnuts, and hazelnuts steeped in honey. This was the sort of cake that used to be served only at christening festivities, but now Valinka baked it for the little girl who was not a blood relative but was now closer to her heart than her own beloved grandson. Alisa shone with happiness as she ate the cake, praised it, and asked for seconds.

"Will you make this exact same cake for me again later?" she pestered her mother. Nastasya had to take dictation of the precise recipe and solemnly promise her daughter to bake a cinnamon cake for Christmas.

"Can you do it right?" Alisa nagged her. The women exchanged glances and snorted. Spending time with the old people had affected Alisa, who had taken on their grumbling tone and manner, standing so she leaned to one side with her hands on her hips, and looking out from under her brow as she craned her neck.

"Oh, you!" Nastasya pulled her daughter's braid. Alisa turned around, snatched a handful of cherry plums off the table, and ran off to her father.

Smiling, Valinka observed Nastasya and Alisa. They bore a surprising resemblance: identically light, slender, and long-legged.

"Our people are different," she drawled out, musing. "We're large, solid, crooked-nosed, and unwieldy. But you flit like butterflies."

"Your people are very beautiful," Nastasya said. "And... it's as if you're made of stone. I think everything's stone in Maran. Houses. Trees. People. And" – she snapped her fingers to remember the word – "carved, yes. Carved from stone."

Valinka would start examining the sketches after Nastasya fed Kirakos, put him to bed, and went out to draw the village. Valinka saw the cemetery, a slanting ray of light in the chapel's narrow window, rain barrels, a cart wheel, a donkey tied to a lone tree, clay jugs, and a mallow plant. Several unfinished portraits of Anatolia lay in a separate pile; Anatolia and Yasaman often stopped by to visit, and Nastasya would sit Anatolia by the window and draw while Yasaman watched the baby, allowing Valinka to rest. Anatolia would unplait her hair. Despite her considerable age, her hair had retained its thickness and astonishing honey color, plus (and here Nastasya would gasp in elation and astonishment) the rare and surprising combination of dark skin and hair that was wheaten with red tints, this was such beauty, such beauty! Anatolia would just shrug a shoulder: "It's nothing special, Stasya-dzhan, I got one thing from my father, another from my mother, so I ended up looking like this."

Yasaman whispered a complaint about her friend, whose health hadn't improved despite herbal treatments.

"I can't make her go to the valley to see a doctor. She won't listen to anybody, not me, not Vasily, not Ovanes. She's so weak, either she's dizzy or her legs won't move. Last week she fainted and we barely brought her around."

"Do you want me to have a talk with her?"

"I'm not sure it'll do any good. She'll do it her way no matter what. And she'll likely be offended that I complained to you about her!"

"Well, what can you do? She's not a little girl, you can't make her go."

"There's nothing we can do, you're right."

Despite her sickly appearance, Anatolia turned out to be a genuine beauty in Nastasya's portraits: young and touchingly luminous. Sometimes Valinka thought Nastasya was deliberately prettifying her, but at other times it seemed there was no prettifying at all and that was exactly how she herself saw Anatolia. In any case, in Nastasya's drawings the whole village came out looking as it hadn't in years. It seemed that Nastasya had deliberately omitted signs of aging and cheerless destruction, leaving Maran with a quiet, happy air of tranquility. Despite the fact that it was alien to her, she seemed to relate to this region with such compassion and understanding that it was as if she was taking personal responsibility for the bitter fate that had come its way. She was remarkably successful at observing or intuitively figuring out things the old people hadn't noticed in a long time.

Valinka fiddled with a detailed drawing of the feeder that stood in Mukuch Nemetsants's yard. It looked like an ordinary feeder, low to the ground, lopsided, and dirtied with chicken droppings. But who would have thought the village siskins would take a fancy to that feeder? They would wait until evening and fly in as a flock, making a commotion. The barn-yard birds observed their swarming from a distance and only one old turkey, a crotchety and clueless bastard whose neck Mukuch couldn't bring himself to wring, would walk circles around them, spitefully clucking and shaking the scarlet snood on his bill. The turkey's indignation didn't concern the siskins, though. After making a scene for a while and eating the feeder clean, they would soar upward all at once and fly off toward the woods. In answer to Nastasya's questions about why the birds flocked to this particular yard, old man Mukuch would throw up his hands: "How should I know, my dear, that's probably how it's supposed to be, since that's how it's always been." The Maranians had grown used to the siskins' strange behavior long ago but Nastasya, who had only been visiting the village for two weeks, didn't just notice it, she even went to the effort of drawing the crooked feeder all covered with birds. She answered with disarming sincerity when Valinka asked her why she was sketching it, saying she herself didn't know.

Then there was the story of the fence at the edge of the bluff, where the peacock lay. Vano had looked out at that fence every evening through dusky sunbeams and Valinka tended the mountain lilies Tigran had planted on the burial mound, but neither of them suspected there were welded seams in the fence's corners where the wrought-iron pattern formed letters that represented the sounds "K" and "Vo".

Nastasya noticed them, drew them, and showed her husband. Tigran couldn't believe his eyes so went out to the fence and confirmed that his wife was correct.

"But how did you manage to make out those letters? You don't know our written language!"

"I saw them on the stone crosses and remembered them!"

Valinka was surprised when she examined the fence pattern in Nastasya's sketch. Valinka and Vano were barely able to put letters together to form words, though they did know what "Π" and "Ч" looked like. They hadn't noticed them and hadn't examined them.

Several sheets of Nastasya's drawings had detailed depictions of the collapsed veranda of Magtakhine Yakulichants's father's home; Valinka had been friends with Magtakhine's mother back before she had completely lost her mind. Nastasya caught the angle where beams that were rotten and long since covered in moss had fallen and formed an old man's profile. If you looked closely, it was Magtakhine's father's face, with its characteristic aquiline nose, knitted brows, and thin lips. Valinka specially went for a walk to have a look. And that's how it was: Petros Yakulichants was lying there, exactly the same as on his funeral day. He was gone, though he remained in the ruins of his home.

Valinka admired Nastasya's drawings for a long time, then she piled them up and put them back on the windowsill. She lifted the canopy on the cradle and listened to Kirakos breathe as he slept. There he was, Maran's last little boy. There were no others, nor would there be more. The young people had gone and the old ones would depart without even leaving behind memories.

"Well, so be it," Valinka said, conceding to bitter reality. "This must just be the way things are supposed to be, so that's how they'll stay."

It was completely by chance that she recalled the forgotten picture in the attic. She was explaining to Nastasya about how laundry needed to be hung out properly, by color and by type of item.

"Who would have thought you could have so many rules for laundry?!" laughed Nastasya, straightening the damp edge of a bedsheet.

"And what did *you* think! People judged a woman as a housewife by how she hung out the laundry. You won't believe it now, but even men knew about those tricks. Even my mother-in-law – may she rest in peace, it's not for nothing that she had princely blood – knew how to hang out laundry properly, even if she couldn't brew tea!"

"Your mother-in-law was a princess?" Nastasya asked in surprise. "Tigran's great-grandmother?"

"He didn't tell you about her? He obviously didn't place any importance on it. That's why their kin are called Melikants, because—" and here Valinka stopped short, started blinking, and slapped herself on the forehead. "How could it have slipped my mind! Let's go, Stasya-dzhan, I'll show you something. This will be interesting for you because you draw." And she hurried off into the house, tossing the laundry aside, wiping her wet hands with the bottom of her apron as she went, and scolding herself for forgetfulness.

The stairway to the attic was in a large corner room on the second floor that Valinka had put to use for storing wool blankets, mattresses, and taut pillows stuffed with goose down. The door to the room had been kept locked ever since the guests had arrived, out of concern that Alisa would get it into her head to clamber up the precarious attic stairway on old steps that reacted to every footstep by creaking with dissatisfaction, spreading detritus, and sagging heavily because the wood had rotted through in places and was threatening to collapse.

"We'll have to ask Tigran to reinforce it," said Nastasya, cautiously examining each step. She was walking in Valinka's tracks, breathlessly holding a hand against the wall because she was afraid to lean against the rickety railing.

Valinka groaned whenever she put a foot down. "I'm too old for this business, my knees ache all the time, I need to use a potato poultice before bed."

"Does that help?"

"A little. You grate a raw potato, add a spoonful of coarse salt, smear it on your knees, wrap it up with a scarf, and put a cushion under your feet." Valinka pushed the little attic door, which opened wide with a squeak and wafted the grim smell of stale things into their faces. "I haven't cleaned up here in a long time, my dear, I don't have the strength. Careful you don't get dirty."

Nastasya peered into the room and gasped: the spacious attic was stuffed full of so many worn-out old items that it felt like a place where time had not simply stopped but become confused and dozed off. The entire space around her was crammed with ancient trunks, large cooking pots, vats, empty clay jugs, and pieces of discarded furniture – a chiffonier, stools, and a broken chair – that were coated with dust and cobwebs. Right in front of her there stood a tall, long-necked copper pitcher with oxidized turquoise spots; its crooked handle was turned toward her. Nastasya couldn't keep from furtively stroking its dusty side and trying to lift its small lid, though her attempt was in vain because the lid held dead tight.

"Here's what you have to do," said Valinka, bending to press a hidden button with her finger. The tiny lid clicked and flipped to the side, opening the pitcher's narrow neck. "You know who made it? Vasily's uncle. Arusyak Kudamants had good sons, they were very good with their hands. Vasily's father was an outstanding blacksmith and Vasily's uncle was a coppersmith. There was a time when all the women in Maran went to the spring with pitchers like that. They had an important quality: water stayed cold in them, no matter the weather." Valinka turned the pitcher to show the holes on its base. "It wore through ages ago and there's nobody to fix it. But I can't bring myself to throw it away."

"How could you? Throwing away something as beautiful as that!"

"To tell the truth, I don't keep it because of the beauty," said Valinka. "It's in memory of people I knew. See those clay jugs? Mariam Bekhlvants's grandfather made them – she's the old woman whose mother-in-law I sent off to the afterworld with Vano's shoes. And Minas, the carpenter, knocked this chest together," said Valinka, slapping its heavy lid. "He was a good old man, conscientious. He died during the war. If he had lived just two days longer, he would have been here when his son's death notice arrived. God was merciful and took him just in time."

Valinka peeked behind the large wooden chest and her hand crept around, groping at the darkened edge of a frame. "Stasya-dzhan, help me get this, I can't do it by myself."

Nastasya grabbed another corner of the frame and cautiously pulled out a very heavy and horribly dirty painting. Valinka took rags out of the chest and held them out for Nastasya.

"Here, you wipe it, my dear, I'm afraid of ruining it."

Nastasya started neatly cleaning off a thick coating of dirt, but that was of little use because underneath the canvas was so grimy it was impossible to discern what was depicted.

"My mother-in-law hid it here," said Valinka, opening the only attic window and starting to cough violently. It was hard for her to catch her breath, and she wiped away tears with the back of her hand. "Dust has made me cough all my life."

Nastasya began feeling uneasy.

"You go downstairs, I'll be right there. I'll just bring the painting into the housekeeping room. Maybe there's a chance I can" – she attempted to think of the Maran word for "restore" but quickly gave up – "fix it."

Valinka nodded. "Whatever you say, my dear. Then I'll finish hanging up the laundry."

"How many years has the painting been lying here?" Nastasya asked as Valinka went.

Valinka stopped in the opening of the attic door. "Well, probably a whole century. To be honest, Vano and I never once saw it. When my mother-in-law was still alive, she wouldn't let anybody near it and by the time she died, we'd completely forgotten about that picture. I'm amazed I remembered it today!"

The frame had crumbled into dead, rotten wood. Nastasya had to take it apart completely, but luckily it came loose easily as the nails that held the canvas had rusted long ago, disintegrating when she pressed them with her finger. After putting the rotten pieces back behind the chest, Nastasya brought the canvas downstairs and placed it so the sunlight beat down on it through the windows. Someone's silhouette appeared on the canvas in the bright afternoon light and a hazy off-white spot showed through on the lower part of the painting.

Kiryusha started gooing and babbling, so Nastasya hurried down to the washstand, cleaned herself up, quickly changed her clothes, and looked in on the baby, whose wet pants Valinka was already changing. He started jabbering joyfully at the sight of his mother and stretched out his little hands to her. She fed him and there was so much milk that Kiryusha could barely take it all in and Nastasya had to take her breast away to let the baby catch his breath. She caught herself thinking that under other circumstances, in another place, she would have considered the return of her milk a miracle. In Maran, though, she regarded it as something to take for granted. "That's probably how things are supposed to be because that's just the way it is," she said to herself, repeating the old people's favorite phrase. She smiled. The simpler the words, the more significant their meaning.

Tigran and Alisa came home, and Nastasya's ecstatic daughter burst into the room announcing they were going to eat lunch and go back out. Then she pecked her brother's round little cheek and kissed Nastasya. "Ma, one of the grannies, I forgot her name, she's teaching me to knit. I already knitted two whole rows, can you believe it?"

While Nastasya entertained Alisa, Valinka sent Tigran upstairs to have a look at the picture, then she started preparing the table for lunch, ladling cold soup with matzoon into dishes and setting out boiled chicken and new potatoes, brynza, greens, fresh cucumbers, radishes, and lightly brined tomatoes with a scent of anise. Tigran came back perplexed because this was the first time he, like Nastasya, had heard of the painting's existence.

"How could it be that you and Grandpa never once recalled it?" he asked.

"I can't figure that out myself!" said Valinka, feeling downcast.

Nastasya spoke up. "I have a rough idea of how to clean the picture. I'll see what I can do. It'll take a long time, but I should be able to manage it before we leave. The only thing I'll need is vegetable oil. Can we find some?"

"I'm sure we can get hold of some."

After lunch, Tigran and Alisa went back to old man Anes's, where Tigran split wood and Anes's wife, whose vision was poor, taught Alisa how to knit a wool sock; Valinka started on dough for an onion and egg pie; and Nastasya went to clean the picture after getting some vegetable oil and a wet rag from Valinka. She set about her work with great caution, fearing that improper storage conditions and the thick layer of dirt had irrevocably ruined the canvas, but the oil paint was preserved fairly well, albeit considerably dulled under a coating of dust, cobwebs, and dark spots left after the fly incursion. In three hours of painstaking work, Nastasya managed to clean a small fragment of the canvas: there was an edge of something striped with dark blue and white, perhaps a crest or a shield, and a chunk of masonry. Another week later, a young Crusader was coming through on the canvas as well; he had a high forehead, deep eyes, a straight nose, and a short, bushy beard. He was dressed in flexible light armor with a heavy crimson and gold velvet cloak over it, and a chain pulled at the neck of the cloak. Each link was decorated with an engraving whose intricate pattern was, unfortunately, impossible to discern.

Nastasya left the white spot for the very end. When she was getting ready to clean it, she thought it was most likely mildew that had irreversibly destroyed part of the canvas. But as years of hardened dirt ceded to the careful touch of her oil-dampened rag, she revealed an image that made the blood drain from Valinka's face. Valinka grasped at her heart and froze, unable to move, when she looked into the housekeeping room with little Kirakos in her arms. Nastasya was afraid the old woman would drop the baby but Valinka calmed her, saying, "Everything's fine, my dear," and handing him to his mother. She took small, uncertain steps toward the painting, gasping and shaking her head mournfully before bursting into tears with such distinct relief it was as if she had received the answer to a question that had been torturing her all her life. At the Crusader's feet there stood a large, regal, frothy-white peacock who was stretching his elegant head with its luxurious crown upward and looking at her with wonderful, transparent eyes the color of pomegranate seeds.

Post Scriptum. Needless to say, Valinka did not leave Maran.

PART III

For the One
Who Listened

Chapter One

Magtakhine came over as night was falling, just when occasional lights began burning in the windows of houses and a merciful September night spread its starry coverlet over the village. She stood on the veranda, arms folded over her chest, and looked at the yard.

Vasily had managed to get used to the visits from his deceased wife. When he first noticed her transparent silhouette set against the darkening sky, he had, despite the irreality of the situation, experienced a feeling of bewilderment and helplessness rather than fear. Anatolia had already gone to bed by that time; she hadn't been feeling well so spent almost all her time away from housekeeping, either on the daybed with undemanding needlework or in bed. The devoted Vasily took care of her by brewing tea, wrapping her chronically chilly feet in a blanket, and not forgetting to bring her herbal tisane on time: she needed to drink it three times a day, strictly before meals. If he had occasion to be away at the smithy, he made sure to warn Yasaman and Ovanes, so Anatolia wasn't left without someone to tend to her. Vasily's caring touched Anatolia to the depths of her soul.

Unaccustomed to affectionate and attentive treatment, she answered him in kind, inasmuch as her health allowed, by preparing his favorite dishes and putting his meager wardrobe in order: she refashioned and resewed an old coat, mended underthings, knitted several pairs of woolen socks, and made two shirts from a piece of light cotton material she had been saving for herself. In the evenings she taught him to read and write. Sticking out the tip of his tongue in his effort, Vasily would trace the squiggles of letters, though he had difficulty holding a pencil in fingers unwieldy and mangled from heavy blacksmith work. Then, frowning and slipping up, he would read, diligently articulating each syllable. Anatolia gave him a chance to rest after the lessons by reading out loud to him from the books she had brought home from the library and saved from destruction during the first of the cold winters. She remembered the contents of those books by heart, but after noticing Vasily's unfeigned interest in literary texts, she read to him with such pleasure it was as if she had picked up the books for the first time. They would fall asleep in a touching embrace. Smiling, she would think about how human happiness can be multifaceted and merciful, too, in each of its manifestations. She grew flustered and blushed when recalling their first awkward night of love, which took place a week after Vasily moved in with her. He had reached toward her, tentatively, and asked if he could hug her. His question greatly surprised Anatolia – her ex-husband had never asked permission to take her, and it had almost always been against her will, incensed as he was by her sullen silence and tears of cowardice. Vasily's disarming request for affection, uttered in a bashful whisper, was such a revelation for her that she reached for him herself and embraced him, embarrassed by her impulse. Despite his unpolished appearance and somewhat coarse manner, Vasily turned out to be surprisingly attentive in bed, accepting her tenderness with gratitude and treating her so cautiously and affectionately that Anatolia realized for the first time that intimacy was something to treasure rather than a degrading ordeal.

By virtue of advancing age, their emotions lacked the ardor and passion that can cloud the consciousness, and their bodies lacked the possibility of loving as often as the young, but they accepted that with understanding and were endlessly grateful to the heavens for the blessed opportunity to share the autumn of their life with someone truly dear.

"If someone had told me I'd need to relive everything I went through with my ex-husband in order to be with you later, I'd agree to that," Anatolia once confessed to Vasily. That touched his soul so deeply that he was overcome and left quite speechless. He then disappeared into the smithy for an entire day and brought her an inexpertly forged rose that same evening, the first flower he had crafted in his many years of work. "I don't know how to say things with words like you do," he confessed to her and then stopped short, not knowing how to finish his thought. "So you decided to forge your feelings in metal?" she said, coming to his aid, and he answered, "Yes."

On the day that Vasily's deceased wife first put in an appearance, Anatolia had gone to bed earlier than usual, after a nerve-wracking thunderstorm. The weather had been stuffy and humid all day, making it impossible to breathe: summer was on its way out, August was acting up and throwing tantrums as it departed, and noon was white-hot, though a thunderstorm had broken out with monstrous power toward nightfall. Demonic sky-dwelling dragonmen tore at the air with spears and rain poured down in hot torrents, failing to bring the relief the villagers had long hoped for. Vasily looked into the bedroom to make sure Anatolia had already fallen asleep, since in addition to overwhelming fits of weakness her legs had been torturing her lately, and she complained of swelling and pain in her joints so slept with a blanket that she would fold into quarters and place under her knees. She lamented that she had gained weight after being as thin as a reed all her life, saying that now she had eaten herself some padding for her hips and then joking that soon she would be as round as a head of cheese. Vasily said that was okay because he loved her fat too, but then had to force a smile since the state of Anatolia's health had been worsening steadily. It was clear she could no longer avoid a trip to the doctors in the valley, something she had been resisting, bursting into tears whenever anyone mentioned it.

Vasily went to the kitchen to make some mint tea, leaving the door to the bedroom ajar so he would hear if she called to him. The front door was wide open for some reason and he saw Magtakhine immediately when he went over to close it. She was standing so that her belly leaned against the veranda railing and she was bareheaded, with her hair cut short for some reason; her arms were crossed over her chest and she was looking at the corner of the yard where Patro's doghouse stood. Despite having lost a lot of weight and being an entire span shorter in height, Vasily recognized her familiar silhouette immediately: once, back in her youth, she had turned around awkwardly, caught her foot in the edging of a carpet runner, and hurt her shoulder after falling from her substantial height. It had often ached after that, particularly when the weather changed, and Magtakhine would instinctively lift the shoulder, holding her arms folded at her chest, fearful she would inadvertently bump something with her elbow and cause herself more pain. That first time, on the veranda, Vasily had wanted to approach her, but then she turned her unexpectedly young and completely unwrinkled face toward him and angrily shook her head. The door slammed shut from a puff of wind, but when Vasily opened it again the veranda was empty.

From that day on, Magtakhine showed up almost daily, always at night, waiting until Anatolia had fallen asleep. Vasily seemed to have a sixth sense for when she would arrive and would peer out at the veranda, where he would see her standing and looking at the yard with her arms pressed to her chest. He had made no further attempts to approach her but knew she had been coming to tell him something, so the only question was why she was lingering.

His deceased wife's visits did not scare him. Her disposition may have worsened with age, but Magtakhine had been a kind and good-natured woman who had selflessly cared for her own parents, people she had accused of insufficient love, though she most likely said that out of habit rather than offense. She and Vasily had married a year after the famine receded and she had accepted and come to love nine-year-old Akop like family. Even after their three sons were born, she made no distinctions between the boys, treating Akop with particular tenderness and not leaving his side when he had inexplicable bouts of fever.

Vasily would grow gloomy and sigh heavily when remembering his younger brother's suffering. Akop's first fit had occurred several months after their mother's death. There had been no answer when Vasily repeatedly called his brother to supper, so he went to search the house for him and found him on the living-room floor. Akop's temperature was so high that Vasily recoiled in fear after touching his forehead. Vasily quickly stripped off all Akop's clothes, rubbed him with mulberry brew, put him to bed, and ran to get Yasaman. By the time she arrived, Akop was lying on the floor again, completely delirious, with his burning body sprawled out on the cool boards. He tried to break away when Yasaman attempted to give him herbal remedies. Then, after being put to bed and covered with two blankets so he would sweat, he cried plaintively, asking them to take away the sword that the evil *dev* Aslan-Balasar had left under his pillow. They had to lift the pillow and show him there was nothing there, but Akop wouldn't calm down. He rolled to the other side of the bed and stretched his arm toward the window, saying, "Look, Aslan-Balasar is waiting so he can find the right moment to come and kill us with his sword."

Vasily carried Akop into another room so he would be farther from the sinister window, but that didn't help. Akop sobbed inconsolably and begged for the sword to be taken away, because otherwise nobody would be saved. The fever held all night, not dropping until nearly dawn. The boy woke up by noon, surprisingly healthy and only a little weak, remembering nothing except that he had lost consciousness from a horror that had immobilized his soul: he had felt the presence of someone scary behind his back and fallen. After that incident, the spells repeated every month, sometimes even more frequently, and it took several days each time for Akop to recover; he was scared of the dark and tried not to be left by himself. Vasily did everything possible to help, bringing Akop to the valley several times for treatment, taking him to dream interpreters and medicine men, and inviting a priest. Unfortunately, all his efforts were to no avail since the doctors could find nothing wrong with him, the incantations of a local medicine man had no effect, the dream interpreters could see nothing no matter how hard they peered into their crystal balls, and when young Father Azaria was summoned to the house, arriving just as Akop was having another seizure, he prayed over him for several difficult night hours until at last he could bear the mental strain no longer and burst into helpless tears, pressing his forehead to Akop's burning hand.

Magtakhine turned out to be the only one able to figure out the reason for Akop's wearying attacks. Unlike Vasily, who tried not to raise the topic of illness with his brother, so as not to force him to relive everything, she gently but firmly drew him into conversation, collecting and assembling fragments of memories into pictures that were initially meaningless. With time, she learned to predict his fits, though she couldn't explain to her husband how she was able to do so; she calculated their approach based solely on intuition, relying on guesswork alone. Akop was at home under her observation on those days, and Vasily was forced to be at the smithy nearly round-the-clock to cope with all the work created by his brother's absence. However, no matter how hard Magtakhine tried to keep Akop within her sight, she hadn't managed to catch the beginning of any of his fits. That dispirited and irritated her immensely because she somehow knew that the solution to the boy's illness lay precisely in the several seconds that preceded his faintings. Vasily regarded his wife's certainty as a whim and sometimes even made fun of her, though deep down he fostered hope that Magtakhine would be able to figure out the reason for his brother's strange illness.

And then one day, two long years later, Magtakhine finally did succeed, after everybody had been driven to despair and disillusionment. Akop had stayed home that day, at her insistence, and was stacking split logs on the woodpile. His one-year-old nephew Karapet, Vasily and Magtakhine's firstborn, was sleeping in a cradle on the veranda, wrapped in a warm blanket. After assuring herself that the child was asleep, Magtakhine went down the stairs to the yard to be closer to Akop, but she hadn't even had a chance to take one step outside before Akop, who was facing away from the veranda, muttered in a quick half-whisper that the child was about to fall. Frightened, Magtakhine turned toward the veranda and gasped because the baby had somehow, against all odds, managed to pull himself free from the blanket and was leaning out of the cradle, dangerously bent over its low plank side and hanging downward. She made it up the stairs in three leaps, grabbed her son in her arms, and clutched him to herself, her heart beating so loudly it seemed it was outside her chest. Alarmed, she somehow slowed her heart and reached the edge of the veranda, where she saw what she had expected to see: overcome by a fit, Akop was lying on the heap of split wood in the middle of the yard, deathly pale and moaning from the horrific heat burning at his insides.

"Maybe you get sick because you're able to see into the future?" Magtakhine cautiously suggested to him the next day.

Akop, who remembered nothing but the fear that had frozen his soul, helplessly closed his eyes. "What's the point if I forget everything right away?" he whispered.

"I don't know."

Some time later, Mariam Bekhlvants witnessed one of his attacks when she stopped by for cornmeal. Magtakhine was bathing the baby and Akop was standing next to her, holding a towel at the ready. He suddenly took a step away from her, attempted to grasp the wall, and leaned against it, his eyes rolling as he slowly sank to the floor, managing only to say, through gritted teeth, "Master Samo", a second before losing consciousness. Magtakhine shoved her son, who was still wet, at Mariam and dashed off to Akop. "Don't ask questions," she said over her shoulder. "Help dress the baby and then run to Serbui's and warn her that misfortune has befallen her father."

They found the shepherd, Master Samo, at the edge of the oak grove. The old man was lying there, surrounded by his devoted and silent herd and sobbing in pain like a child because he had stumbled, taken a bad fall, and broken his ankle.

News quickly spread around the village that blacksmith Vasily's younger brother could foresee misfortune. People began coming to learn about their future but Akop helplessly threw up his hands, since even if he could see something, he might not remember. The Maranians treated his muddled explanations with mistrust and took offense, accusing him of insensitivity and an unwillingness to help. Old Parandzem, whose barnyard birds had all fallen dead from a mysterious illness, went even further than the rest. After somehow deciding that Akop's fits were responsible, she spread a rumor that he was no mere fortune-teller but in fact the cause of people's misfortune. Everybody disliked Parandzem because of her mean disposition and abominably nasty tongue, but some Maranians believed her gossip anyway and began treating Akop like a leper. They hid their children from him, didn't come to the smithy when he was there, and if they ran into him on the street they timidly made the sign of the cross, averted their eyes, and walked away.

Although Akop took all that with a composure and even a good humor uncharacteristic for his young age – people could think what they wished, so long as they didn't annoy him with their pesky attention – Vasily took their treatment of his brother as an offense and a wound to the heart. He attempted several times to talk this through with his fellow villagers, arguing and persuading, growing incensed, and even getting into fights, though his efforts ended up having the opposite effect since the Maranians now avoided him too. Work at the smithy, however, did not decrease; fear is fear, but a high-quality hoe that will serve long years and not break from constantly smashing apart clods (there was at least as much rocky material at the top of Manish-kar as dirt) was something you couldn't get from just any blacksmith. And so the Maranians kept going to the smithy and Vasily silently took their orders despite their hurtful behavior, doing his work the only way he knew how: diligently, painstakingly, and often on credit, never refusing payment in installments from a neighbor who wasn't in a position to pay for the labor immediately.

The tension that had arisen between Vasily's family and their fellow villagers would probably have lasted for many long years, eventually turning the blacksmith and his brother into pariahs, if not for an occurrence that spring that literally turned Maran's relationship with Akop upside down. His fits had become more frequent than ever by that time, and they were now so exhausting that it seemed as if any one of them might be his last. Yasaman, who was always right there, helped the young man fight his illness as best she could. She made a special mix of herbs whose extracts were supposed to help him get through the worst of the attacks more easily. Akop assiduously followed all her instructions: he drank bitter tinctures, slept with the window wide open in any weather, took cold showers, and breathed as she had taught him, taking fifteen deep breaths in and out each morning immediately after waking up and then again before bed. The treatment undoubtedly helped because he never had a single serious illness all those years, not even a common cold. Even the chicken pox epidemic that overran the village, something that nobody had been able to dodge, not even the old people, passed him by unnoticed. Coping with the fits, however, was not within the power of Yasaman's prescribed treatment. The fits were excruciating and severe, and they became so unbearable over time that Akop instantly lost consciousness when he was caught off guard, leaving him with no time to warn of the coming disaster or even recognize what was happening.

Despairing because he was unable to do anything to ease his brother's condition, Vasily brought Akop to the valley once more. This visit to the doctor also yielded nothing. Not only did they fail to uncover any abnormalities in the young man, they couldn't think of anything to suggest apart from sending Akop to a clinic for the mentally ill. Infuriated, Vasily brought Akop home with the firm intention of never returning to the valley. "If he's fated to die from an attack, better that it happen in my arms than there, among the insane," he declared.

Akop was more worried about Vasily than himself, so he never moaned or groaned. Akop tried not to feel dejected, and after recovering from each fit he would help at the smithy, where he worked deftly and enthusiastically, expecting no leniency and getting very offended if Vasily left the most difficult part of the work to himself or suggested that Akop take a short rest. Akop was endlessly grateful to Magtakhine for her care. He loved her like a sister and was courteous and affectionate with her parents, old people who were keenly worried about their younger daughter Shushanik's precarious health and were themselves severely weakened: Petros's left leg no longer worked properly and his wife had taken to her bed after being driven to exhaustion by insomnia and a depressive malady, the illness of dusk, also known as *zhimazhanka*. Akop willingly helped around the house by tidying up, laundering, cooking, and fussing with his adored nephews who had been born in rapid succession; the eldest had turned seven by that time, the middle one was five, and the youngest was three. The little boys already knew about their uncle's illness and it was touching to see them walk around the house on tiptoe, allowing Akop to catch up on his sleep in peace after his most severe attacks. Vasily's heart bled when he observed his sons, brother, and unfortunate Magtakhine, who was torn between her family and her parents, all of whom needed her care. He breathed a sigh of relief at the start of each January, hoping the new year would be happier and more merciful than the last, but each December he always reflected with bitterness that life's hardships had not eased. The past year had only presented the family with new ordeals to endure.

The incident that changed the Maranians' treatment of Akop was later called "the day Arusyak Kudamants's youngest grandson saved us from ruin." On one of Manish-kar's cliffs, on the opposite side from the one that had collapsed into the void during the earthquake, there gaped a broad, deep bare spot. This was where a mudslide came down each year, just after the snow melted, crushing the wild plum bushes that stubbornly grew there. People had long become accustomed to the din of the fast-moving avalanche cascading into the very heart of the chasm; its flow always followed the same worn path, leaving behind a damp, muddy scar that smelled of moist earth and cold. A huge volcanic pinnacle stuck out like a fang, a little higher than the houses closest to it, and protected the village from the mudflow because, time and again, the mucky avalanche had stumbled against its indestructible asbestos side, turned right, and departed completely, preventing any harm from befalling Maran. People devoutly believed in the indestructibility of the stone pinnacle that had even withstood the infamous earthquake and regarded the mud with carefree indifference because they saw no point in fearing something that would never reach them.

One day, Akop foresaw that the tooth-like pinnacle would not remain standing. This was the only time that he regained consciousness after an attack and remembered a detailed picture as it had appeared before his eyes. Mud rushed forward in a lethal icy flow, smashed the protective block to smithereens, and devoured the village, house by house, with a horrendous squelching sound as it swept everything away into the abyss, leaving no one among the living.

Akop had never been able to remember a prediction, so he initially placed no importance on this one either, deciding it was just a typical trick of his memory. But the next day, weary from indistinct worry, he went down to the eastern slope simply to reassure himself that everything was all right there. It took an entire hour to walk around the perimeter. The huge asbestos outcrop towered at the edge of the village, solidly wrought, without a single crack, and appeared absolutely indestructible. What Akop saw had calmed him, so he spread his short caftan at the sunny base of the pinnacle, stretched out in relief to have a rest, and directed his gaze at the sky. The ground was cold but already covered in tender shoots of grass and snowdrops that had finished blossoming and were ceding their place to pale blue alpine violets that had opened their meek leaves but were still biding their time before blossoming. It was serene and still, and a leisurely low cloud floated past overhead, hooking the crown of Manish-kar as if it were the snow-white hem of a bridal dress, before slowly pouring a milky quiet all around. Akop placed his hands under his head, smiled, inhaled a chestful of weightless air scented with melted snow, and closed his eyes, only to be struck by a vision on the inside of his eyelids of two vast moving craters. They were churning at tremendous speed, using their icy power to pulverize Maran's stone-sided chapel to dust. If you were to squint, you could make out the cross on the cupola, glimmering in the midst like a bird that has fallen into a trap and is straining upward, spreading its thin wings in pointless flight.

Akop snapped out of his icy haze with the firm certainty that the volcanic pinnacle would not hold up this time and that the only possible way to save the village was to build a stone barrier between the peak and the houses to the east. Vasily believed Akop unconditionally, so there was no need whatsoever to persuade his brother of the danger threatening Maran. But how could they convince the other men, particularly those who were categorically disposed against Akop, when pitifully little time remained and every pair of hands was needed to build the barrier that would save them?

After thinking for a while, Akop went to see Vano Melikants, whom the Maranians regarded with particular reverence. How else could one regard the person who had done everything in his power to multiply the herd from Noah's Ark and save the village from ruin by doing so? Vano heard Akop out without interrupting and didn't ask questions either, though he also made no promises. After seeing Akop off, Vano went to the smithy to have a talk with Vasily. That same evening, he gathered Maran's entire male population in his yard. The Kudamants brothers didn't know what Vano said to convince them – Vasily and Akop both refused, point-blank, to go to the gathering, since Vasily still hadn't forgiven his fellow villagers for their biased and superstitious treatment of his brother, and Akop didn't see the need.

The Maranians spent nearly a month constructing a protective wall along the eastern side of the village. By the beginning of Palm Week, the wall encircled the stone pinnacle from the side where the three farthest yards were nestled together. At Akop's insistence, they reinforced it with additional solid beams and surrounded it with earth-filled sacks. The mudslide came down on the eve of Palm Sunday, at *enbashti*, the most wordless and frightening time of night. People couldn't make out anything in the dark because of a blizzard that had consumed the village, and in the early morning they found only the lower part of the protective wall. Its upper half, which had taken the horrendous force of the blow, was smashed to bits and had collapsed into the chasm, taking the wooden beams and sacks of earth with it. Only a rough ditch remained on the spot where the stone fang had stood, protecting the village for many centuries. It was as if someone had gone along Manish-kar's slope with a huge plow, using a broad cutting blade to rip the flesh off its surviving shoulder.

Akop walked up to the half-collapsed wall, pressed his palm against it, and listened to it. He turned to his fellow villagers: "We have the entire year ahead to restore the wall. I hear the din of other mudslides that won't be as strong and won't cause damage to the village. But we need to re-inforce the wall anyway. Just in case." The Maranians parted silently, letting their savior through, some extending a hand in apology. Akop shook his head. "No need to apologize." He walked through the crowd, looking thin and emaci-ated; he was rapidly turning pale and his restless eyes were the color of cooled ash. Vasily's gaze followed Akop and he immediately sensed something amiss so hurried off, elbowing people out of the way and reaching his brother in time to grab him a second before he fainted. Akop's body was burning with a horrible fever, his legs were convulsing, his head was helplessly thrown back, and a hoarse, drawn-out moan escaped from his throat. The villagers were at a loss and froze in fear because they were witnessing one of his fits for the first time, but a moment later they lifted Akop and helped carry him home. Magtakhine brought her sons to her parents' so their uncle's moaning wouldn't frighten them, and when she returned she found Vasily at Akop's bedside, exhausted from worry, repeating, "How can I help you? How?" and grasping the hand of his brother, who was thrashing in delirium. Magtakhine embraced her husband and pressed his head to her chest, but Vasily made a weak attempt to break free before going limp and bursting out in helpless sobs, saying he couldn't take it, couldn't stand it any longer.

Unlike previous attacks, this one didn't end the next morning and Akop kept drifting in and out of consciousness, tossing and turning in bed, his head splitting from unbearable pain and his eyes burning so much it was as if two fiery rods had been driven into his pupils. By ten o'clock Vasily had carried his brother out of the house; the April sun was flooding the village from end to end with its curative light and a holiday service had begun at the chapel. Magtakhine walked alongside him, telling him which way to go. Years later, when she was completely broken by adversity and had turned her husband's life into unrelenting torment with her displeasure and never-ending complaints and lamentations, Vasily never once permitted himself a single defiant word. He tolerated all that to the bitter end, and when it became completely unbearable he would lead his wife by the hand to the far room, lock her in, and then, stealthily checking that the wooden ladder was set under the window, go to the smithy to while away a long, empty day. Magtakhine would complain bitterly about her fate, her ungrateful parents, and the intolerable pain that had settled in her soul after her sons' deaths, but never once did she mention Akop's name and never once did she reproach her husband for twelve long years of night vigils when she had sat by the patient's bed, not in order to help – what sort of help could there be with an incurable ailment? – but simply to be with him.

That holiday morning, Vasily had gone out to the veranda to ask his wife to change bed linens soaked with Akop's sweat and she was standing, leaning against the wooden railing, with her hands pressed to her chest, gazing at the corner of the yard where Vasily would install a doghouse thirty years later. Magtakhine turned at the sound of his footsteps and said she knew why Akop suffered so much: it was because he was battling death each time, tearing someone's life from its clutches, but death couldn't forgive that of anyone, so it was torturing him with the fits. Vasily was at a loss as to how to answer and looked at her as if he had been hit by lightning, gasping for air as Magtakhine kept silent, though she added that Vasily needn't worry, she had realized what needed to be done. She ordered him to wrap Akop in a blanket and take him out of the house, down to the meidan. Vasily did as she asked, carrying his brother out of the house just as he had carried him out on the chilly night of the famine when he was five years old and learned at the precipice that the whole valley was gleaming with dark blue lights. Magtakhine walked silently beside him, pressing her hands to her chest. Maran seemed deserted because people had gone to the holiday service; only pets and flying birds witnessed them carrying the haggard, dying young man to the meidan. The square, which had been washed clean for Palm Sunday, shone in the sun like highly polished shards of glass that children use to catch sunbeams, and Magtakhine led Vasily to the center of the meidan, where she asked him to take off the blanket and lay Akop on the ground. Akop came to immediately from the cold, and opened his eyes.

Magtakhine knelt beside him and stroked his cheeks and forehead, saying, "Akop-dzhan, say you don't want this to happen anymore."

And he whispered, barely moving his pale lips, that he didn't want it.

"But don't tell that to me," Magtakhine said angrily. "You know who's torturing you, tell them you don't want that anymore, shout once but loudly so they hear you," and Akop nodded ever so slightly, closed his eyes, inhaled deeply, and forced out an unbearably frightening wail that damaged his larynx. That wail transformed into thousands of icy slivers that pierced his soul, turning it inside out, immobilizing it, and taking its will, directing it toward the unbearably cold breath of whatever was spinning inside his eyelids and then it exploded in a blinding flash, filling up absolutely everything with itself and leaving not even the slightest hope of rescue. Akop's soul hung over the cold abyss like a wretched, ragged shred and then it floated down into the chasm's permanent frost, into a boundless and ghastly darkness. At the very last moment, though, when all the heavenly vaults had collapsed and its last supports had crumbled, when time had been covered with hoarfrost from the soulless breath of the visions, Akop's soul dodged, turned, and broke loose for a fraction of a second so that it could exhale, burning with the cold as it did: "I DON'T WANT THIS ANYMORE." His soul was stunned, knocked down, dragged into the chasm, beaten against its thistly shores, sucked into the reeking darkness, and pierced by such horrendous pain that it spilled everywhere like drops of mercury that burned glowing, fiery labyrinths in Akop's miserable body. And all at once, at the very edge, when there was nothing left but a hopeless sense of doom, when the suffering had erased the line between life and death and the last light had gone out, absolute silence set in.

"Stand," someone ordered in a voice that brooked no objection.

And Akop opened his eyes.

∿

Anatolia's condition had been worsening steadily since the day Magtakhine began visiting and now, in addition to her overall weakness, a horrendous nausea was sapping her strength and any crumb she ate came straight back up again. If in August she had been complaining of getting fatter, by October she had lost so much weight that you could count all her ribs with the touch of your fingers, and there was one night when Vasily woke up because she hadn't been able to reach the privy: her weakened legs had given out and she was sitting on the floor, sobbing uncontrollably, lamenting her bitter fate. He helped her handle her business, put her back to bed, and plumped the pillows to prop her up, in the hope that this would settle some of her nausea. He put on the kettle and sat beside her, caressing her hands while the water heated. Anatolia cried, both from shame over her feebleness and from having landed on his shoulders as such a heavy burden. She attempted several times to apologize to Vasily but he cut her off, asking her not to offend him by apologizing. He brewed some strong, sweet tea and fed it to her from the saucer, blowing carefully before each sip to cool the boiling-hot liquid; Anatolia drank a third of the cup and could drink no more, so lay back on the pillow and closed her eyes. Vasily lay down beside her, cautiously embraced her shoulders, and kissed her temple.

"I feel so guilty for what I'm doing to you," whispered Anatolia.

"Don't start that again," Vasily interrupted her.

"Let me finish," she begged.

Vasily silently heard out her sorry story. She confided in him about the sudden blood flow, how she had hidden it from Yasaman, how she'd half-heartedly agreed to the suggestion of moving in together in order to get him out of the house that day but hadn't been able to find the right words later to change his mind. "I knew this escapade would end in disaster, but I couldn't tell you the truth," she ended by saying.

"Do you regret that we're together?" Vasily asked.

"What do you mean?" Anatolia buried her face in her hands, distraught. "I regret that I complicated your life."

"You complicated your own life, not mine. If you'd told Yasaman about the blood in time, she'd have known how to cure you."

"She wouldn't have thought of treating me. She'd have asked Satenik to call for an ambulance. But I didn't want to go to the valley. I wanted to die."

"Why?"

"Because I was tired of living."

"Do you want that now?" Vasily asked with a half-smile that barely concealed his hurt.

Anatolia burst into tears. "Now I want to live as long as I can."

Vasily waited until she had fallen asleep then carefully got up, threw a short caftan over his shoulders, and went out on the veranda. Magtakhine was waiting for him by the railing. This time she was facing him rather than standing with her back to him and she was exactly the same as he had seen her on her wedding day: young and beautiful, in a fancy pearl and silver *mintana* dress and a lacy wrap that framed the delicate oval of her face. She smiled but raised a hand in caution, not allowing him to approach her.

"Why do you come here?" asked Vasily.

She didn't answer.

"She's been getting worse and worse ever since the day you started showing up. Are you coming for her?"

Offended, Magtakhine shook her head, looking almost like a child.

"I beg you to help her. Since you saved Akop, you can save her too."

Magtakhine began flickering and shimmering, transforming into little golden sparks at the mention of Akop's name. She disappeared a second later, dissolving into the air without a trace. Vasily went over to the spot where she had been standing and touched the railing. It was warm, as if someone really had been leaning against it. He stood a little longer, inhaling lungfuls of sharp autumn air. Daybreak was catching hold in the east, chasing off the night's gloom, and a first meager dew was falling. By morning there would be an abundant second dew that smelled of grass and damp earth. The protective wall towered over the edge of the village: ever since the day Akop had renounced his gift and rid himself of the fits forever, twenty-two mudslides had come down from the crown of Manish-kar but they had all passed by, causing no damage to the village.

Satenik sent a telegram to the valley early that morning. And so, two hours later, after an initial but thorough examination, an ambulance carried Anatolia to the hospital, sounding its siren and leaving the village stupefied by the sensational news. In her fifty-eighth year of life, after outliving the last of her relatives by nearly a half-century, surviving famine, cold, betrayal, and war, but being able, despite those dire ordeals, to preserve a kind heart and a sensitive disposition, the youngest daughter of Kapiton Sevoyants and Voske Agulisants turned out to be in her fifth month of pregnancy.

Chapter Two

After the ambulance departed, the old people of Maran waited, all atwitter, for news from the valley that would come either when Mukuch returned after a trip for groceries or when postman Mamikon, who stormed up the long, gently sloping path to the village with the obstinacy of a ram once every two weeks, came to deliver insipid periodicals and advertising flyers to the post office.

Unfortunately, there was little news because entry to the specially equipped ward where Anatolia lay under medical supervision was closed not just to outside visitors but also to Vasily. He was only permitted to ask a nurse to pass along clumsy little notes scribbled in block letters that Anatolia answered by writing long messages filled with assurances that her treatment was excellent and the food was delicious, but that she wasn't allowed to get up for fear that, at her age, she might lose the baby. *But everything will be fine, my beloved*, wrote Anatolia, and each time Vasily deciphered her letters syllable by syllable, he would get stuck on that affectionate address and repeat "beloved, beloved" to himself. He was staying at a remote hotel and it took three hours to get to the hospital; he had taken a job at the hotel as a yard worker to pay for his cheap, unheated room. They had been reluctant to hire someone of his advanced age, but had eventually agreed to offer him work. So now Vasily wasn't sleeping nearly enough because he was up early every morning hard at work, clearing autumn leaves off the streets on the outskirts of the city and then sitting until late under the windows of the ward where Anatolia lay, safeguarding her restlessness until the overhead lights were shut off inside the hospital. He could have stayed in Maran and ridden to the valley with Mukuch Nemetsants, of course, but he was wary of leaving the city, thanks to a superstitious fear that something catastrophic might happen to Anatolia if he was not nearby.

Oddly enough, he didn't think about the child at all, and didn't even especially believe in its existence since the haste with which Anatolia had been hidden away in the hospital and the strict secrecy that surrounded her had moved him to think she most likely had some sort of illness unknown to medicine, as Akop had, except that in Akop's case he had been able to trick them. This time, however, they had won and taken the only person who was dearer to him than life itself. Vasily didn't tell anyone about his concerns and didn't even write to Anatolia about them, just in case a nurse happened upon his note and showed it to a supervisor, after which he would be banned from showing his face on the hospital premises. He had already attempted to free her from captivity once: he visited the head doctor to call for her immediate discharge, taking the doctor aback with the force of his demands. The doctor, however, showed Vasily a number of pictures and papers covered in incomprehensible squiggles, then proceeded to put Vasily to shame. Vasily, however, wouldn't listen, demanding to be let into the ward instead. When he was refused, he called the doctor a mangy young whippersnapper, whereupon he was immediately restrained by the guards and removed from the hospital, and now he was only allowed to hand over notes and sit under the window of Anatolia's ward.

Each week, Mukuch delivered groceries that the old villagers gathered for Vasily: bread, cheese, nuts, dried fruit, some brined vegetables and clarified butter, and simple baked goods like *sali* bread or a sweet nut-filled *gata* pastry. Vasily was endlessly grateful for their concern, so he went to a craft store with a tiny amount of the money he had saved and purchased eight embroidery kits with fabric and various colored silk threads to send along to the village. Vasily explained to Mukuch that the men would do just fine but he wanted to thank the women. Mukuch wanted to refuse, but he took the little gifts and then two weeks later brought eight identical little embroidered pillows that the old women wanted him to pass along to Anatolia so that she could rest comfortably. They rejected the little pillows at the hospital, though, on the grounds that Anatolia was in a sterile ward and they couldn't risk bringing in anything that might cause contagion. Insulted, Vasily left them in his hotel room to bring back to Maran later.

Toward the end of November, a bank transfer and a large parcel of supplies arrived from beyond the northern pass. Wiping sweat from his brow, Mamikon dragged it to the hotel, where Vasily decided the parcel was for Valinka Eibogants and needed to be sent to Maran with Mukuch. But that offended Mamikon: "I'm a postman! Delivering packages is what I do! I brought a dispatch to Valinka just last week, nearly broke my back. But anyway, this one's for you from Tigran and his wife...what's-her-name there, right, nearly forgot, yes, Nastasya."

The package contained canned fish and meat, condensed milk and several packages of cookies, as well as a little snow-white blanket, delicate and soft, made of some kind of weightless yarn and carefully wrapped up in fancy paper.

"And who's that for?" asked Vasily, taken aback.

"It must be for the baby," said Mamikon, clicking his tongue with delight.

Vasily just shrugged his shoulders without objection. He put the little blanket away under the embroidered pillows and laid the canned goods on the windowsill. He attempted to give several items to Mamikon, who waved him off and backed toward the door. "You've lost your mind," he told Vasily. "You have nothing to live on but you're tossing food around like you're rich!"

The money Tigran sent turned out to be exactly enough to pay two months in advance for his hotel room. Vasily was deeply touched, and went to the post office to send a telegram with thanks and an assurance that he would return the money as soon as he earned it. He didn't have to wait long for an answer: two days later the maid delivered a sheet of paper folded into quarters, which Vasily was unable to read on his own, so small was the print. He went to ask for help from the doorman, who turned the telegram over in his hands, put on his glasses, cleared his throat, and read, pausing significantly at the end of each sentence. When he read the line *Uncle Vaso, you don't need to return anything. One request: await my arrival. I should be the child's godfather*, the doorman tore himself away from the telegram.

"What child?"

Vasily scratched the back of his head, groaned, and surprised himself by telling this stranger about the trouble that had befallen Anatolia, about how everybody was glad about her pregnancy, but that he didn't believe it because he wasn't used to believing doctors. It would be one thing if they put the child in his arms, because that would mean they hadn't lied, but if not, he would have to battle the hospital, something he didn't yet know how to do.

"Whose child is it?" The doorman didn't understand.

"Mine," growled Vasily, annoyed that the other man was so slow on the uptake. He took the telegram, headed to the post office, and dictated an answer: "God willing, Tigran, God willing."

When he returned that night from keeping watch under the windows of Anatolia's ward, he found a fidgety young man at his door. He was so white that it looked as if he had been sprinkled with flour. He stuck a little metal box with wires in Vasily's face and started jabbering about the old lady's pregnancy.

"What old lady?" Vasily said, squinting.

"Well, your spouse," the young man explained. "Tell me how you managed to conceive a child at your age. And why did they lock your wife in a hospital ward? Maybe she has some sort of disease that's dangerous for people around her? Or maybe something's not right with the child?"

Vasily cuffed him on the ear and sent him down the stairs, prodding him along with kicks, then went down to see the doorman. He lifted him by the front of his shirt, shook him in the air for a good few minutes, threatened to pull out his spine if he blabbed about Anatolia to anyone else, and then placed him neatly back on the floor. The doorman's hand groped at the back of a chair, where he sat down, mixed himself a sedative, and drank it through chattering teeth. The next day, Vasily demanded his money back for the advance he had paid on his room and moved to another hotel, though the press picked up the news, which quickly spread around the valley. Articles about the hundred-year-old resident of a mountain village who had miraculously become pregnant made a splash in all the papers. The news grew more harebrained and nonsensical with every passing day: the old woman, they said, was the last resident of the village and she had been impregnated by an evil spirit and was locked in the hospital because the child she was expecting was none other than the incarnation of evil, which would come alive again in human form and destroy the whole valley before long. Other papers disagreed, in an obvious attempt to undermine the first article. According to their pieces, the child was conceived by the Holy Spirit and a new Savior was finally on the way to lead all mankind to long-awaited peace and prosperity. A tight ring of gaping onlookers, religious fanatics, and journalists now surrounded the hospital premises, giving the medical workers no peace. The hospital had to triple its security staff and its personnel needed to leave the workplace through basement corridors, so it was a good thing they were connected to the neighboring building, which was home to a bustling law office and therefore offered a fairly easy means for hospital staff to blend in with legal clients and leave unrecognized.

One November evening, when Vasily was observing the gawkers from behind a corner, he happened upon the head doctor, who had pulled a bowler hat over his eyes, raised the collar of his coat, and popped out of the legal office to hurry away from the hospital. When the doctor recognized Vasily, he grabbed him by the elbow and led him up the street for some time without slowing his pace. A while later, he turned into a passageway, where he assured himself that nobody else would hear, and announced in a loud whisper:

"It's dangerous for you to be here. I don't know how the journalists found out about your wife, but they won't leave anyone alone now. I'll give you my home address. Stop by for news once a week – it would be unwise to come more often, in case they track you down."

Vasily didn't have the heart to admit that his incautious candidness was the reason for the commotion that had arisen around the hospital.

"How's my wife?" he asked.

"She's struggling a little, actually." The doctor pulled his hat toward the back of his head. Only then did Vasily notice that the man was young, thirty-three or thirty-five at most, but looked much older than his years because of the dark bags under his eyes and an expression of interminable exhaustion on his face. "Her blood pressure's falling, the tests aren't positive, and we're holding on for the seventh month to do a cesarean section."

"What do you mean, seven months? What do you mean by 'cesarean section'?"

The head doctor cast a tired look at Vasily, drew his hat firmly over his eyebrows, and buried his nose in the collar of his coat. "As I understand it, you still don't believe your wife's pregnant? Well fine, you'll change your tune when the baby's handed to you." He hurriedly scratched out his address on a sheet of paper and melted into the darkness.

When Mukuch arrived several days later, he told Vasily that people from the valley had shown up in Maran for the first time in a half-century, curious about Anatolia. The Maranians were lucky that the people from the valley, who had introduced themselves as journalists, stopped in first at Yasaman's where, unfortunately for them, Ovanes, who read the valley gutter press until he was blue in the face, kept his wits about him and swiftly showed them out, tapping a finger at his temple and assuring them there had never been a resident of Maran with that name. After roaming the village for half a day longer without receiving any comprehensible answers from the other old people, the emissaries from the lower reaches had left safely for home and not shown up again.

A week later Vasily wrapped a can of sprats and a package of cookies in a scrap of newspaper and set off to see the head doctor. He had used a safety pin to attach the piece of paper with the hastily scratched address to the lining of his jacket, more likely for certainty than for prompting since he had memorized the address when he first read it, meaning there was no need whatsoever to glance at the note: Brick Quarter, White Jasmine Street, number 8. The doctor's house was nestled at the bend of a lane paved with cobblestones. It was so narrow that you could touch the cast-iron fences on either side of you if you were to walk down it with both arms outstretched.

Despite the street's name, there were no jasmine bushes to be found nearby, the small yards were soundly lined with concrete slabs, and branchy stems of artificial plants stuck out of squat planters standing here and there along the walls. Vasily felt miserable and stifled by this impersonal drabness, amid unsociable gray houses where the windows were securely hung with impenetrable, heavy drapes. He walked along, gasping for the cold November air and stopping occasionally to clear his throat and free himself of the flavor of city smog that had attached itself to the roof of his mouth.

A pleasant-looking young woman opened the door and led Vasily into the living room, where the modesty of the decor surprised him: the furniture was old and the upholstery on the armrests of the easy chair into which he carefully lowered himself was so worn that the coarse calico lining sometimes peered out. The woman introduced herself as Maria and apologized that her husband wasn't at home because he was on duty today. She held out a letter from Anatolia, turned on a plastic-shaded overhead lamp that blinked a few times before filling the room with a dim yellow light, and then tactfully went out, leaving Vasily on his own. He unfolded a sheet of paper covered with block print letters (Anatolia wrote that way so it was easier for him to decipher), sighing heavily when he found the word "beloved" in the very first sentence and then getting on with his reading, soundlessly moving his lips. Unfortunately, he learned nothing new and Anatolia told him that everything was fine but the main thing was to hang on until she reached seven months, when they would be able to operate.

He peered out into the entryway but didn't see anyone because the doors to the other rooms were tightly closed.

Afraid of disturbing people, Vasily decided to leave without saying goodbye. Maria was surprised to return a minute later to an empty room, carrying a cup of tea and some little sandwiches, though on the coffee table she found a can of sprats, a package of cookies, an envelope, and a scrap of paper with the clumsy instructions: LETER FORR ANATOLIA AND FOOD FORR YOU.

Vasily wept from happiness as he walked through the dusky November evening. He finally believed Anatolia was in the hospital because she was carrying a child beneath her heart, rather than owing to some serious illness. Oddly enough, the thing that had convinced him of his wife's pregnancy wasn't her letters. It wasn't the gaze of the ambulance doctor when his short fat fingers pressed carefully at Anatolia's belly before he looked up at her all of a sudden with surprised eyes, muttering uncertainly, "That can't be!" It wasn't even the medical records the hospital's young head doctor had fanned out for Vasily the day he had made a scene. No, what had convinced him was the meager decor of the doctor's home. To Vasily's mind, someone who supervised a large clinic yet lived in such humble conditions was incapable of deception. And of course he was right: someone with a multitude of opportunities to be on the take but who never gave in to temptation could not, by definition, lie.

Exactly seven days later, Vasily wrapped a can of sauries and a package of cookies in a scrap of newspaper and prepared to visit the doctor again. He had spent the last week in painful reflection: a lingering, gloomy fear had fettered his soul as soon as his initial joy had dwindled. He and Anatolia had long been aging and would soon depart this world. Who would they leave the child with? Maran was not fit for a baby: it couldn't provide anything a small child needed. There was no school, no games, no other children to play with. Who would the baby grow up to be, among old people it would be seeing off to the great beyond, one after another?

Vasily shared his fears with Mamikon and Father Azaria when they stopped by to visit. Although they had held diametrically opposed opinions on every issue from time immemorial, they were in surprising agreement on this occasion, though the way they expressed their views was as different as ever.

"One does not find God in despondency—" Father Azaria uttered solemnly.

Mamikon interrupted before letting him finish: "The rooster finally had an egg laid in your chicken coop and you're upset. You should be happy!"

Father Azaria looked at him askance then gazed up at the ceiling. Mamikon winked at Vasily and broke into a gap-toothed smile. "I seem to have embarrassed you, Holy Father?"

"It's not as if you and I just met! I know what to expect from you—"

"Your life only began to take on real meaning the day you came to know me!"

Father Azaria snorted but kept quiet. He clicked his rosary stones and put them in his pocket. "I will tell you this, Vaso," he said, coughing. "A moment of human happiness does not become days or weeks without God's knowledge and desire. A moment will remain a moment, it is fleeting and short-lived. Happiness has been granted to you, so accept it with gratitude. Do not offend heaven's good intentions through mistrust. Be worthy of the gift that has been conferred upon you."

"I already had a gift like that. An entire three gifts, three sons," Vasily objected hoarsely. "God gave them to me, then took them away—"

"That means it was fated to be that way."

"Father Azaria, is that meant to console me?" asked Vasily, offended.

"He sees no further than his Holy Scripture, which is why he consoles in a way that makes us want to lock him in the cellar and bury the key so he can't get out," snorted Mamikon.

"Oh, be quiet, you nitwit!" the priest snapped good-naturedly.

"Vaso, let me put this simply for you," said Mamikon, brushing the priest aside. "I'll tell you honestly: if I'd ended up in a situation like this, I wouldn't know what to do with myself either. But a real man has to rise to the occasion. He may be unsure of himself, but he can't retreat. Does that make sense?"

"It does," said Vasily.

"Well, if I'm talking sense, then you'll cope. So stop doubting. And wipe that sour expression off your face. People will think you have a toothache," said Mamikon.

Vasily smiled lopsidedly. He couldn't say the conversation had taken a load off his mind, but it had certainly helped him come to terms with the unexpected changes in his life and put him in a happier mood.

The doctor turned out to be at home for Vasily's second visit. He opened the door himself and stepped aside, letting Vasily into the tiny hallway. A wooden chair stood to the left of the door, apparently so that one could sit down to put one's shoes on. The can of sprats and package of cookies lay on the seat.

"You're not empty-handed today, either?" said the curious doctor, taking the newspaper bundle from Vasily. "Ah, sauries. And cookies again. Leave them here, you'll take them with you later."

"It's in all sincerity... Don't you be thinking—" said Vasily, beginning to justify himself.

"I'm in all sincerity too. Thank you, but you don't need to bring us anything. Come into the living room and make yourself comfortable. We need to have a talk."

They had barely sat in their chairs when Maria came in carrying a tray of snacks. Vasily stood, flustered, and started shifting from one foot to the other.

"Sit, sit," she smiled at him and set the tray on the table. "You two serve yourselves and I'll leave, I won't bother you."

The doctor poured tea into cups, served pie for Vasily, and moved the sugar bowl closer. Vasily thanked him and looked at him questioningly.

"Eat, it's a delicious pie, Maria baked it herself."

"I won't be able to get anything down."

"Fine then, we'll talk and then you'll eat."

The conversation didn't last long, but it was alarming. The doctor started by telling Vasily about the state of Anatolia's health. Vasily didn't understand much of what the doctor said, but judging from his worried tone, things weren't looking good. Anatolia's low blood pressure troubled the doctor, as did some kind of protein in her urine, and then there was the general weakness that they just couldn't shake.

"There's a month left to hang on. But if her condition doesn't improve, we'll have to do the operation earlier." He clasped his hands on his knee and immediately unclasped them. He was obviously nervous. "In any case, Anatolia's life remains our priority, so we'll do everything in our power to save her."

"What does prioror...ity mean?"

"Important. When we're presented with choices about who to save, we'll choose the mother. But I assure you we'll bend over backward so they both pull through."

Several times Vasily clenched and unclenched his huge fists that hard blacksmith work had maimed so badly. He didn't look up, so as not to betray his despair and pain.

The doctor bent across the table and cautiously touched Vasily's hand. "Everything will be fine, I promise you."

"How can I repay you for your kindness?" Vasily finally uttered when he regained control of himself.

"There's no need. I'll be extremely candid with you. Your case is unique. And if everything goes well, that will raise our clinic's prestige, understand? This story is advantageous for all of us, since we're providing your wife excellent and – this is of no small importance – free care and treatment. In return, when everything's over, we'll receive additional bonuses in the form of state financing, the opportunity to open a research laboratory, and an increased number of patients who want treatment specifically from us."

Vasily was listening attentively, trying to grasp the doctor's train of thought, while ignoring the excessive number of incomprehensible words that the doctor sprinkled in because he was carried away and was showing no mercy for his partner-in-conversation.

"You mean it's important to you to save the child?" Vasily clarified, cautious now.

"Yes."

"And you'll do everything you can for that?"

"Yes."

"And we don't owe you anything for that?"

The doctor faltered before continuing. "The only thing I'd like to request of you is to agree to be interviewed. By a good, serious newspaper. When all this is over, we'll hold a meeting where we talk about your case in detail. And you'll corroborate that information. At the same time, we'll convene a research panel and familiarize colleagues with the treatments we used. After all, we've been maintaining your wife's condition using new methods that one might say we've developed during the course of our observation. And if all goes well, that will give us the basis for treating other women using those methods. All this means you've already helped us, above and beyond, so thank you very much for that."

Vasily listened without interrupting. Encouraged by his silence, the doctor continued:

"Mother and child will remain under observation for two or three weeks, maybe a month, since we need to be sure they'll be all right. Don't worry – you'll be able to visit them after the birth. I'm not going to give a prognosis, but I think that if all goes well we'll discharge them in mid-February."

Vasily nodded curtly. "Then so be it."

The doctor sighed with relief. "You should understand that I'm not doing this for my own financial enrichment." He started speaking faster, attempting to justify himself. "I—"

"I believe you, son," Vasily interrupted him. "And nothing is more important than trust."

❧

Snow did not wait for the official start of winter but began falling in earnest in late November. It covered the valley from end to end in a silent, heavy blanket, flattening the light and blotting out colors so only the odd hint of black cautiously framed the valley's white covers.

Anatolia fell asleep on the twenty-third of December and did not wake up the next morning. The frightened doctors circled the ward like a swarm of flustered bees, but they couldn't manage to rouse her. The patient's overall condition had not worsened but had, to their universal astonishment, even stabilized a little, so they made the decision not to undertake anything drastic but to keep a close eye on any changes in her physical state. Nurses changed her intravenous drips, turned her from one side to the other every hour to prevent bedsores, sponged off her body, which was emaciated to the point of transparency, and gave her massages to encourage blood flow. Anatolia slept for seven long days in a deep, heavy slumber, and on the eighth day Patro's voice awakened her. The dog was digging with abandon at the ground under the old apple tree, barking insistently, and running up to Anatolia, cautiously nipping at the hem of her dress and pulling her. She followed him without complaint, but then she stopped a few strides short of his goal, where Patro began howling as if chiding her, and his outraged bark woke Anatolia, who opened her eyes and attempted to sit up. She immediately felt dizzy and lay back on the pillows. They operated that same day and the next noon Mamikon, frozen to the very core after surmounting, on foot, the entire snow-covered path from

Manish-kar's base to its crown, brought the chilly village the news that thirteen old women and eight old men had been awaiting, all atwitter: in his sixty-seventh year of life, the grandson of Arusyak, Vasily Kudamants, who was as harsh as a cliff and soft-hearted as a lamb and had buried everyone he loved – father, mother, brother, three sons, and unfortunate wife – had been rewarded for his sufferings in the sunset of his life with the salvatory feeling of true love and had become the father of a wonderful, healthy little girl.

They named her in honor of her grandmother. Voske. The golden one.

Chapter Three

February, which was usually merciless and bitingly windy, happened to be snowy and benevolent that year. The mornings were silent, drowsy, and wrapped up to their very eyes in icicle-covered scarves, and they arrived late, their weak breath apparently reluctant to drive away the last of the nocturnal gloom. Roosters hardly crowed because they weren't in the mood. One would cock-a-doodle-doo and go silent, impassively listening for a response that seemed to come from the other end of the earth. The yard dogs didn't bark, they just snarled as they stared, dissatisfied, at big fluffy snowflakes circling in the air. Large flakes meant the snow wouldn't last long and would quickly subside. February was cunning, though, magically shaking bits of grainy snow out of its sleeves, sprinkling endless generous handfuls of it on sleeping yards.

The houses showed their awakening with chimney smoke. It stretched upward, dissolving in the swirling snow and leaving behind the warm smell of burning logs and the aroma of slices of spongy homemade bread toasted on the stove. Cattle that had been milked and fed were dozing in sheds, chickens who had successfully survived the regular morning torment of laying eggs rummaged around in their feeders, and turkeys in love with themselves clucked their pretensions as the guinea fowl quarreled and wouldn't share the area by the water.

Four paths only the width of two footprints had been trampled in the snow. They branched from Ovanes Shalvarants's veranda, extending in various directions. One led to the shed and chicken coop, another to the cellar, the third to the outhouse, and the fourth to the gate. The remainder of the yard was resting under a layer of crumbly (though dry and unmelted) snow that would obviously stay for a long time. Despite the uproar from the bustling yard birds, there was such quiet all around that it seemed as if someone had purposely muffled the sound, leaving nothing but the wind's barely perceptible breath and falling snowflakes that whispered among themselves.

Ovanes Shalvarants had clambered up on the wooden storage bin by the kitchen door and now sat there, beating his customary breakfast of two raw egg yolks and six tablespoons of sugar into a luxuriant froth. The teakettle had boiled on the stove and its peeling spout whistled with hot steam. On the table, large slices of bread that had toasted slightly on the stove were cooling, their crispy, singed sides leaning against the edge of a thick-rimmed clay dish.

"Are you going to take the kettle off, or may I approach it?" Ovanes asked rustily.

Yasaman rinsed her burlap floor rag in soapy water and angrily snorted, "Stay where you are. I'll do it myself."

"I can't even take a step in my own home without permission!"

"Don't make things worse!"

Ovanes tried his sugared eggs and clattered the fork all the harder, irritated at feeling grains of sugar in his teeth.

"They're large sugar grains this time, they just won't dissolve. We'll have to tell Mukuch not to get that kind anymore."

"Large doesn't necessarily mean bad," Yasaman told him. She had thoroughly washed the floor under the table and was moving toward the door, wiping the runner rug.

"The sugar might be good and all that, but my hand fell off stirring."

"Well, at least you're not wiping the floor!"

Ovanes clicked his tongue in anger. "But I offered to help you!"

"Whenever you help me I have twice the work to do later, cleaning up after you and straightening things out!" Yasaman was trying to save energy by speaking between mop strokes.

"It's one thing to tidy up at their house. But why does ours have to be spotless?" grumbled Ovanes.

Yasaman finished cleaning the rug, rinsed the burlap in fresh water, and wiped down the kitchen again, then sat next to her husband. Her work-worn hands, reddened from cold water, were clasped on her knees as she waited for the floor to dry.

"So sickness doesn't get brought in by accident, got that?" she said, recovering her breath and condescending to answer. "Did you forget what a small child is?"

"I didn't forget. But if you're afraid of sick people, there's no need to wipe the floor – just don't go and see the child," chuckled Ovanes.

Yasaman slowly turned toward her husband, raising her brows. "Eighty-five years old and a brain with the capacity of dog poo!"

Ovanes wanted to come back with an answer but thought better of it. His wife had been worked up all morning, so it was best not to antagonize her.

"So, can I go to the table yet? It's time to brew the tea, otherwise the water will cool completely," he said peaceably.

Yasaman cast her exacting gaze at the kitchen floor. "Looks like it's dried off. You take out the dirty water and rinse the bucket. And I'll get started on breakfast."

She picked up his bowl with the sugary, frothy eggs and slowly stood up. The clock over the dish cupboard rang nine with a senile rattle. There was still plenty of time, though there was a lot to do today since the village's old women were gathering by eleven at Satenik's house to work on food for a festive table. And the old men were going to arm themselves with shovels and clear the road to Maran. It was a futile effort because the snow kept falling and falling, but something had to be done to ease the way, if only a little, for Mukuch Nemetsants's cart, because today he was supposed to pick up Vasily, Anatolia, and tiny Voske from the valley, very early in the morning, and bring them home through the blizzard. An attempt to transport them in an ambulance had failed because it had got stuck on the snow-covered mountain road's hairpin bends and the vehicle had had to return to the clinic without reaching its destination. After being awakened from yesterday's midday nap, Mukuch insulated the cart with woolen blankets and loaded up heavy fur cloaks so there was something to wrap Anatolia and the baby in, then he took another old man with him to help and set off into the blizzard. If everything went favorably, they should arrive in Maran today, by three in the afternoon.

It was Valinka Eibogants who had suggested they greet the new family with a festive table. After the Maranians saw Mukuch off for the valley, they decided to stop at someone's house rather than dispersing. They spent the evening in leisurely conversation around a hot burning stove, washed down baked potatoes with cherry plum compote, and tried not to start talking about the next day, out of a superstitious fear they would inadvertently bring bad luck. After having a bite to eat, the men sat down to backgammon and the women cleared and washed the dishes before getting down to mending and knitting. Only then did Valinka cast a glance at the quiet room and suggest they set a celebratory table for Anatolia's arrival. The old people didn't like her idea very much.

"Let them make the trip without any misadventures, then we'll think about a celebration," said Mariam Bekhlvants, expressing the general misgivings and throwing up her hands in fright.

Valinka Eibogants snorted, though. "What kind of thinking about it can there be when Anatolia's given birth to a child and given us a new lease of life at the same time? Don't look so surprised, that's exactly what's happening. We'd been slowly readying ourselves to die but how can you die now, when there's this responsibility of raising a child and bringing it into the world?"

Silence reigned in the room for a minute, broken only by the crackling of logs in the woodstove.

"Let Satenik say what she thinks, she's Vasily's direct relative after all," said Yasaman, finally speaking up.

The old people fixed their gaze on Satenik. She chewed at her lips a little then cleared her throat. "I think Anatolia and Vasily would like it a lot if we were to greet them properly, with love and respect and refreshments befitting that kind of celebration."

They spent the rest of the evening approving a list of dishes. They wanted very much to set a table that would make the brand-new parents happy. They settled on turkey with onion and pomegranate seeds, bean pâté, goose baked with dried cornelian cherries, and salad made from boiled chicken with ground walnuts, as well as fried slices of lightly brined brynza in cornmeal and white wine batter. For dessert, they decided on *krkeni*, a special *gata* baked solely in cinders and served only on the most important dates.

By eleven in the morning the men had gone out, bundled in cloaks and wielding shovels, to clear snow from the approaches to Maran and the women had started on the cooking. Some were browning a turkey so they could braise it with golden sautéed onion and pomegranate seeds; others were fussing over the goose, salad, and appetizers. They had entrusted the *krkeni* to Valinka and Yasaman, Maran's handiest housewives. While Yasaman groaned from the strain of clearing snow from a corner of the yard to free up a place for the fire, Valinka made two kinds of dough and mixed up a filling of clarified butter, sugar, vanilla, and roasted hazelnuts ground to a fine powder. After that, she and Yasaman worked together to roll out the buttery pastry dough, spread it with the filling, assemble everything, and pinch the edges together, forming two large pies that they carefully pressed with their fingertips. After that, they rolled out a plain flour and water dough, generously sprinkling it with more flour and folding the buttery dough rounds into it, attempting to completely cover them, before they buried the whole thing in hot ashes.

The *krkeni* dessert was ready by three in the afternoon, when Mukuch Nemetsants's cart, its wheels squeaking, delivered Anatolia and the baby to Maran, wrapped in the warm woolen blankets. Yasaman and Valinka pulled out the pies, brushed off the ashes, and knocked them with a wooden rolling pin so the burned outer crust completely cracked and broke. There was just one small thing left – removing the remnants of the plain dough casing and carefully releasing the core: crumbly, delicate, golden rounds of the tenderest buttery pastry. It was at that very moment that Mukuch and the village's old men rolled up to Satenik's house. Valinka and Yasaman had just thrown dressy shawls over their shoulders and proudly raised their heads as they brought out sunny rounds of blazing-hot *krkeni*, carrying them through swirling snowflakes. Two steps behind them was Satenik, illuminated by a smile, walking with small steps and holding the bundle of photographs of Vasily's sons that had once been given to her. The time had come to return them. Her cousin now had the mental strength to look into their beautiful, dear eyes.

Epilogue

By six months, Voske could sit, had learned to crawl by comically placing her chubby little feet and hands on the floor, and would even attempt to stand by grabbing at her mother's legs but became very angry when she was unable to do so. She took after her father in terms of appearance: gray eyes the color of cooled ash, high eyebrows, and long, dark lashes. From her mother, the girl inherited hair with a very rare honey tinge that was whitish in infancy, though Anatolia knew it would darken with age, filling with the same wheaten gold that was iridescent in her own braids even now that it had grayed after giving birth.

Despite a lack of sleep, Anatolia felt younger and full of energy. She tirelessly busied herself around the house by cooking, laundering, and tidying up. Vasily had taken the kitchen garden and animals upon himself, so he watered, weeded, sowed and harvested crops, and milked the goats and sheep. He had even grown so adept at making cheese that Anatolia jokingly complained that his brynza was coming out more delicious than hers, though he had barely learned to make it yesterday.

In the evenings, after sitting the baby in the carriage – which Vasily had made himself, tinkering on it for quite some time at the smithy, so it turned out heavy but surprisingly maneuverable – Vasily would go out for a walk around Maran, stopping at every gate to greet the old people. Voske chirped and babbled, allowed herself to be lifted out, and laughed infectiously whenever someone recited the little rhyme about granny's butting goat, acting it out on their fingers.

Tigran and Nastasya came for Easter vacation and Father Azaria solemnly christened Voske. The child sat straight up, ruffled and proud in her godfather's arms for the whole ceremony, but let out an enraged howl when being dunked and nearly knocked over the font, which was the very same brass basin in which Valinka had made her first strawberry jam of the season the night before and then brought for the sacrament the next morning after cleaning it to a shine and tying lacy ribbon on it. The Maran chapel's walls shook from the child's scream then began groaning and shrugged their numbed shoulders, after which year-and-a-half-old Kirakos, who had peacefully dozed off on his grandmother's knees, woke up and readily chimed in with Voske's howling, filling the whole area with such powerful roulades that even Suren Petinants, who was completely deaf, heard them and Mamikon, laughing into his beard, couldn't resist joking that the infants were already singing together harmoniously, and, oh, now what might that mean!

The day before the summer solstice, Anatolia went out to the yard and found Patro under the withered apple tree that Vasily had left standing at her request because it had been

Babo Maneh's favorite tree, meaning it should stand in her memory. The dog was digging with abandon under the dead tree, throwing around damp clumps of earth, but when he sensed Anatolia's presence he began barking loudly, darted over to her, grabbed the hem of her dress with his teeth, and pulled her after him. Flabbergasted that her dream had become reality, Anatolia let Patro lead her to the shallow pit he had dug, and peered inside. She tried to calm the dog, telling him there was nothing there, but Patro whined and whimpered, tossing soil with his paws and then, joyfully yelping, pulled something out and placed it at her feet. Anatolia leaned down, examined a half-rotted clump of fabric, and carefully unfolded it, discovering inside a heavy silver ring that had darkened with time and was set with a large dark blue stone she didn't know the name of. After carefully cleaning off the dirt and the dingy patina, she put it away in her jewelry box with the only other jewelry left from her mother, the cameo made of genuine shell, light pink and beige-tinged with an elegantly carved young woman sitting half-turned and peering out at someone in the distance. When Voske grew up a little, she would wear it.

In the evenings, as she rocked her daughter to sleep, Anatolia sang lullabies that her mother had once sung to her, about rain that helps mushrooms grow and falls the day a wolf mother gives birth, about her seven wolf pups who scatter around the world but return on the day she has given up hope of seeing them as powerful wolves; about a wind whose fast-flying wings bring news from those long gone; about a grapevine that stretches to the heavens and the birds of paradise that sleep on its branches…

∾

Voske listened, holding her breath, and Vasily lay next to her, his nose buried in her soft curls: she didn't know how to fall asleep any other way. Her mother had to sing her a lullaby and her father just had to be next to her, and that was as it should be, since Voske knew nothing about the big wide world. She had her own tiny little world: a stone house, a withered apple tree, a couple of dozen old people, one chapel where a visiting priest led services on holidays, and a solid wall that protected the village's eastern side from avalanches, though the western side had collapsed irretrievably into a chasm; the only road leading to the valley was becoming more impassable from year to year, overgrown with tall weeds and thistles, and only the tracks from the cart of Mukuch Nemetsants, who went for groceries, kept it from becoming completely impenetrable, leaving two narrow white furrows the length of the entire track from Manish-kar's crown into the wider world. On the veranda of Anatolia's home, arms folded across her chest, stood Voske's guardian angel Magtakhine, unseen by all; the crack in the wall of Valinka Eibogants's home still breathed, either coming apart or joining back together but not healing, as if it were a heart that had split in two from grief and was ill but continued to live; in a linen trunk, neatly wrapped in a calico pillowcase so they wouldn't fade, lay Nastasya's drawings: everybody had already forgotten about the letters she had spotted by the white peacock's gravestone, but Maran had recognized them long ago as the initials of its only offspring, a boy and a girl who were fated to either cut off the village's history or think up a new page for it – but who could know how that would work out, who could know; in a wooden doghouse, his long-eared head resting on his big paws, slept Patro, a loyal dog who had found, among the roots of the withered apple tree, the ring hidden on Anatolia's birthday by the gypsy woman Patrina; and over little Voske's tiny world there stretched an endless summer's night that told stories about the power of the human spirit, about devotion and nobility, about how life is like the ripples left by raindrops on the surface of a pool of water, where every event is a consequence of what came before it and it's just that nobody is fated to guess those events other than chosen ones who appear on this earth once, never to return, because they drain their cups all the way to the bottom the first time. But that's not what this is about. This story is about how exactly one year and one month ago, on a Friday just past noon, after the sun had rolled past its lofty zenith and begun sliding sedately toward the western edge of the valley, Anatolia Sevoyants had lain down to breathe her last, not knowing how many wonderful things awaited her, and there they were, they had come, those wonderful things, breathing easily and affectionately, and may it be thus for a long time and may it always be thus, so the night will cast spells, protecting her happiness, and three apples will roll along night's cool hands and later, as has been established in Maran legends since time immemorial, the night will drop them to earth from the sky: one apple for the one who saw, another for the one who told the story, and a third for the one who listened and believed in what is good.

TRANSLATOR'S ACKNOWLEDGMENTS

Translating *Three Apples Fell from the Sky* was a wonderful experience, starting with my first reading of Narine Abgaryan's lively text and ending with proofreading. I enjoyed the opportunity to work with Narine, who was unfailingly good-natured and quick about answering all my queries. My colleague Liza Prudovskaya reviewed an early draft of my translation, offering hundreds of suggestions, corrections, and answers to questions. *Three Apples* is my sixth translation for Oneworld and it was, as always, a pleasure to work with Juliet Mabey and her team. Juliet's edits and queries forced me to re-read and re-evaluate many of my decisions, inspiring revisions that result in a much more readable book. Copy-editor Sarah Terry's work on *Three Apples* helped me to further refine the text and smooth out the most intractable (and mysterious!) rough spots in my translation. It was also a pleasure to work again with proofreader Helen Szirtes. Thanks go to Laura McFarlane, Production & Editorial Manager, and Paul Nash, Head of Production, for keeping everything on schedule. Finally, I'm grateful to Julia Goumen and Natasha Banke of Banke, Goumen & Smirnova Literary Agency for sending me two of Narine's books, including *Three Apples*, several summers ago.

LISA C. HAYDEN